Praise for
VENGEANCE *at the* VINEYARD

The Charming Characters Win Our Hearts Instantly

"*Vengeance at the Vineyard* is a cozy mystery with a jaw-dropping final twist. Tana L. H. Boerger crafts a captivating blend of family drama and suspense with a thrilling touch of the paranormal … The author gives some clues to the thoughtful reader, but with so many suspects, it is impossible to predict the outcome of this riveting novel. I highly recommend it!"

Nino Lobiladze, Readers' Favorite

Sharp Writing

"Tana L. H. Boerger's *Vengeance at the Vineyard* is a wonderfully immersive mystery that introduces some genuinely fresh, unexpected twists within the luxurious and privileged backdrop of a château. I love the paranormal elements, and Boerger's sharp writing offers a menagerie of characters. This a read that will undoubtedly be roundly well received. Very highly recommended."

Jamie Michele, Readers' Favorite

Didn't Know Anyone Could Be That Hateful

"Full of mystery and intrigue, the story captures your interest 'til the end."

coyotecactus, Amazon

Love This Series

"Beautifully written and love the plot and characters! This leaves you anxiously waiting for the next book in the series!"

Wanda Wilson, Amazon

Finished The Book Before I Knew It

"The ending was absolutely SUPERB! Totally loved the ending and love Wallace the butler as well. Fantastic read! Cannot wait until the next book!"

Debbie L. Campbell, Amazon

The Beauty And Allure Of French Life

"This is a delightful read for mystery enthusiasts and Francophiles alike. The novel's blend of suspense, humor, and rich cultural details will keep readers engaged from the first page to the last."

Hassena, Goodreads

Wine And Crime, What A Great Combination!

"… As entertaining as the first two books in the series …"

Valleri Sullivan, Goodreads

Celebration

"These books just keep getting better and the characters are coming to life. Tana L H Boerger has created a good mystery with good sleuthing."

Cooper2208, BookBub

Riveting Read

"This book grabs you right from the first page. Love how the characters interact and are developing. Look forward to book 3."

Booklover, Amazon

C'est magnifique!

"Thoroughly enjoyed Tana's 2nd book. Never knew about giclee,
counterfeit wine and la chanteuse, Zaz. Quelle merveilleuse lecture
but it's over so quickly. I hope the 3rd edition is coming soon!"

CLG, Amazon

Fun Characters

"Book 2 is a delight. Great characters follow the new Lord and Lady
on their next journey to their wine estate. Mystery follows.

Tazmania, Amazon

What a delightful book!

"From the very beginning, I was so caught up in the story that I could not stop reading! *Money, Murder, Mayhem* checks all the boxes for a great movie, as well! I am anxiously awaiting *Art, Wine, and Crime* in France."

G. Bowers, Amazon

Many Twists and Unique Characters

"Super loving couple Philip and Genevieve provide insight into becoming extremely wealthy suddenly in England. Owning an estate with a ghost and then having their closest friend nearly murdered changes their lives even more. Trying to be accepted into the life of being royalty while there is a murder investigation adds humor and excitement to the story…. Many twists and unique characters keep the mystery exciting."

KSHYDOG, Goodreads

Cannot put it down!

"To me, the sign of a great book is when you come to the end of it and you want to know what happens next to the characters! That is how I felt after reading this book! I have to say that I am not a reader of mysteries, but *Money, Murder, Mayhem* held my attention all the way through…. The characters were so well developed that by the end of the book you felt like you knew them…. But best of all, Ms. Boerger is writing a sequel to this book and I can assure you that I will be among the first to buy it! Enjoy!"

Steven L. Amazon

Agatha Christie couldn't have done it better!

"A delightful read with just the right mixture of humor and mystery. Can't wait for the Warwick's next adventure!"

Janice Daniel, Amazon

Finished the book

"WOW! Wish I could give this book ten stars. Author keeps the
reader not only engaged but makes them feel like they are a part of
the story line. Fantastic read!"

Debbie L. Campbell, Amazon

"I love mysteries, and this one did not disappoint!

"Greatly enjoyed this debut novel, and true to genre I was kept
guessing as to whodunit until the secrets were revealed! Great and
accurate descriptions of the English countryside and the trials,
tribulations, and delights of inherited treasures! I liked getting
to know these characters, they were quite obviously written and
created with love and care, and I look forward to the next install-
ment of the Crosswicks!"

Mark Haggerty, Amazon

A Lord and Lady Crosswick Mystery

FORTUNE'S FINAL FRENZY

Tana L.H. Boerger

Altta Publishing
2 The Pointe
Sanford, NC, 27332

Printed in the United States of America

Paperback ISBN: 979-8-9919220-4-3
Hardcover ISBN: 979-8-9919220-5-0
Ebook ISBN: 979-8-9919220-3-6

First Edition

*To my spectacular ancestors who forged
their futures in Germany and England
then braved the unknown when they
crossed the Atlantic. Thank you for
your sense of adventure, your courage,
and your extraordinary genes.*

AUTHOR'S NOTE

For all of you who occasionally lose track of who's who like I do, fear not! Flip to the back of the book and you'll find a *dramatis personae* (a character list for those of us whose Latin is limited to *E pluribus unum* or *et cetera, et cetera, et cetera*). I hope it helps.

FORTUNE'S
FINAL
FRENZY

The Butterfly Effect is a funny thing. It's the kind of phenomenon that can start with a grouse shoot in York, and weeks later, people are dead in an Alpine blizzard.

PROLOGUE

Sun Valley, Idaho, 1958

H E SCRUNCHED HIS eyes closed, then opened them wide, trying to steady the waving image before him. Leaning his elbows on the table, he steadied himself and wished he hadn't thrown back the last Apfel Korn, or three. The schnaps went down so easily but hit so hard. His stomach churned and he tugged his thick black turtleneck away from his throat. It was too warm and his armpits felt clammy. Across the table, the younger perfect specimen of an Austrian swam in front of him, his thick blond hair swooping across his forehead. *What an arrogant wanker*, he thought, mesmerized by the white racoon marks left by the man's goggles on his otherwise sun-bronzed face.

"You really are a pompous git, aren't you?" he slurred, his English accent making the insult almost elegant.

"Und du, mine freund, bist ein Warmduscher."

The Brit barked a laugh, unable to believe the Austrian had no better insult to hurl at him than a warm shower; what a wimp.

The two men had known each other for decades. Sometimes they were mates and sometimes they were foes. At the moment, the loathing ran deep between the two alpha males. Over the years they had competed on some of the world's poshest ski slopes, bid in the best auction houses for the same art acquisitions, and occasionally—with their hearts on the line—chased the same women. And today, one of those women stood squarely in the middle. They pierced each other with dagger-like stares, jaws clenched and hands fisted on a table littered with beer mugs, shot glasses and half-empty chili bowls. They were deaf to the din of voices, laughter and the sound of clattering dishes that bounced off the soaring glass walls of the Roundhouse Restaurant, 7,700 feet up Sun Valley's Bald Mountain. They saw nothing but the anger from each other's glare. After an age, the man in black broke their eye lock and said with a thick-tongued slur, "We'll settle this on the slope. We'll race to the bottom and whoever gets there first wins it all. Agreed?"

"Ja. Bestimmt." The blond skier bobbed his head and mumbled, "Yes, definitely." He pushed himself to stand and extended his hand, wobbling as he did so.

The challenger rose and grasped the outstretched hand. "I'll meet you at the top of the run in ten minutes," he said, wondering if, in his woozy state, he would be able to find his skis.

"Zehn Minuten," the other skier confirmed. "Ten minutes."

Nothing sobered a man faster than hurtling down a black run when the late-afternoon shadows stretched long and the frigid air froze his nostrils. From the sting of the wind slapping his cheeks, he knew they were schussing toward the finish line at a reckless speed. He sensed his nemesis gaining on him and eased forward ever-so-slightly, coaxing more speed from his skis. If he could keep his lead as he edged into the turn coming at him, he could streak to the bottom of the run, hockey stop in front of his fiancé—the woman the Austrian was trying to woo away from him—and send a spray of snow ten feet into the air, blasting anyone who was near, her included.

Just as he leaned into the curve, his right binding wobbled and his ski clattered on the mix of ice and snow, treacherous this late in the day. He tried to drive his edge into the rough mix, but his heel lifted in the loose binding, and he had no control over his ski. He missed the turn and headed straight for the edge of the run. The last thing he remembered, he was weightless, flying through the winter air. He felt his lips curl into a smile and heard himself laugh at the absolute freedom of his flight. And then there was nothing.

CHAPTER 1

"You cannot be serious!" Philip bellowed through his mobile into David Weatherington's ear. "That man is unbearable."

"He may be a pillock, Philip, but he put ten million euros into your pet project, The Art of The Vine, last year with the promise of more to come. Every euro he puts in is a dollar you and Genevieve don't have to. I think that's worth a few days grouse shooting at Wilmingrove Hall, don't you, mate?"

"I think this is where you call me Lord Crosswick," Philip deadpanned.

If David hadn't known Philip Warwick, the 13ᵗʰ Earl of Crosswick, so well, he might have thought the recently minted peer was serious. "Look, *my lord*," David wrapped the title in his poshest accent. "I know I am your solicitor, and this is really Lillie Langdon's area, but let me remind you: not only did Baron von

Bassewitz make a huge donation to your nonprofit, but he is also eager to build a Laney Museum in Berlin and willing to donate a large collection of his family's German Expressionists for the privilege of doing so. I don't have to tell you this will increase your artistic reach dramatically and will give the Laney museums three locations, only two short of The Guggenheim's. I'm pretty sure when Genevieve hears about this, she is going to insist on throwing this shoot for him."

"Of course, you're right, David." Philip loathed the idea of the too-handsome, too-boisterous, too-overbearing Austrian stinking up Wilmingrove Hall with his thick cigars. He deplored that Friedrich von Bassewitz and his family used the title of Baron, even though the Abolition of Nobility Act in 1919 had abolished all privileges for the aristocracy in Austria. It was absurd that the von Bassewitz family still embraced the titles of Baron and Baroness, but, Philip thought, it said so much about their arrogance. He hated the idea of the sporty Wiener shooting his birds and flirting with his wife, but he knew inviting him for a grouse shoot at The Hall was a small price for what the Baron was willing to do for the Laney museums. "All right," he said, "but you have to be here. And Becca, too, if she can manage it."

"Crikey! There's no question. You won't be able to keep Becca away. She finds Friedrick von Bassewitz absolutely charming. He has that effect on women, doesn't he?"

"I don't know that his recently divorced wife would agree, but I'm sure his new one would. It's disgusting," Philip growled. "He's an excellent shot, plays a wicked game of tennis, skis like Jean-Claude Killy, and looks like a young George Clooney."

"Rather like you, my lord."

Philip imagined David smirking at the other end of the phone as he tipped back in his chair behind his centuries-old carved desk at the London law firm of Weatherington Holmes Fitch Smythson Morrow, where he was managing partner.

"Exactly like me, David. Except for the fact that I'm, as you Brits would say, a rubbish shot, and I look more like Clooney's dad than Clooney. Thank god I'm a decent skier."

"Now you're just fishing for compliments."

Philip barked a laugh. He loved David like a brother. He, Genevieve, David, and his newish bride, Becca, had become fast friends when Philip inherited his cousin's title and vast fortune almost two years ago. He blew a puff of air from his cheeks, as his mind flashed back over the last twenty-four months, marveling at how much had happened to change their lives. With his inheritance, Philip and Genevieve had stepped from comfortable wealth and a joyful marriage into a life few would ever experience. They now lived in a world of billion-pound privilege where not everyone wished them well and where one misadventure seemed to follow on the heels of another. But in the last few months, they finally felt on an even keel.

"Let me talk to G and I'll get back to you with a date. You know I don't have anything to do with our social calendar. I just show up when and where I'm told. Having said that, I guess we'll have to get it done soon. The season's over December 10TH, isn't it?"

"It is, so you're right. Better sooner than later, because you're running out of later. And, by the way, where *is* the good Lady Crosswick?" Of all the people in Philip and Genevieve's close circle, David was like family. Though they hadn't known each other over the course of many years, the three of them had been through intense times in the last two years and had become close as kin.

"She's at Chateau Beaulieu meeting with the Cité du Vin board about next year's The Art of The Vine class." He sipped his coffee and winced when he found it was cold. "Timely, wouldn't you say? She's trying to convince them to double their commitment to the program. I'd say if we can assure them more money is coming from the von Bassewitz family, they would be enthusiastic about devoting more of their resources."

"You made my point," David gloated.

"She'll be home tomorrow." Philip glanced at his vibrating phone. "In fact she's calling right now." He felt his lips pull up at the corners when Genevieve's picture flooded his screen. Forty-four years of marriage had only made him adore her more. "I'll give you a call after we've decided on the particulars for the shoot."

"Cheers, mate," Philip heard David say as he switched the line to Genevieve.

He smiled at the lilt in his voice as he said, "Hi, darling girl."

"And hi to you. What are you doing on this beautiful early fall day?"

"How do you know it's beautiful in York?"

"I asked Google, of course."

Philip's laugh rang through the line. "How did the meeting go?"

"It was fine." Normally brimming with energy, Genevieve sounded tired.

"You okay?"

"Sure," she said, with no conviction. "I'm just anxious to get back to the Hall. Everyone's busy here. You know the Ban des Vendanges is next week, so Duncan and Julia are working like mad on the harvest festival. Alex and Ella are in school all day and the staff is preparing for the harvest. Now that I've finished my business with Cité du Vin, I feel superfluous. It isn't nearly as much fun to be here when you're not." She sighed. "I'd leave now, but Captain Bruni has everything set to leave in the morning. Besides, I'll have dinner with Duncan, Julia and the kids tonight so that will be jolly."

"What time are you leaving tomorrow?"

"Ten o'clock. I should be home by noon with the hour time difference."

"Do you want me to pick you up at the airport?"

"No, I'll take the helicopter, save you a trip."

"When you get home, we need to talk about organizing a grouse shoot and inviting Baron Friedrich von Bassewitz."

"Really?" Her surprise cut through the distance. "You don't like the Baron, even if he insists you call him Freddie. Why would you invite him to join you shooting?"

Philip recounted his conversation with David, ending with, "The Baron called David to talk about a few details for the Berlin museum and let it drop that he wants to come for a shooting weekend. Talk about blackmailing his way into that!" Philip's shoulders slumped. "I guess sometimes we have to do things for the greater good."

Genevieve coughed a laugh. "Don't you mean, 'our soul is for sale for the right price'?"

"That, too. Anyway, if you look at our calendar and tell me what dates are available, I'll get with Sean and we can get this organized and over with."

"I suppose he'll bring his newish Viennese wife with her perfect English, her perfect blonde hair and her flawless Teutonic face. You know, darling, we really should like this couple. They're handsome, accomplished, love our wines and want to give us lots of money for our projects. Why in the world do we find them so annoying?"

Philip shifted in his leather desk chair, uncrossing and recrossing his legs. "I suppose we find them irritating because they're charming, they give to Art of The Vine so generously, support our favorite causes and seem to like spending time with us. Could that be it?"

"Yup," Genevieve said. "It's a pisser, isn't it?"

On the other end of the phone, Philip heard someone speak to Genevieve. "Philip, I need to go. Delphine needs to talk to me. Don't do anything fun until I see you. À demain, chéri."

"See you tomorrow, darling girl." The connection went dead and Philip stared at his phone, unhappy to let Genevieve go. *What a lucky scoundrel I am*, he thought. Feeling his throat tighten, he shook his head and pushed back from his desk. "Jeeze, Philip, get a grip," he said as he walked out of his study toward the kitchen.

"Excuse me, my lord. What did you say?" Elsie Lomax startled Philip out of his deep concentration.

"Elsie, I didn't see you there. I was just talking to myself." His eyes crinkled at the corners as he smiled at the head cook. "I just got off the phone with Lady Crosswick. She'll be home tomorrow and should be here in time for lunch about one o'clock if you could arrange that please. It will just be the two of us."

"I believe it is supposed to be a lovely day tomorrow. If it's nice enough, would you like to lunch on the terrace?"

"I know Lady Crosswick would love that." Philip rested his hand on her arm. "Thank you, Elsie. We won't have too many more days we can do that, will we?"

"No, my lord, we won't, so we should take advantage of every day the sun shines and the winds don't blow."

"Those are words to live by." Philip flashed Elsie a grin, strode out the French doors and headed toward the estate office to talk to Sean Harrington about the upcoming shoot. As he walked across the back terrace toward the stairs leading to the office, he smelled the sweet scent of Rose Otto, Charlotte Chaubert's subtle way of letting only a chosen few know that the Laney ghost was near. He stood on the top stair and sniffed, hoping he wouldn't scare her away.

"So you're here with me," Philip whispered into the autumn air, looking around for another sign that would confirm her presence. He was surprised she wasn't at Chateau Beaulieu keeping Genevieve company. Over the last two years, Charlotte and Genevieve had become close, as close as a spirit can be to a living, breathing human being. Since the beginning when the newly minted Lord and Lady Crosswick arrived at Margrave House, their Kensington manse and the scene of Charlotte's tragic death, Philip had never encountered her. He smiled at the idea that Charlotte was privileging him with her presence and couldn't wait to tell Genevieve. "To what do I owe this honor,

Charlotte?" he asked, enjoying the warmth of the sun beating on his cheeks. But just as the words left his lips, an icy slap of wind smacked him so hard he staggered back several steps. Rose Otto flooded his nostrils, then, in an instant, the fragrance was gone. Philip put his hands on the stone wall and, for several seconds, leaned his weight on his palms trying to chase away the dizziness churning in his head.

He plopped down on the top step, cradled his head in his hands and closed his eyes.

"My lord. Are you all right?" Sean Harrington stood on the terrace looming over his boss.

Startled by the estate manager's greeting, Philip turned his head to look up at Sean's face but instead squinted into the sun blazing over the estate manager's shoulder. With Charlotte's assault lingering in his memory, it took Philip a moment to compose himself before he said, "Sean, I was just coming to see you." He extended his hand and Harrington pulled Philip to his feet.

"What can I do for you, my lord?"

Philip patted his estate manager on the back. "Oh, you're going to be thrilled when I tell you. Let's go to your office, fortify ourselves with a whisky, and I'll fill you in on what's about to happen." He couldn't help looking back over his shoulder as they started down the long staircase to the estate's headquarters.

CHAPTER 2

THE MOMENT THE House of Crosswick helicopter touched down on the Wilmingrove Hall pad, Genevieve unsnapped her seatbelt and shoved herself out of her seat in one agile move. She grabbed her tote and handbag and was at the door even before William, the young purser. Waiting anxiously, she bounced her shoulders to the rhythm of "Stop in the Name of Love," playing through the cabin speakers, and mouthed the words.

"It will be just a moment, my lady," William said, smiling at his boss's anxious dance and feeling pressure to get the hatch open.

"By all means, William, do proceed at a glacial pace," Genevieve rolled her eyes, then smiled, teasing the young man who was eager to please.

At last, he heard the "okay" in his earbuds. He turned the lever, the hydraulic door slid silently up and the stairs dropped into place.

"Thank you, William, Captain Bruni," Genevieve called over her shoulder as she dashed down the two steps to the ground. Philip did not disappoint. When she saw him sitting in the golfcart waiting for her arrival she felt her smile stretch across her face. With the blades still slowly rotating, Genevieve reflex-stooped, strode to the cart, and slid onto the seat beside Philip. The electricity sparked between the two and it was a draw who kissed whom, but the embrace was long, deep, and warm.

Philip squeezed Genevieve's knee, then pressed the accelerator and the cart sped up the hill toward the Hall. "I'm so glad you're home."

Genevieve loved that it hadn't taken either of them long to embrace Wilmingrove Hall, the generational House of Crosswick family seat, as home. She kissed Philip again, on the cheek this time. "So I've checked the calendar and have two dates for the great Baron von Bassewitz grouse shoot. Are we going to have to go through with it?" Genevieve had her fingers crossed in her lap hoping the answer would be no.

"I know you're hoping it's not going to happen, but David convinced me that if we want the Baron to continue to support the Art of The Vine and possibly finance a museum in Berlin, it's worth a little courting."

He glanced at her and she nodded. "It's hard to argue with that." She shrugged. "It'll be fine. I'm sure they can be a lot of fun," she said, trying to convince herself. She pulled her phone from her jeans pocket and tapped the calendar. "The two dates we have open for this grand event are—"

"Actually, G, they've already been invited."

"What? I thought you were waiting for me to give you some dates."

"I was but…" He didn't finish his sentence.

"Philip?" She waited. When she spoke again, there was an edge to her voice. "Philip, when is this shoot?"

"Um," he stalled. "Um," he said again. "We're doing it this weekend. It was the only weekend David and Becca could make it," he rushed to explain, "and I knew you'd want them to be here. Becca's coming to see Olivia. That's the upside to having her chronically felonious daughter institutionalized so close to us. We get to see Becca and David often."

Olivia had been the bane of their existence not once but twice since Philip inherited his fortune and title. She now resided in Blaine Lodge, a psychiatric hospital only a few miles from Wilmingrove Hall and, though the courts and the hospital insisted she would be there well into the future, those who knew her would never underestimate her ability to wriggle her way back into society.

He braced himself for Genevieve's tongue lashing over such short notice, but it didn't come, so he pressed on. "And one more thing—"

Genevieve rolled her eyes.

"—Freddie is bringing his brother Gabriel, and Gabriel is bringing Michael, his current partner."

She said nothing until they were at the top of the hill and stopped at the side entrance of the centuries-old Hall.

She slid out of the cart, turned to grab her things, and looked at him with one eyebrow raised. "Is that all or will King Charles and Queen Camilla be joining us as well?"

"No, they sent their regrets, but Lillie and Finn will be here."

He splashed an irresistible grin across his face and in spite of her annoyance she chuckled and leaned back into the cart to kiss him on the lips with a loud smack. "Well, at least we'll get it done. With David, Becca, Lillie and Finn here to ease the pain, how bad could it possibly be?"

CHAPTER 3

AT THE STROKE of seven, eight guests joined Philip and Genevieve in the library, filling the room with laughter and conversation. In addition to the guests, Wilmingrove Hall's estate falconer, Andrew Frasier and Sean Harrington, the estate manager, joined the jolly group to talk about the next day's shoot and to regale everyone with tales of birds of prey and shoots at the grand estate over the centuries. Lively storytellers, both men kept the conversation sparkling and the guests hanging on their every word.

The group was an entertaining mix of Americans, Brits and Austrians, and though English was the language of the evening, conversations were flavored with multiple accents.

Windswept from the Scottish Highlands, as magnificent as a fierce Scotsman should be, and adding his Scottish burr to the mix, the falconer raised his hand in greeting when the Baroness von Bassewitz called out, "Andrew Frasier," delight ringing in her voice.

As she crossed to him, he stood a bit taller, prepared to extend his hand if she offered hers. Instead she grabbed his shoulders and kissed each side of his chiseled face.

"How marvelous that you are here," she said, as color pinked his cheeks.

"'Tis grand to see you, Baroness," he said, a shy smile reaching his eyes.

She turned to the group. "Andrew came to Schloss Friedrichstein to work with Freddie's papa and his beloved falcons." She patted Andrew's tweedy lapel and said to Philip, "Mr. Frasier is amazing, isn't he?"

"He is indeed," Philip said, chuckling at her enthusiasm and enjoying Andrew's unease.

Genevieve's smile crinkled the tiny lines at the corners of her eyes. "At the risk of embarrassing you, Andrew, I have to tell everyone that our granddaughter Ella is madly in love with our falconer. She and our grandson Alex call him 'Hawk Man'. A perfect name, don't you think?"

"Now that's a name we could brand," said Lillie Langston, the executive director of the Laney Foundation that supported the Warwicks' art museums. "And what a product!" She gestured toward the embarrassed man. "If you're game, Andrew, we could build an entire campaign around you." Lillie never missed an opportunity to create revenue streams for the Foundation, and she instantly visualized the exhibit. "Can't you see it?" she said, sweeping her hand through the air. "*The Ancient Art of Falconry:*

From the Bedouins to the Brits, with Andrew standing on a rock in full Scottish regalia: a kilt, sporran and dagger, his hair blown back and a peregrine falcon on his gloved hand."

"It's either a poster for an exhibition or"—Genevieve patted her heart—"a perfect cover for a bodice ripper."

"Bodice ripper?" David's confusion made Becca laugh.

"A torrid romance novel," she said, fluttering her hand to cool her feigned rising temperature. "Remember Fabio, the blond god on the cover of all those paperbacks in the grocery store?"

"I certainly do." Michael's smile bloomed onto his chubby cheeks.

"Why, you little tramp," Gabriel gasped, pretending shock.

Still David appeared clueless.

"Never mind," Lillie said. "What do you think, Andrew? Are you up for it?"

Crimson from his white starched collar to the roots of his thick, copper-colored hair, Frasier said with the thickest Scottish burr, "I live but to serve and would lay down my pride for the right price. Use me how're you wish. But pay me grandly" His cheeky sarcasm escaped no one.

Laughter and applause filled the room just as Wallace, the Warwicks' consummate butler, interrupted and announced, "Dinner is served."

Philip took Adelheide Christiana Hauffman's arm—the Baroness von Bassewitz—and escorted her into the imposing dining room, made cozy by the fire crackling on the hearth.

She was a beauty, and he had to admit he felt a flush of pleasure when she flashed him a radiant smile. "Lord Crosswick, what a lovely gift you have given us," she said, looking up at him through thick lashes. "The Baron and I are delighted to be included in the shoot." She tilted her head toward Philip and lowered her voice to a whisper. "You know about his terrible divorce, I'm certain. But it was much worse than the tabloids reported. Things between Angelina and the *elder* Baron had become toxic. This is the perfect tonic to help him get over that awful business."

Not quite sure how to respond, Philip cleared his throat. "I'm sure we'll have a terrific weekend, Baroness," he said as he held the chair for her to sit.

"You must call me Heidi. And may I call you Philip, Lord Crosswick?"

A boyish grin pulled his lips wide. "Of course, Heidi. I think that's appropriate. I was Philip long before I was Lord Crosswick, and since we'll be slaughtering birds together I think we should be on a first-name basis."

Genevieve followed Philip into the dining room on the arm of Friedrich Gerhardt Hauffman, the Baron von Bassewitz; Freddie to his friends. They were having a delightful conversation about a new artist they had both recently discovered.

"I first met him at Art Basel Miami," Freddie said. "*He's* a terrible bore, but his work is extraordinary. Have you seen it?"

"Actually, Lillie brought him to our vineyard in Bordeaux." She glanced in Lillie's direction. "We're thinking about buying some of his work for our museum in Paris and perhaps for the Berlin museum, when it's finished." She glanced at him to see if he was smiling at the mention of Berlin. "So Lillie asked him to join us at a gala at Cité du Vin last month. I found him to be a delightful conversationalist"—She leaned toward Freddie until their foreheads were almost touching—"as long as he was talking about *his* art or *him*." She threw a dazzling smile his way and they laughed together at the fact that they had both found the brilliant artist an insufferable bore.

Much to her surprise, Genevieve was having a wonderful time with the Baron. He was not at all like she remembered him. The few times they had been together at events, his first wife seemed stuck to him like chewing gum. Genevieve remembered the bosomy blonde, an art curator for a new-money gallery in Munich, often tipsy and unpleasantly vulgar. Perhaps it was the boorish Baroness she had disliked, not this attractive, charming man beside her. Now, the weekend held more promise than she had expected. She felt a glow warming her face.

Ah, she thought. *The prospect of a delightful party.* Then realized it was probably the Champagne and wine she had been drinking.

Glorious at any time of year, tonight the dining room boasted all that a room dressed for a special autumn evening should. Adorning the Hepplewhite sideboards anchoring each end of the room, twelve-taper candelabras blazed on either side of imposing vases, scenes of grouse shooting covering their smooth porcelain. Soaring from the vases, hydrangeas, pheasant feathers, and branches of red berries stretched toward the coffered ceiling.

Set for twelve guests, the table groaned with faceted crystal awaiting the finest wines, Royal Crown Derby bespoke bone china hand-painted with the House of Crosswick coat of arms, and rows of sterling-silver flatware. In the center of the round table, more hydrangeas filled a vintage brass pedestaled bowl. Encircling its base was a bed of moss tucked with tangerines, crabapples and clusters of pyracantha. Votives twinkled everywhere on the table.

The rest of the guests sauntered in without breaking the thread of their conversation, Lillie between Michael and David, and Sean bringing up the rear.

Much to her delight, Becca found herself sitting between Gabriel and Finn, who held her chair while she slid onto the upholstered seat, ready to engage the two younger men in lively conversation. She knew Finn well, and though she hadn't met the devilishly handsome Gabriel before, his social media preceded him. He was a man with a reputation for living well, and until recently he had been considered one of the most eligible gay men in the world. And she could see why. He moved with the easy elegance of a natural athlete and Becca was quite certain he was equally at home on the ski slope, the tennis court or his polo pony—with whom he was often featured on the Instagram pages of his latest companions. But according to TMZ.com, his heart now belonged to the unlikely-looking American man across the table.

Though he was a bit round and always rumpled, Michael Andersen's dimpled face belied his sharp mind and shrewd business acumen. When he was twenty and still at Stanford, he bought a faltering study guide business from a fellow student and turned it into a multimillion-dollar online enterprise before he graduated. Now, with four successful tech companies behind him, he was about to receive a patent that would revolutionize the art museum experience. Sitting between Lillie and Finn, he smiled around the table, enjoying the beautiful surroundings and the sparkling array of dinner guests. When his keen eyes landed on Gabriel, they softened and lingered there until Gabe glanced back at him, pressed his hand to his heart, and returned his grin.

With everyone seated, Wallace began to pour the Château Beaulieu grand cru, which he had decanted two hours earlier. As it swirled into glasses, it caught the candlelight revealing an elegant garnet that promised greatness.

"Is this Bordeaux from your vineyard?" the Baron asked, anticipating his first sip.

"It is, Freddie. Nothing but the best for you, my friend."

Genevieve caught Philip's eye and rolled hers as if to say, *That was a bit much.*

Lottie and Claire, the kitchen maids, served each person an elegant bowl of orange carrot soup with a dollop of crème fraiche in the center and offered each guest a hot mini baguette to start the meal.

When everyone was served, Philip stood. Tall and magnetic, he commanded the room. "I want to extend our warmest welcome to all of you. Genevieve and I love filling Wilmingrove Hall with interesting people and everyone here certainly fits that description, some more than others." He pointed at Finn, raised an eyebrow and laughter rippled around the table. "For those of you who don't know Finnegan Mountbatten, you'll find that, though he is a responsible adult now, he has a bit of a checkered past. And I will never understand how he wriggled his way into Lillie's heart. I mean, she's known for her exquisite taste."

"Everyone's entitled to a mistake." Lillie's smile lit up the room as she poked fun at Finn.

"Finn, we tease because we love; we love in spite of— or perhaps because of—your youthful bad behavior," said Genevieve, taunting the international security expert they thought of as a second son.

"But we digress." Philip regained his train of thought. "My point is we're pleased you're all here and we're sure that tomorrow will be a splendid day. In the meantime, let's raise our glasses and toast our Austrian friends. Zum Wohl. Cheers."

The room was quiet as everyone drank. Genevieve picked up her spoon and the meal and lively conversation began.

With his wine glass still in his hand, the Baron perused the splendid room, drinking in the House of Crosswick's generational family seat. His eyes wandered over the buttercup-silk walls, admiring the family portraits of former earls and countesses, until he arrived at an early postmodern portrait commanding the space over the fireplace. He leaned toward Genevieve so their arms were touching. "Genevieve." He gestured across the room with his wine glass. "Who is that?"

"Aha," she said. "You mean the portrait demanding pride of place over the mantle?"

"Ja." His eyes bore into the canvas. "That man looks very much like Philip."

"Doesn't he?" A smile lit Genevieve's face. "That's Philip's cousin, from whom he inherited the House of Crosswick estate. Jonathon William Wallace Laney, the 12TH Earl of Crosswick. He looks exactly like Philip did twenty years ago. The portrait was painted when Jonathon was thirty-six, six months before he had a tragic skiing accident." Her eyes misted. "He had just become engaged to Katherine Robeson, the daughter of an American media mogul. He gave up the love of his life because he was paralyzed and didn't want her to spend her life caring for an invalid. Isn't that a tragic story?"

Freddie continued leaning into Genevieve's arm. "You know, Genevieve, my father and the 12TH Earl were friends for many years before the Earl's accident. In fact my father spent some wonderful times here at Wilmingrove Hall when the two were very young. The Hall is where my father discovered he had a passion for falconry. To this day he keeps birds of prey."

Genevieve sat back in her chair and stared at the Baron. "I didn't know that until I heard the Baroness say that Andrew Frasier had come to your ski chalet to train your father and his falconer." She leaned her elbow on the table and cradled her chin, never taking her eyes off the Baron. "And to hear that your father and Jonathon were boyhood friends…. Well, I love that." She thought for several seconds then clapped her hands. "It makes the two families joining forces to create a museum in Berlin an even better idea," she said, unable to resist the opportunity to promote the von Bassewitz's involvement.

Hoping she wasn't taking things a step too far, she raised her glass, which Wallace had replenished. "I have a toast I want to make." She stood, knocking over her chair as she did so.

Wallace righted it before anyone knew what had happened.

"Thank you, Wallace," Genevieve said and went on. "Everyone, I've just learned that Baron von Bassewitz, Freddie and Gabriel's father, and the 12TH Earl of Crosswick, Philip's cousin, were close friends for years and that Baron von Bassewitz the elder spent time here as a boy. As you all know"—her eyes swept around the table—"we have been discussing the possibility of the von Bassewitz family funding the Laney Musée des Beaux Arts, Berlin. It seems like kismet that our two families should go forward with this project and I would like to toast that alliance." Beaming at Freddie, she bent down, put her lips close to his ear, and whispered, "I hope that didn't make you uncomfortable."

"Certainly not," he said, his broad smile confirming his words. He stood next to her and raised his glass. "To the Laney Musée des Beaux Arts, Berlin."

"Here, here," everyone approved and held glasses high.

Before he drank, the Baron said, "But we might have to reconsider the name."

"What did you have in mind?" Philip asked, a faint smile playing at the corners of his mouth.

"I was thinking—" He stopped as they heard a ruckus in the hall.

"Get your filthy hands off me!" The shrill voice of a woman cut through the closed dining room doors.

Everyone around the table watched as Philip strode toward the entrance, but before he got there, the double doors burst open and a frazzled blonde stood with a hand on each knob, eyes wild and rimmed red. Her black cashmere coat hung open, revealing a red wool jumpsuit cinched with a wide black belt and gold buckle enameled with the von Bassewitz coat of arms.

Normally unflappable, Wallace, who minutes before had tried to usher the fierce woman back out the front door, now stood behind her, with no idea how to control the situation and no intention of touching her again.

"Freddie, du Schwein!" she shrieked, then whispered, "You pig. You filthy pig."

All eyes turned to the Baron, who rose and walked toward his raging ex-wife. He did not seem surprised to see her. "Sissi." He kept his voice low and approached her slowly. "What are you doing here?" he purred.

A growl rolled from deep in her throat. "I have come to tell Lord Crosswick about your thieving, treacherous family and you can't stop me." She bared her teeth, snarling like a rabid dog.

With his hands chest-high, palms out, he took several cautious steps forward. When he was a few feet from her, she flew at him, holding her long red nails like talons. He stepped to the side and she hit the floor with a scream and a thud.

The Baron heaved a deep sigh as all the feelings flooded back from her unbearable behavior the last two years of their marriage. He bent down beside his disheveled former wife wondering how he could ever have been so in love with this sad, vengeful woman. He laid his hand on her shoulder and she wrenched away from him.

"Shatzie," he soothed as he stood, then bent to help her up, taking firm hold of her arm. When their eyes locked, he saw the pain, the embarrassment, the regret that haunted her. And then she began to sob.

"Let us help you, Freddie." In an instant Philip and Genevieve were at his side.

"Angelina, are you all right?" Genevieve handed the weeping woman a linen napkin to wipe the tears streaming down her cheeks. "Did you hurt yourself?" she said, hoping the interloper hadn't badly bruised herself when she fell.

Weeping uncontrollably, Angelina couldn't speak. Her body shook with every new cry.

"Why don't you come with me and we'll get you sorted." She wrapped her arm around Angelina's shoulders and started to guide her toward the door, but Freddie stopped them.

"Thank you, Genevieve, but I'll escort her back to her car."

"But…" Genevieve started to object but the Baron held up his hand. She backed away from Angelina and stood next to Philip, who slid his arm around her.

With his hand on Angelina's elbow, Freddie led the intruder toward the open double mahogany doors where Wallace still stood, his usual rigid propriety in shambles.

The diners watched Freddie guide the bedraggled former Baroness through the doorway and into the great salon. The room was silent until the sound of the front door opening then closing echoed through the vast hall. Then the room erupted and everyone talked at once.

As the uproar bounced off the dining room walls, Genevieve returned to the table and sat down next to Freddie's brother. "Gabriel, do you have any idea what just happened?" She rested her hand on the sleeve of his loden jacket.

He looked at Genevieve with wide eyes. "I have to say, over the five years Freddie and Angelina were married, I saw her behave badly—drunk, flirty, nearly naked in the Trevi Fountain—but I've never seen her like this." He picked up his wine glass and emptied it in two gulps. "Was zum Hölle! What the devil. She was savage." Then he looked across the table. "Heidi, are you all right?"

The Baron's current wife suddenly became the center of attention. Startled, like a doe in the hunter's crosshairs, she froze.

"Heidi, were you surprised by Angelina's behavior?" Philip asked.

She held Philip's gaze and her cerulean eyes misted. "No. Not really." She inhaled, closed her eyes, then exhaled. When her eyes flickered open, they were clear and focused and she went on. "Since their divorce was final six months ago, Angelina has been angry, lashing out, sending Freddie vile texts. When we married last month, things got worse. She stalked him through social media, threatening to reveal family secrets that would ruin him and his father. We couldn't imagine what she could possibly do to cause him trouble. Then she began to threaten to hurt me. That worried Freddie more than anything." She massaged her temples then her neck.

"Did you report all of this to the police?" David jumped into attorney mode.

"We spoke to a friend of his from university who is the Federal Minister of the Interior, the head of Austrian law enforcement. He advised us to take out a restraining order, which we did. You can see how much good it did. Angelina doesn't care. I feel rather sorry for her."

"After what we just witnessed, I'd say that's more than kind." Lillie sat forward in her chair, elbows planted on the table. "I think I would have had her locked up."

Heidi's mouth pulled up at the corners. "I must admit, picturing Angelina sharing a cell with a big, burly roommate brings a smile to my face."

Wilmingrove Hall's heavy front door creaked open then closed, capturing everyone's attention and the room went silent again. All eyes focused on the dining room door and each person listened to the sound of boots approaching.

"War das nicht etwas?" Freddie filled the doorway with his energy.

"Ja," his brother confirmed. "Indeed, that was really something."

The Baron rubbed his hands together as he headed toward his seat at the table but before he sat, he walked to Heidi. He took her chin in his hand, tipped her head back and said, "Liebling, are you all right?"

"I'm fine but Angelina was a bit out of control, wasn't she?" Heidi said.

"Ja, stimmt. She was." He kissed his wife's lips then looked at the dinner guests. "Es tut mir Leid. I am terribly sorry Angelina crashed our lovely party but she's taken care of now. Philip, please carry on with your toast." He walked back and slid into his chair between Genevieve and Lillie.

Genevieve put her hand on Freddie's arm. "Before we go on, I have to ask. What did Angelina mean when she said she had come to tell Philip about your, um… I think she said, 'thieving, treacherous family'?"

His brow knitted. "Genevieve, I have no idea what she was talking about. She has been a bit of a mad woman for these last months." He covered her hand with his. "But let us not allow her wild disruption to ruin our wonderful time together." He raised his chin toward the head of the table. "Philip, please continue."

"Pardon me, my lord." Looking at his phone, Andrew Frasier interrupted. "Before you carry on with your toast, I need to excuse myself. I just received an alert from the mews. It's probably a false alarm, but I need to see if there's a problem."

"Of course, Andrew. Let me know what's going on and please come back if you can."

"Thank you, my lord," he said and was out the door.

As he stood, Philip caught Genevieve's eye and they exchanged annoyed looks before Philip held his glass high. "Never let it be said that an evening at Wilmingrove Hall is dull. I'm not certain where we were before we were so… um… dramatically interrupted with Angelina. And now with Andrew's departure…" his voice trailed off. "But suffice it to say, we're pleased you're all here and are sure that tomorrow will be an extraordinary day. Please raise your glasses as we drink to our unwitting partners in tomorrow's shoot. To the grouse."

"To the grouse," everyone toasted, still unnerved by Angelina's unpleasant interruption.

As she drank, Genevieve felt an icy prickle on her neck and Charlotte Chaubert's scent, Rose Otto, flooded her senses. Then it was gone.

CHAPTER 4

And so the glorious day dawned. Crispness snapped the air as four Land Rovers rolled down picturesque back roads and bumped over the rutted lanes that led them from Wilmingrove Hall to the grouse moors.

Spirits high, the shooting party emerged from the vehicles, laughing, chattering, anxious for the shoot to begin. It was a tableau from *Country Life*—men in tweeds and breeks and women in wool flat caps, the bills pulled low against the morning sun. Their boots were well-worn and well-cared-for, their guns expensive, and their well-trained English pointers raced around the shooters barking with excitement, anxious to point, anxious to flush the grouse from the safety of their nests in the undergrowth.

Fortnum & Mason picnic baskets filled the backs' of the Rovers, ready to spill their sumptuous spreads onto tables covered with starched cloths and set with crystal goblets, sterling flatware and pretty pots of rust and yellow mums. There was no roughing it at Wilmingrove Hall. It was all elegance and civility… until it wasn't.

The group encircled Sean Harrington, pressing close, waiting to hear his instructions. "We'll be shooting four brace today," he began. "That's a total of eight birds. When we see a pack of grouse, we'll try to take a few of them out but if there is just a pair, we're going to honor them and let them go." His eyes lasered in on Baron von Bassewitz. "Is that quite clear?" He seemed to ask the Baron directly.

"When you hear this sound"—he blew a shrill tweet through a silver whistle—"stop shooting immediately and return to this location." Harrington ran the shoot as he ran the estate, with precision and loyalty to Mother Nature. Under his expert care, the birds were plentiful and the estate an ecological paragon.

He continued, a smile stretching from ear to ear. "As Lord Crosswick knows all too well, the ground we're walking today is uneven and will do its best to trip you up, so be careful and stay upright if you can."

Laughter rippled around the circle, all eyes focusing on Philip as the shooting party waited to hear the story behind Harrington's cautionary words.

Philip rolled his eyes. "Jeeze! I fall flat on my face and nearly blow my foot off one time and the man will never let me live it down. Thanks a lot, Sean."

The group roared.

"And that was only the half of it," Genevieve said, continuing the story. "The night before, the rain was torrential so when Philip stood up, he was plastered with mud and looked as if he had been frosted with chocolate icing!"

"Wie lustig, so funny." The Baron gasped. "I can just imagine how hilarious you looked."

Philip bowed from the waist. "I'm delighted to be the source of such mirth but"—he jerked his head toward Harrington, who was still smiling—"I believe Sean is ready to get on with the shoot."

"Sorry everyone, but we don't want to laugh away this perfect weather, do we?" Harrington pointed to the west, where a bank of dark clouds marched toward them. "It looks as if our fair morning is about to turn drizzly so we'd better get cracking. Are there any questions before we head out?" Heads shook. "If not, remember: the day is about safety. Stay in line, communicate, and don't think of this as grouse shooting so much as extreme dog walking." Harrington chuckled at his own joke then strode forward, his gun broken over his shoulder. The red and white setters began to work, wiggling their way into the heather, their tails whipping back and forth with elation for the hunt. The shooters stretched out, forming a long line on either side of the estate manager and the shoot was on.

Genevieve looked down the advancing row of eager guns and smiled at the idea that she and Philip were now a part of a centuries-old heritage filled with country sports, fine art, and men and women who had shaped English history. Now, the challenge for the most recent Lord and Lady Crosswick was to ensure that the House of Crosswick continued to flourish.

Some days the idea that they were out of their element haunted Genevieve, but on days like today she was absolutely certain that the house would thrive well into the years ahead and their good fortune would allow them to leave a positive imprint on the world.

Just as Harrington predicted, the day darkened and a mist settled over the moor. Except for the full-throated crack of shotguns, the occasional bark of a pointer, and the rustling of wings when the dogs flushed a covey into the air, silence blanketed the moor. The guns tromped forward, careful to find even ground with every step, each shooter taut and ready to bring shotgun to shoulder, focus down the elegant barrel of their Fabbri over-and-under or Purdey Damascus, and squeeze the trigger, the exhilaration of dropping a wily grouse a singular thrill.

In front of Genevieve, Jax—a spirited five-year-old English hunter—raced back and forth, dashing to her, racing out ten yards, barking, then dashing back. The third time he shot away, he stopped dead still and pointed. Expecting a rush of grouse to burst from their nests, Genevieve snugged her Purdey shotgun into her shoulder and waited for the grouse to explode from the heather. She took in a sharp breath and held it. No grouse. She exhaled through barely parted lips. Still no grouse. Jax held steady, his nose pointing into a sprawling clump of bog myrtle and heather.

After several seconds, Genevieve lowered her gun and eased forward just as another pointer shot to where Jax stood, statue-still. Instead of pointing, Rosco, the latecomer, circled around

Jax, barking furiously. Out of the corner of her eye, Genevieve saw Harrington move toward the two dogs. She broke her gun and moved forward, wiping the mist from her eyes. A gun cracked on her far left. She saw a bird drop from the sky and Philip lowered his shotgun. So engrossed were the other shooters with a covey of grouse flushed from their nests, they didn't seem to notice what was going on just down the line.

Nearly at Sean's side, Genevieve whispered, "What do you think's going on with the dogs?"

"A dead animal, maybe a fox." He drew his lower lip over his teeth, emitted a shrill whistle, and the dogs instantly heeled. "Stay," he said and strode to where Jax and Rosco had been focusing their attention, with Genevieve right behind him. He stopped so abruptly that Genevieve smashed into his rock-hard back. "What is it?" she gasped, trying to recover the air he had knocked out of her.

"Stay back, Lady Crosswick." He spread his arms wide so she couldn't get past. Even on her tiptoes, she couldn't see over his shoulder.

"Sean, what is it?" she asked again, her voice brittle with growing concern.

"It's a body, my lady." He squatted and reached towards the body, pausing for a moment before he felt the carotid artery. "I'm afraid she's dead."

Desperate to see, Genevieve stretched over Harrington's back as he knelt on the ground, nearly knocking him over. Though the woman's blonde hair was matted with blood and the face distorted by the early stages of rigor mortis, Genevieve still recognized the once-elegant profile. That and her black cashmere coat confirmed without a doubt that Angelina Hauffman, the former Baroness von Bassewitz who had exploded into the dining room last night and made a dramatic scene, was dead on the moor.

CHAPTER 5

IN THE TWO short years since Philip and Genevieve became the Lord and Lady of the House of Crosswick and its massive responsibilities, this was the third time emergency medical teams had raced down the long Wilmingrove Hall allée and Yorkshire police had swarmed the estate's grounds.

Far too often, Genevieve thought. *To say nothing of what's happened at Chateau Beaulieu. Will we ever be free from mayhem?*

Philip's cool palm squeezed the back of her neck. Their eyes met—his clear, the corners crinkled with fatigue, hers misty with emotion. She nestled into the crook of his shoulder and he pressed his lips to the top of her head. They watched together as the coroner's van crunched its way down the gravel-covered lane away from the grand house, until it slowed to a stop before moving onto the road to York.

Genevieve heaved a sigh of exhaustion and burrowed deeper

into Philip's solid chest. She never wanted to leave the safety of his strength. For a moment, she didn't think they could possibly face what was coming next, but when Philip gave her a last squeeze, she knew it was time to muster their courage and press on. She looked up at her husband. They shared a sad smile, eased apart and, intertwining fingers, walked into the Hall.

A uniformed officer stood guard just inside the massive oak front door that opened into the grand salon. The pleasure Genevieve normally felt when she entered their generational family home was supplanted by a sense of dread for what might be discovered about the death of Angelina Antonia Hauffman. Did she die of a tragic accident or did someone murder her on their estate?

Bustling across the vast reception room, Mrs. MacIntosh, Wilmingrove Hall's head housekeeper, made a beeline for Philip and Genevieve. "Lord and Lady Crosswick," she said, her voice strained by the onslaught of unexpected people in the house. "What shall we do with all these officers? No one has told me and Elsie is asking me questions I cannot answer. Do they need to be fed? Wallace is anxious to know how long the Hall will be in a state of disruption. He's concerned the police are not respectful enough of the furnishings and they are leaving dirty footprints everywhere."

In spite of the gloom that hung over the house, Genevieve couldn't help but smile. A woman was dead and Mrs. MacIntosh and Wallace were most concerned about their duties and the state of the house for which they were responsible. It was so typical of their dedication. More than once they had proven that they would never let Philip and Genevieve down and they were doing it yet again.

Grateful for the distraction, Genevieve took Mrs. MacIntosh by the shoulder, spun her around and they headed to the kitchen. "Philip, if you need me I'll be with Elsie figuring out how to feed all these officers," she said over her shoulder.

"And I'm going down to the mews. I'm meeting with Andrew.

As Genevieve and Mrs. MacIntosh walked into the hall, DCI Cecil Fields emerged from Philip's study. "Lady Crosswick." His eyes filled with warmth and he extended his hand.

"Ah, DCI Fields." She turned to the housekeeper. "Mrs. MacIntosh, I'll be in the kitchen in a minute." When she turned back to Fields, her smile sparkled into her eyes. "I didn't know you were here." She grasped his hand in both of hers and felt oddly comforted that he was still rumpled and disheveled, his thinning hair sticking out in all directions, just as she had remembered. "I feel so much better knowing you're in charge." She paused. "You are in charge, aren't you?"

"I am, my lady. It looks like you and the Earl are up to your old tricks." His chuckle was followed by a phlegmy cough.

"And it sounds to me, Cecil, as if you're still smoking."

He shrugged. "What can I say?"

"I thought when you were here two years ago investigating Sir David's incident, Philip convinced you to stop."

"And I did," he said, his eyes wide and innocent.

Genevieve squinted. "For how long?" she asked, suspicion dripping from her words.

"Until I left Wilmingrove Hall that day."

They shared a laugh and Genevieve squeezed the detective's shoulder. "Behave yourself." Noticing a spot of food on his tie, she grinned and shook her head. "Obviously, Cecil, anything Philip and I can do to get to the bottom of the former Baroness's death, we're anxious to do. We're hoping it was a terrible accident." She watched his pale grey eyes for any clue but he gave her nothing.

"I'm sure you can appreciate that we will be gathering information from all your guests for the next couple of days. Thank you for the use of the Hall. It's much more comfortable for everyone to answer questions here than at the station."

"Of course." Genevieve nodded. "Anything you need, just ask. Now, let me go organize a buffet for all your people. We want them to keep up their strength, don't we?"

As Genevieve left DCI Fields and headed to the kitchen, she marveled at how his messy, bumbling demeanor belied his keen intelligence and his sharp deductive skills, and was relieved that he was in charge.

When she pushed through the kitchen doors, she was startled by the chaos swirling around her. Elsie Lomax, the head cook, barked orders at Lottie and Claire, her two helpers. Mrs. MacIntosh stood by the back door, wringing her hands as she watched Wallace and Sean Harrington argue about what happened the previous evening when the former Baroness burst into the dining room.

"Wallace! She was absolutely pissed. She was so plastered she fell down."

Pulling to his full height and using his most stilted diction, Wallace said, "Mr. Harrington, I would appreciate if you wouldn't use vulgarities in these hallowed halls. I do not believe the previous Baroness von Bassewitz was inebriated. I believe she was extremely angry but perfectly clear-headed when she said she had come to tell Lord Crosswick about the Baron's murderous family, wasn't she?"

Sean bit his lower lip. "I suppose you're right about that." He plopped down on a stool next to the marble-covered island in the middle of the room. "What do you suppose she meant by that?"

"That's a very good question," Genevieve said, startling everyone. Elsie stopped yelling at the kitchen staff. Harrington jumped off the stool and almost stood at attention. No one had noticed her standing in the kitchen watching the bedlam and nearly everyone flushed with embarrassment as Lady Crosswick finished, saying, "A question I hope will be answered over the next couple of days."

Always composed, Wallace was the only one who changed nothing. He still stood erect and looked noble. "I'm so sorry, my lady, for all the chaos here in the kitchen. The staff is a little out of sorts and trying to make some sense of what happened last night and earlier today.

"Of course, Wallace." Genevieve laid her hand on his arm, comforted by the feel of his sturdy wool sleeve. "This sort of thing seems to happen to us a bit too often, doesn't it?"

"It is certainly through no fault of your own, my lady." Elsie was emphatic.

"Thank you, Elsie. It's very kind of you to say." She gave the cook a smile of thanks then clapped her hands and said, "Okay, everyone. It appears that for the next two or three days,

Wilmingrove Hall will be the center of the investigation into Angelina Hauffman's death. In an effort to make everything run smoothly I think we should set up a buffet in the dining room for breakfast, lunch and tea." She noticed Wallace's forehead furrow. "Wallace, do you have other thoughts?"

He hesitated.

"Please, Wallace. What are you thinking?"

With Genevieve's nudge, he was off and running. "Well, my lady. I don't expect most of these… um, police officers are used to being in a stately home and I'm just concerned that we protect all the treasures in the house. I mean, can you imagine if one of them put a wet glass on a Hepplewhite sideboard?" His eyes flashed wide as if he had been slapped.

Genevieve struggled not to laugh. "I suppose you're right, Wallace," she said, coughing to disguise a giggle. "I'm sure you have an idea. Where would you suggest we set up food for these good people?"

Without missing a beat, he said, "I think we should set up food right here in the kitchen, on the island."

"What!" Elsie's voice was several octaves higher than normal. "Absolutely not, Wallace. I'm not going to have people in and out and in and out of my kitchen all day. That is not going to happen." Her face flushed so red she looked sunburned.

Genevieve felt her phone vibrate in her pocket and glanced at the screen. "Philip needs me," she said to the room, not expecting anyone to notice when she left. "I'm sure you'll all be able to sort this out and whatever you decide will be perfect."

Glad to make her exit, Genevieve strode to the library.

When she entered, DCI Fields and Philip were deep in solemn conversation.

"I thought you were going to the mews," she said to Philip.

"I was but Cecil sidetracked me." Philip patted the loveseat next to him and she sat. She felt his firm thigh against hers and squeezed his knee.

"So what is it?" she said, sensing the news wasn't good.

"You tell her, Cecil."

Philip nodded at Fields just as the officer plucked a cookie from a plate in front of him and popped it into his mouth. He chewed as quickly as he could, swallowed, then began. "These coconut shortbreads are delicious." As he spoke, crumbs sprayed from his mouth down the front of his rumpled jacket, a few clinging to his lips.

"They are, aren't they? They're one of Mrs. Lomax's specialties." Genevieve laughed out loud, amused that, in the middle of the investigation of a death, this seasoned detective was smitten with Elsie's cookies. "I'll let her know you like them. Now, what is it you were going to tell me? What's the news?"

"I just got a call from the coroner."

Genevieve's stomach clutched. "That was fast."

"It didn't take long for them to determine that Angelina Hauffman died of a single bullet entering through her forehead," he pointed to his hairline, "and exiting through the cranial floor." He tapped the back of his head where the skull met his spine.

Philip covered Genevieve's hand with his and pressed it into his knee. Her leg vibrated against his. When he looked at her, he saw she was struggling to keep tears from streaming down her cheeks. She swiped her eyes with the back of her hand then asked in a shaky voice, "Did the medical examiner have a time of death?"

"She estimated the time of death between 8:00 and 9:30 last night."

"Hmm," Genevieve hummed, feeling her composure return as she began to analyze the events of the previous night. "She left the dining room at 8:15." "Do you remember, Philip? The clock struck the quarter hour as Freddie took Angelina out of the Hall?"

"I do. That means she was killed soon after she left us."

"Exactly," the detective confirmed. "But the strangest thing about the gunshot wound. The angle at which the bullet entered was above the Baroness." He held the tip of his pen on his forehead and angled the shaft so it would come out the base of his skull if it traveled through his head. "I'm not at all sure what that means, but our forensic people assure me it's significant."

"Have you talked to Freddie, Baron von Bassewitz, yet?" Genevieve couldn't imagine he had anything to do with Angelina's death but the Baron was one of the last people to see her alive.

"Our best interviewer is with him now." Fields was anxious to join the young interrogator. "In fact, I need to get in there. I'm interested to hear what he has to say."

"Yeah. I think we'll all be interested to hear what he says," Philip mumbled.

Deep in thought, Genevieve stared out of the tall library windows without seeing.

"What is it, G?" Philip said.

"I was just going over everything that happened last night in the dining room. Angelina came in then Freddie took her out. I was thinking no one else left the table but that's not true, is it?"

"It isn't? Philip stared back at Genevieve. "Ah, you're right," he said after a second. "Andrew got an alert that something was going on at the mews. But, G, he was back within half an hour. I hardly think he's a suspect."

Curious, Fields said, "Was there a problem with one of the birds?"

"No. Andrew said it was a technical glitch. He rebooted and got everything back online." Philip snapped his fingers and stood. "That reminds me. I've got to get down there. I told Andrew I'd meet with him shortly." He kissed the top of Genevieve's head, nodded at DCI Fields and was out the door.

CHAPTER 6

EVERY ROOM AT Wilmingrove Hall buzzed with police interviewers questioning each guest and every person on the Wilmingrove Hall staff. The news that Angelina's death was a murder unnerved everyone and the versions of her uninvited presence at the house were as varied as the tellers. Some said she was falling-down drunk. Others said she was sober as a judge. Some said she socked Wallace in the nose and drew blood when he tried to keep her from entering the dining room. Wallace insisted, though her fists were flailing about, she missed him by a mile. Some said the Baron dragged the ex-Baroness out of the Hall by her hair and others insisted he was the perfect gentleman, kind and courteous as he ushered her to her Jaguar. The only thing the staff agreed on was that there was a dog in the Jaguar who barked the entire time the Baroness was in the house. The only dinner guest who heard the dog was the Baron, who encountered the yapping Maltese when he escorted Angelina to her car. Dinner guests and staff all agreed the Baron was gone no more than ten minutes. Wallace had watched from the front door as the Baron waited for his ex-wife to lower the top on her car before she drove down the lane and turned onto the main road. After his return, the Baron didn't leave the dining room again until eleven o'clock when he and his current wife said their good nights. It was, the police concluded, highly unlikely—if not impossible—that Baron von Bassewitz killed the former Baroness.

And so it went hour after hour until by nine-thirty the last of the interviews was over, DCI Fields and his crew had left the house, and guests and staff had retired, exhausted from the emotion of the past twenty-four hours.

Philip and Genevieve climbed the stairs and made it to their room with barely an ounce of energy left between them. Jade leather walls surrounded them in quiet luxury. Each fluted bedpost on their four-poster bed pushed ten feet towards a coffered ceiling, light glancing off the goldleaf burnished into the mahogany. The linen sheets had been turned down over the pale green silk duvet and were waiting for the exhausted couple to snuggle under the deep pile of bedding. Plumped against the headboard, down pillows waited to cradle weary heads.

Dragging out of the bathroom, Philip ruffled his damp hair with a thick white towel.

"What did DCI Fields ask you?" Genevieve said fragrant from the shower. Sitting at her dressing table, she opened a jar of cream that smelled of lavender and marjoram and dotted her freshly washed face with the thick moisturizer.

"Before we talk about that, I have something to tell you that is not going to make you happy."

Genevieve turned from her dressing table mirror to look at Philip, slumped in an overstuffed chair by the dwindling fire, eyelids drooping. She knew that tone and braced herself for more news she was not going to like. "What is it?"

"It's about Andrew Frasier."

"What about Andrew?"

"He's leaving."

"What do you mean he's leaving?" She sat a little straighter.

"I mean he's not going to be our falconer any longer." Philip raised his hand to stop the barrage of questions he knew was coming. "He wants to travel."

"Well that stinks." Genevieve stuck out her lower lip in a full blown pout. "I thought he'd be here forever. This is absurd, so sudden."

Philip gave her a sympathetic smile. "Genevieve, he's young and wants to experience life. It'll be fine. We'll find someone even better than Andrew."

"But, Philip." She looked as if she were going to cry.

He knelt by her and wrapped her in a hug. "I know you and the our grandchildren think he's magical." He held her at arm's length and knuckled away the lone tear trailing down her cheek.

Genevieve turned back to her mirror, saw her face wrinkled into a scowl and sighed at the thought of Andrew leaving them. "I really can't believe he's leaving so abruptly," she mumbled and patted the remaining cream onto her cheekbones massaging her face with gentle upward strokes.

Philip stood and pulled on his bathrobe. "Now, back to your

question of what DCI Fields asked me. He asked how long we've known Freddie, did we know Angelina, where did we meet, were we close friends, had he been to Wilmingrove Hall before, had he been here to shoot—you know, that sort of thing."

"Did he ask you if you had ever given Freddie a tour of the estate?"

He shook his head. "No, but it sounds like that's a question he asked you."

"He did."

"And what did you say?" he asked, one eyebrow raised.

"I told him to talk to Sean. Didn't he send Freddie a drone tour of the grouse moors last spring to show to his shooting club?"

Nothing registered, then a light began to dawn and Philip cocked his head. "I think you're right. I vaguely remember Harrington mentioning he had done that. Didn't Freddie want to bring his club here for a shoot?"

"I'm surprised you've forgotten. As I remember it, you were pretty emphatic with Sean that you weren't interested in having groups here. I think your words were something like, 'I don't want a bunch of gun-happy lager louts crawling all over Wilmingrove Hall.'"

"That sounds like something I would have said." Philip pulled a log from the copper wood box and tossed it onto the fire's glowing embers. He stabbed at it twice with the poker and the fire danced to life. Drained by the day's events, he slumped back into his chair, crossed his long, elegant legs and drained the last splash of scotch left in the bottom of his crystal tumbler. "I have to say, Freddie has been a real surprise this time. He's a different person than I've seen before."

Genevieve left her dressing table stool and walked to the revived fire, holding her hands to the warmth. "I was thinking exactly the same thing last night. I was having such fun and a delightful conversation with him until Angelina appeared. The whole thing is just so strange. And what in the world was she talking about when she said she came to tell you about his murderous family?" She snuggled into the down-filled wing chair opposite Philip and pulled her legs up under her.

"I wonder what Fields is thinking. There's no way Freddie could have been responsible for Angelina's death. He was with us the entire evening. And how in the world did she get all the way up to the grouse moor? It's at least a mile from here."

"It's actually two-and-a-half miles." He rolled his empty glass between his hands then set it on the table beside his chair. "Where is her car and where is her little dog?"

Genevieve straightened her legs out in front of her, reached her arms over her head, stretched from her fingertips to her toes then collapsed. "I would kill for a massage right now." Realizing what she'd said, she slapped her hand over her mouth. "Bad choice of words."

She heard the faint strains of La Marseillaise, the French national anthem, and watched Philip pull his cell phone from his robe pocket. He looked at her. "Speak of the devil, it's Fields," he said and noted that it was 10:45.

Genevieve groaned at the prospect of a conversation with the officer, as Philip tapped "Accept" and put the phone to his ear.

"Cecil?"

"Lord Crosswick. I'm sorry to call so late but I think you're going to want to hear what we've discovered."

"That's quite all right, Chief Inspector. I'm putting you on speaker so be careful, Genevieve's listening."

"Good evening, my lady."

Genevieve smiled at the phone sitting on the table between Philip and her. "It's been a long day for you, Cecil."

"It has, but I thought this was important, so here we are."

She could hear him take a drag on what she assumed was a cigarette, then exhale. She envisioned smoke clouding from his nose and mouth and nearly coughed.

"Today, while part of our team interviewed all of the guests and each of the Hall staff, the other officers were on the moor searching the area where the former Baroness was killed. They were also looking for the dog and the Baroness's Jaguar. Late this evening, they found the car about three-quarters of a mile from where the Baroness was found. And the puppy was asleep in the front seat." Philip and Genevieve could hear him take another drag on his smoke. "He was filthy and matted and there were muddy pawprints on the side of the door that would indicate that he'd jumped back into the car. My lads think it's probable that, as the Baroness was driving along with the top down, the dog saw a rabbit, a fox or a deer, and jumped out of the Jag to chase the animal through the field. The Baroness pulled over, got out and ran after her dog. It was dark. The dog went one way, she went the other. They got separated. He eventually returned to the car. She did not."

Genevieve leaned toward the cell phone on the table, her elbow on her knee, her chin on her fist. "That's an interesting theory. How plausible do you think it is?"

Fields cleared his throat before he answered. "I like it," he said. "It explains why she was on the grouse moor but it certainly doesn't shed any light on the strange angle of the bullet or who the shooter was."

"Ah, yes, two small details." Philip picked up his glass and walked to the small chest next to the fireplace. "Are you confident that the person who murdered Angelina isn't here, at the Hall?" He raised his voice to be certain he could be heard. He splashed two fingers of Macallan 18 into his glass, held up an empty glass toward Genevieve, raising his brows in question. She nodded and he gave her a generous pour.

"We're still reviewing some of the interviews so I can't yet tell you with absolute certainty no one at Wilmingrove Hall was involved. I will say, however, it looks very unlikely that anyone associated with the House of Crosswick had anything to do with Angelina Hauffman's death."

Genevieve took a sip of her scotch. "So, Cecil, do you think by tomorrow our guests will be free to leave?"

"Since we have everyone's information and no guest is under suspicion, there's really no reason to keep any of them here. And, of course, all the staff live here at Wilmingrove Hall so if we need to ask them any further questions, we know where to find them. I'll be back tomorrow morning to wrap up everything. After that they're free to go."

"That's good news, Cecil. It will be nice to have everyone gone and the house to ourselves again." Philip smiled at Genevieve as she blew a puff of air from her cheeks. "I suppose you'll have people on the moor for a while, won't you?"

"We will. I'll let you know when it's no longer considered a crime scene. As you might imagine, we've got to find evidence that will help us solve this puzzle. So far we have found bugger all. Oh shit." Philip and Genevieve heard Fields gasp on the other end of the line then there was an abrupt silence before he said, "My lady. I'm so sorry. Forgive me."

"That's quite all right, Cecil. I think that's a most appropriate phrase under the circumstances." Genevieve didn't try to keep the amusement out of her voice.

"What I meant to say was we have discovered nothing. No footprints, no foreign fibers, not even the bullet, which makes zero sense. If someone were there to shoot the Baroness, there should be footprints. We know someone shot her, so there should be a bullet casing unless they picked it up. But if they picked it up, where are their footprints? If no one was there to pick up the bullet, then it should be there. At any rate, somebody had to be on the premises to shoot this woman, ergo"—Genevieve chuckled to herself at his use of the Latin word—"they had to leave behind some evidence. But we have found none at this point. Not one scrap."

"I'm certain your police department has drones but if you don't, we have a couple that Andrew Frasier uses for training our birds." Philip wanted to help in any way they could. "Would they be useful in surveying the scene?"

"That might be useful, my lord. I'll check with our tech people in the morning. We need all the help we can get."

Genevieve stifled a yawn then said, "DCI Fields, don't be

discouraged. I'm sure that within the next few days, you will have this mystery wrapped up and tied with a pretty red bow. I'm just relieved that no one at Wilmingrove Hall is a suspect."

"Thank you for your confidence, my lady. By the way, would you ask Mrs. Lomax if I could have the recipe for her coconut shortbreads? Don't tell anyone but I stuffed a few in my pockets before I left this evening. Those biscuits are magic, absolutely brilliant."

"I'll ask her tomorrow, Cecil. Good night."

The moment Philip hit "End," they both burst into laughter.

"What a fitting finale to a strange day." Genevieve stood and arched her back in a stretch. "I'm going to bed."

"Oh, I'm up for that." Philip rubbed his hands together. "I'm right behind you," he said.

"I should have said I'm going to sleep." Genevieve unbuttoned her navy wool robe, slid it seductively down her pajama-clad shoulders and batted her eyelashes.

"We'll see about that," Philip said and swatted her bottom as he walked by. "I seem to have a second wind, how about you?"

She drew the corners of her mouth down and rolled her eyes to the ceiling as if checking to see if she had any energy left. "Hmm, maybe," she said as she jumped onto the bed, giggling, and pulled the covers over her head.

CHAPTER 7

Genevieve felt herself smiling as she wafted from the warmth of a lovely dream toward wakefulness. The memory of last night's playful lovemaking would keep her twinkling throughout the day. After forty-two years of marriage, how could Philip still make her feel like a bride? She giggled and reached for him under the duvet but felt nothing but cold sheets. She forced her left eye open and was surprised to find her watch said 9:07. "Jeepers. The day's practically over," she said to no one, closed her eyes, and made no attempt to get up.

The creaking of the door hinge announced someone's arrival—*Philip,* she assumed. She lay still as a stone, her only movement the twitching of her eyes under her lids. *Maybe he's bringing coffee,* she hoped, just before she smelled the rich aroma.

"Okay, sleeping beauty. Stop faking it. Up time." He was too chipper. He was always too chirpy in the morning. "I come bearing coffee and croissants—English croissants, but croissants nonetheless."

He set the tray on the table in front of the sofa and just as he turned, a pillow thumped into his chest. "What the…? I bring you treasures and this is how you repay me?" He held the pillow over his head, menacing her as he approached the bed with a Frankenstein's monster gait.

"Actually, darling boy, I threw before I thought." She tittered and snorted a giggle as she watched him approach. She tilted her head down á la Diana, Princess of Wales, looked up at him through naturally thick lashes and fluttered them with all the coquettish charm she could muster with her bedhead and unbrushed teeth. He still trod forward. She dove under the covers, curling into a ball, clenching the edge of the duvet in her fist, shrieking with nervous anticipation of what would happen next.

He continued to lumber to her side of the bed, making low groaning noises with each step. When he arrived, he stood and breathed loudly, hoarsely—in, out, in, out. "You must get up." His voice was low, gravelly and his accent Transylvanian.

Paralyzed with suspense, she froze under the covers but couldn't quiet the snigger gurgling in her throat.

"You must get up," he repeated. "People are waiting for you and you must not disappoint them."

She waited but he said no more and nothing happened. Seconds ticked by. When she thought it was safe, her muscles eased and her fist relaxed its grip on the duvet and at that very moment, the covers flew off her fetal form and fell at the foot of the bed. Philip loomed over her. She screamed. He scooped her up and threw her over his shoulder, Genevieve squealing all the while. Continuing his monster stride, he plodded into their bathroom. He opened the door of their marble shower, turned on the side jets and set her down on the marble floor in the stream of cold water, pajamas and all.

"There you go, Lady Crosswick. Special delivery." He put a hand on either side of her face, leaned in and kissed her mouth that was open in a silent scream as she began to shiver from the cold water.

He backed away from the shower, chortling at his wife, her pajamas plastered to her body, her eyes still wide with surprise. She held him in her laser stare as she groped for the faucet lever and turned it from cold to warm. "When you least expect it, I will take my revenge, you wicked man," she called after Philip's retreating back.

He turned and with his most charming smile stretched across his face, said, "I can hardly wait, G. Everyone's gathering in the dining room, cute girl. Hustle up."

And he was gone.

CHAPTER 8

Overnight, a storm had moved in and rain pelted the tall windows looking out over the back terraces and down to the river. Every light and lamp in the dining room bloomed with a warm, yellow glow, so rather than gloomy, the room sparkled as if it were a sunny day.

Except for DCI Fields, Genevieve was the last to arrive. She breezed in looking very much of the nobility, her purple-heather jacket cut to perfection, the waist nipped in and the collar popped. Her taupe twill trousers fit her butt and long legs like a second skin and she felt her color rise when she saw Philip look at her with a lusty smile.

"Good morning, everyone," she said and walked to the sideboard to see what Elsie Lomax and her crew had prepared for breakfast. She salivated at the smell of freshly baked pastries. A bowl of fresh fruit was dotted with mint from the garden. Sautéed tomatoes, grilled mushrooms, sausages and bacon filled a large platter and golden pieces of toast stood like soldiers in a sterling silver toast rack. "I see Mrs. Lomax hasn't spared any calories this morning."

"Guten Morgen, Genevieve." Freddie, waited to see where Genevieve would sit, then made a beeline to hold her chair for her.

"Did everyone sleep well?" She nodded a thank you to the Baron and he returned to his seat. "After yesterday, I bet everyone either slept like a log or couldn't sleep at all."

"Here's a better question: is everyone all right this morning?" Becca asked with a snicker.

"What do you mean?" Genevieve stopped midway through pouring herself a cup of coffee from the silver carafe and frowned at Becca.

Becca glanced across the table at David then the two of them focused back on Genevieve. "Well, we heard a lot of…" Becca looked at David for help.

"We heard a lot of laughing and a couple of screams coming from your room as we were on our way to breakfast."

"Oh, that," Genevieve said. "That started with me miscalculating a pillow throw and ended with Philip depositing me in a cold shower with my pajamas on."

"Are you serious?" Baroness von Bassewitz's mouth gaped in disbelief.

"Completely. Now Philip has to live in fear until I take my revenge," she deadpanned and brought her coffee cup to her lips. Before she drank, she looked at Philip over the rim with wild, crazy eyes. "There's no telling what I might do," she said, then punctuated the threat with her best witch cackle.

Returning from the sideboard with a sausage and muffin, Philip faked a yawn. "You're terrifying, darling." He walked behind her, stopping to pat her on the shoulder and kiss the top of her head.

She squeezed his hand and was down to business. "So what did I miss? Have we heard anything from DCI Fields?"

She'd directed her question to Philip, but David answered: "I spoke to him about an hour ago. Philip and I decided as your solicitor, I should step in."

"Makes sense," she said through a mouthful of croissant, a bit of raspberry preserves oozing out of the corner of her mouth. "Sorry," she said and swept up the red goo with the tip of her tongue. "What did he say?"

"He'll be here." David looked at his watch. "Actually, any minute."

As if on cue, the dining room doors opened and Wallace stood there, regal as ever. "My lord, DCI Fields." He stepped to the side and the officer entered.

Genevieve was certain he was wearing his suit from the previous day and, she feared, the same rumpled shirt. But, she noticed, he had changed his tie.

Philip was out of his chair and across the room in a flash, his hand extended. "Chief Inspector, good morning."

Fields grasped the outstretched hand. "Good morning, my lord." He turned to the group at the table and nodded. "Good morning. I hope everyone was able to get a decent night's sleep after yesterday's long, difficult day." He scratched the top of his head, which, as usual, left a few strands of his wispy hair standing straight up.

Genevieve moved to the buffet and poured coffee into a cup with the House of Crosswick crest on the side. "Cream, sugar, Cecil?" she asked.

"Both, please." He looked grateful at the prospect of a good cup of coffee. It had been a long night, as the shadows under his eyes hinted, and he welcomed anything that would help him get through this meeting with Lord and Lady Crosswick and their lofty guests.

Genevieve brought his coffee to the table and pulled out a chair for him. "Please, DCI Fields, sit."

He eased himself onto the seat next to Lillie Langdon, the beautiful sprite who ran the Crosswick foundation. He recalled her name from the previous day's interview and remembered her vibrant energy. He returned the smile she offered him, hers radiant, his heavy with fatigue.

Genevieve returned with a plate filled with sausages, grilled tomatoes, mushrooms, and two pieces of toast. "Please, Cecil, help yourself to anything on the buffet," she said. "This will get you started." She set the plate in front of him and returned to her seat.

"Chief Inspector," David began. "We're anxious to hear your conclusions from your interviews yesterday. Though most of us didn't know the former Baroness, finding oneself in proximity to death is never a comfortable situation. Can you tell us anything about what you discovered?"

Fields had been shoveling food into his mouth at a rapid pace so it was several long seconds before he could clear his palate and answer. He took a drink of water and wiped his yellow linen napkin across his lips. "Thanks to everyone's cooperation, we've come to several conclusions that I'm happy to share with all of you." He put his wadded napkin next to his plate and took another sip of water. "After interviewing everyone here at Wilmingrove Hall, we have concluded that no one here is a person of interest. As a result, everyone is free to leave whenever you like."

A collective sigh rippled around the table.

"That's excellent news. Michael has meetings in London tomorrow and we need to get back." Gabriel said. "So, DCI Fields, not even my brother is under suspicion?" He leaned forward, put his elbows on the table and left the question hanging in the air for DCI Fields.

Michael shot him a warning glance from across the table. "Gabriel, what are you doing?"

Fields narrowed his eyes at the younger of the two von Bassewitz brothers, glaring at Gabe for a moment before answering. "In your opinion, is there any reason the Baron should be a suspect?" He shifted his gaze to Freddie, then back to Gabriel.

Gabriel sat back in his chair. He pursed his lips and shrugged his shoulders. "Of course not," he said. "I just wondered since he probably was the last person to see Angelina."

"What the hell, Gabriel?" Freddie stood abruptly, slapped his hands on the table and leaned toward his brother. "What is the matter with you? Are you suggesting I killed my ex-wife?"

"Calm down, Freddie." He smirked. "Of course I don't think

you killed Angelina. I just think it's interesting the police don't suspect you. I mean, honestly, Freddie. You had every reason to want her dead. She really was a bitch to you." He looked at Heidi. "Am I not right, Heidi?"

With her jaw clenching and unclenching, the stunning blonde chose her iciest glare and frostiest voice. "Gabriel, why do you always choose to be such a kleines Stück Scheiße?" Her voice softened, regretting that she had called him a little piece of shit. "You know better than anyone, your brother is one of the kindest men on the planet. He has shown you that many, many times. He could never hurt anyone, much less someone he once loved."

Captivated by the exchange, the others around the table watched the back-and-forth as if it were a play and the three people speaking were actors. The tension was palpable. Eyes wide, mouths closed, the onlookers wondered what would come next.

"All right. That's enough, Mr. von Bassewitz." Fields sat as tall as he could in his chair. "Your brother is not under suspicion. If you have any evidence that he *should* be and you do not present that information, or you lied during your interview, you could possibly be arrested, prosecuted and potentially imprisoned. Do you have any such information?"

Gabriel raised his hands chest-high, palms out. "I do not. I was just teasing my brother. I guess the joke was not so funny." He tilted his head. "Freddie, forgive me. I am sorry."

The Baron balled his napkin and threw it across the table at his brother. "Arschloch!" he said, shaking his head and allowing the corners of his mouth to draw up as he called his brother an asshole.

Anxious to get on with his presentation, DCI Fields stood,

which made him feel more in command. As he walked around the room, he shared the theory of how and why Angelina was on the grouse moor and posed the conundrum of how she was shot and who shot her.

"Last night we had no bullet but this morning we do," he told his rapt audience. "It was found deep in the soil just behind where the ex-Baroness fell. With the aid of metal detectors we were able to locate it."

He studied the carpet. "Even if we work backwards and find the owner of the gun, how did he or she commit this murder without leaving any footprints or tire tracks? Nothing disturbed the ground." He seemed to be talking to himself. Everyone watched as he lumbered to the windows. He stood looking out for what seemed a very long time. At last he turned back to the room. "You see my dilemma?" he asked the room.

Everyone nodded and waited for him to speak again. "I'm stymied. We're all stymied. It's like this poor, sad, angry lady is thrown out of a lovely dinner party, goes out on the moor to chase her dog who's chasing a fox. They lose each other, then an alien flies by and shoots her in the head. We'll never find the alien because it sped back to Tatooine at warp speed."

Everyone sat spellbound.

"You see my problem. That is the only explanation I can come up with but it isn't quite plausible, is it?"

No one responded.

Fields's gaze searched from person to person. "I'm really asking," he said, "is this explanation at all possible? Because I can't come up with anything else."

A hush settled over the room, the crackling fire the only sound.

At last Becca's voice cut through the silence. "What about an assassin bird? Harpy eagles can be vicious."

All heads whipped around, everyone focusing on her to see if she was serious. Her stony face couldn't conceal her laughing eyes. "Well," she said, "it's every bit as likely as aliens from Tatooine, don't you think?"

"Very clever, Lady Weatherington. I'll certainly take that under advisement." He went to the sideboard, plucked a bite-sized sausage roll off the platter and began to walk slowly around the table, pausing behind one person's chair or another. He stopped behind the Baron, popped the roll in his mouth, chewed, and swallowed. "There is one more thing our forensic people discovered late yesterday that you might be able to help me with." He pushed a crumb from his lip into his mouth. "They found a planner in the Baroness's car. On her calendar, she'd made an entry for this coming Monday at ten o'clock. It's simply marked 'SY'. Would any of you have an idea what that might mean?"

"Mein Gott, it could be anything," Heidi said. "It could be her stylist, her masseuse, ein Freund she's meeting for coffee. The list could be endless."

Having arrived back at his chair, Fields plopped back down beside Lillie and took a gulp of coffee. "Exactly," he said. "But I thought it would be worth asking. If anything occurs to you, please give me a call. You each have my card."

CHAPTER 9

W ITH HIS ARM around her, Philip squeezed Genevieve as close as possible so the umbrella he held would cover them both. The storm front that had moved in yesterday during the shoot had settled in overnight and showed no signs of departing, but much to their relief, their guests were. The last to leave, the Baron and Baroness lingered in the rain even though Philip and Genevieve did their best to usher them on their way.

"So you'll come to us at the chalet in Lech the first week in December. That's just a few weeks away." He seemed unbothered by the sheeting rain. "I regret that David and Becca can't join us but am pleased that Lillie and Finn can be there. And of course, Gabe. Too bad Michael has to be in New York. You know his new product could be extraordinary in our Berlin museum. Let's hope his meeting with his patent attorneys goes well. With Papa coming, we can talk seriously about the museum. And maybe we can give you a specific commitment—when we're not on the slopes." His smile bared his white teeth.

While Freddie stood in the pouring rain confirming ski holiday plans with Philip and Genevieve, Heidi kissed both their cheeks, gave each of them a hug, and slid onto the front seat of the Mercedes-Benz AMG GT 63, its copper-orange mango color so intense it shone through the dreary day like a beacon. "Freddie, steig ins auto. Get in the car," she ordered him.

"It's on the calendar, Freddie. We look forward to it." Genevieve linked her arm through his and ushered him to the driver's side, with Philip covering her with the umbrella as best he could. "As Heidi said, get in the car before you drown." Before he let her hand go, Freddie brought it to his lips. She wiggled her fingers from his palm, took a step back, waited for him to pull his leg into the car, then slammed the door after him.

Immediately, the window eased down. "Vielen Dank für eure Hilf. Thank you so much for your kindness and all your help." Though his thanks were for both his hosts, his eyes were only for Genevieve. "I am so sorry for the dreadful business of Angelina. I hope you are not inconvenienced too much in the days to come, with the police still on the moor."

Philip shook his head. "It'll be fine, Freddie. I have every confidence that DCI Fields and his team will figure out how Angelina was killed and who killed her. Roll up your window. You're getting soaked."

Finally, Freddie blew a kiss to Genevieve, rolled up his window, and the elegant automobile backed up and headed down the allée. Philip and Genevieve trotted up the wide stairs, through the front door, and closed the massive oak slab with a satisfying thud. Damp, chilly, and exhausted, they leaned against the door, their eyes closed in relief. At last they were alone.

"Well you two, it looks like you need to change into some dry clothes and have some hot soup and a stiff drink."

"Oh, good lord!" Genevieve's eyes flew open and her hand slapped to her chest to keep her heart from jumping out. "Mrs. MacIntosh! You startled me."

Philip winked at Mrs. MacIntosh and she smiled back.

"So sorry, my lady. That certainly wasn't my intention." The housekeeper was already walking away. "A little table has been set by the fire in the conservatory. A light lunch will be served in half an hour."

"I guess we have our marching orders, don't we?" Philip couldn't think of anything nicer than a rainy afternoon and lunch by the fire, just the two of them.

Genevieve strode across the grand salon toward the staircase. "I can't wait to get out of these wet clothes," she said over her shoulder and was halfway up the stairs before Philip caught up to her. "I didn't think Freddie would ever leave, did you?"

"He has quite a crush on you, doesn't he?"

"What?" Genevieve stopped, her hand on the banister and her foot on a riser, mid-step. "What are you talking about?"

"Oh, come on." Philip swatted her bottom as he passed her on the stairs. "Surely you noticed the entire time he was here he was fawning all over you."

"Philip, that's ridiculous." They hit the top stair at the same time. "Freddie's young enough to be my son—*our* son."

"So? What's your point? You know the saying, 'The heart wants what the heart wants?'"

She rolled her eyes and charged ahead of her husband down the hall and into their bedroom. She marched straight into her dressing room, pulling off her Harris tweed jacket that now had more of a wet-doggy smell than its usual rich, earthy aroma. She sat on her step stool and peeled her soggy twill trousers down her legs, tugging them over her feet. What she really wanted to do was crawl back into bed, pull the covers over her head and pretend that everything that had happened over the last two days was nothing but a bad dream, a nightmare.

When she looked up, Philip stood in her doorway wearing his oldest, softest jeans, pulling a sweatshirt over his head.

"Ooooh. That's perfect," she sighed. "Jeans and a comfy top. Cozy, cozy, cozy."

"Isn't that a little dramatic?" he laughed.

"No, silly." She threw her wet jacket at him. He made no attempt to catch it. It hit his chest and fell to the floor.

"Careful. You know what happened the last time you threw something at me." He shook a finger in her direction.

"I do. Sorry." She bent down, snatched up the jacket, eased it onto a padded hanger and hung it on a valet rod to dry. "This is much too nice to be throwing at you anyway." She gave him a flirty smile and bent over to pick up the slacks she had dropped to the floor.

Philip watched as she tidied her damp clothes then pulled on a pair of faded boyfriend jeans and shoved a tartan flannel shirt into the waistband.

"I had a thought," she said.

Philip groaned. "That's never good"

"Very funny."

"What's your thought, pretty girl?"

"As I was saying before I was so rudely interrupted, I was thinking. All the other times we've been involved with a murder—" As she talked, she shoved her hands into the sleeves of a navy sweater and raised it to her head. "—the murders have involved us in some fashion." Her head went into the depths of the sweater and popped out the top of the turtleneck.

"What do you mean?" Not understanding, Philip's forehead wrinkled.

She ran her hands over her hair to tame the static electricity. "Since we became Lord and Lady Crosswick, we've been in a vortex of murders, attempted murders, fraud, theft, an endless string of events. This, my friend, is the first crime that has absolutely nothing to do with us. No one killed or tried to kill us or anyone we love. So that's a good thing, right?"

"Oh, my darling. I wish you hadn't said that." Philip puffed his cheeks and blew the air out. "Why in the world would you say that? It's like the minute you say you haven't been sick for years, you're going to get the worst case of the flu you've ever had in your life."

Genevieve sat back down on her step stool, put her elbows on her knees, and cradled her head in her hands. "Yikes! You're right. I take it back. I take it back!"

Philip slowly shook his head. "Too late, G. Too late," he said.

CHAPTER 10

"Mrs. MacIntosh, have you seen my black Bogner ski jacket?" Usually an organized and efficient traveler, as she packed for their four-day ski trip to the von Bassewitzes' baronial chalet in Lech, Austria, Genevieve could find nothing.

Perhaps it was because she really didn't want to go. Leaving Wilmingrove Hall just as Christmas preparations shifted into high gear was the last thing she wanted to do. Granted, it was only for a few days and was critical in securing the donation from the von Bassewitz family that would help turn the Musée des Beaux Arts, Berlin from dream to reality. But still, she wanted to be here draping pine boughs up and down the stairs, unpacking and admiring the hundreds of ornaments collected by generations of Crosswicks, helping Elsie Lomax plan menus, drinking hot cider, and sitting by the fire writing personal notes on the few Christmas cards she and Philip still sent.

"Buck up, Genevieve," she said to herself. "When did you turn into such a simpering wimp?"

"What did you say, my lady?" Mrs. MacIntosh walked out of Philip's dressing room carrying a black ski jacket with a red lightning bolt emblazoned across the front.

Genevieve's eyes flashed wide. "You found it! My favorite jacket. Where was it, Mrs. MacIntosh?"

"It was in with Lord Crosswick's ski clothes. I suppose it has been there since the ski apparel went to the dry cleaner's last spring."

"Aren't you clever to think of looking in Philip's things. When I wear that lightning bolt, I can ski so fast." She yanked the plastic off the jacket, took it off the hanger, and slipped her arms into the sleeves. She tugged it up around her shoulders, then hooked the bottom of the zipper and slid it almost to the top. As she walked to the cheval glass, she flipped up her hood. All of a sudden, a prick of excitement caught her by surprise. "Maybe this won't be so bad," she said. "Maybe it will even be fun."

"You'll have a wonderful time, my lady. And when you get back next week, we'll have everything in place so you can put the finishing touches to the decorations."

"How's it going in here?" Philip's flushed cheeks and sweaty forehead suggested he had been two floors down in the gym, working out.

"Well, aren't you the poster boy for fit and fine!" Genevieve sidled up to him, put a hand on his soggy T-shirt, and planted a kiss on his moist lips. She screwed up her face. "Ew! How can somebody so yummy be so yucky? Go shower, will you please?"

"Mrs. MacIntosh." Philip turned to the head housekeeper, arms out, beaconing a hug. "You won't reject me, will you? I've been working so hard to keep myself appealing for all the women under my roof. Surely you can—"

The commanding Scot cut him off. "Surely you can peel those disgusting clothes off and get in the shower as Lady Crosswick suggested." She started to leave then turned around. "And don't put those wet, smelly togs in the basket. Leave them on the bathroom floor for Lottie. She'll pick them up and put them directly into the wash." She turned around. "Poor Lottie," she mumbled as she pulled the bedroom door closed. "I hope she brings tongs."

"I think you just received a verbal spanking. What do you think?"

"Bertie MacIntosh would have made a good clan chief. She's tough as gorse."

"I love that about her. She's certainly not afraid of you, is she?" Realizing she was roasting, Genevieve unzipped her jacket and threw it on the bed. "Are you taking your tux?"

Philip pulled his T-shirt over his head. "Hard to imagine putting on a tux right now," he said, smelling his shirt and wrinkling his nose. "I guess I should toss one in, shouldn't I? There's no telling what kind of evenings Heidi will organize. From all reports, their chalet isn't just a charming little ski lodge. It's more of a baronial castle."

"If you're a descendant of the Habsburgs, no matter how far removed, I would imagine your ski-in-ski-out residence is more than a log cabin."

Philip stood naked in the center of the room, showing no signs of moving toward the bathroom and into a hot shower. Even knowing his body as well as she knew her own, Genevieve couldn't help admiring his well-toned physique, broad shoulders and long, tapering legs—a result of a lifetime of serious swimming.

He winked at her, enjoying the fact that he could still catch her eye. "You can't tell me you haven't googled their little ski hut, Schloss Friedrichstein?" he teased.

Dragging her lusty look from Philip, she walked back into her closet to search for more clothes to pack. "Well, I'd be lying if I said I hadn't sneaked a peek online." She looked back at Philip then took out a cashmere sweater and laid it carefully in her Tumi suitcase. "It makes our little properties look quaint."

"Damn," he said and headed to the shower. "I'll take a tux."

CHAPTER 11

WITH THEIR SIX suitcases filled with skiwear, casualwear, eveningwear, and their skis, boots, and poles tucked in the belly of their Bombardier 6000, Philip and Genevieve agreed this trip was a long ride for a short slide. But if they were successful in getting funding for the Laney Musée des Beaux Arts, Berlin as well as a commitment from the von Bassewitzes to donate their collection of German Expressionist paintings to the museum, it would all be worth it. And, they were anxious to learn more about Michael's patent, new technology that might revolutionize the experience for museum-goers. What a boon it could be for their new Berlin museum. The more Genevieve thought about it, the more buoyed she became. If everything came to fruition, it would be an extraordinary trip. If nothing came to fruition, the skiing would still be excellent.

She clicked her seatbelt just as William, dressed in his navy-blue uniform, set a flute of Champagne in front of her.

"Ooooh. Thank you, William. Just what I had in mind."

"My pleasure, Lady Crosswick." He turned to Philip and placed a glass on the table next to Philip's leather-covered armchair. "My lord," he said. "I'll bring hot hors d'oeuvres as soon as they're ready."

"It can't be too soon. I'm famished." Genevieve reached toward Philip with her glass. "Here's to wrenching two hundred million euros from the posh pockets of the von Bassewitz family." They touched rims and she eased back into her chair, closed her eyes and took a sip, enjoying the bubbles tickling her nose. "I hope this trip is going to be worth the effort."

"It's a good thing Lillie and Finn are joining us. If anybody can close the deal, Lillie can do it. We've seen her pry millions of euros out of the pockets of the most miserly patrons imaginable, haven't we?"

Genevieve nodded. "I would not want to be the one in Lillie's crosshairs when she sets her sights on a donor."

He drained his Champagne glass and put it back on the table. "Remember the first party we gave in Paris? That night she announced four French bankers had committed to giving a million euros each to our foundation's education fund, not just once, but on a recurring basis. And they were grateful to her for taking their money."

Genevieve chuckled at the memory and smiled a grateful smile as William returned, a bottle of Veuve Clicquot in one hand and a silver tray of hot morsels in the other. "Just in time," she said. "My glass is empty and I was about to faint from hunger."

"I'm glad I could come to the rescue." He beamed at Genevieve.

"I'll keep a better eye on those Champagne glasses, I promise."

Philip nodded. "You don't want to face Lady Crosswick's wrath if her glass goes empty again, do you?"

"Certainly not, my lord. I am British, you know. We have quite a tradition of heads rolling and I do not want to be separated from mine." He topped off the glasses and a cheeky grin showed the gap between his front teeth. "Is there anything else I can get you?"

"Genevieve?" Philip said.

"Just a smooth flight and a quick return home."

"I'll do my best, my lady."

"Thank you, William."

"He's a darling kid, isn't he?" Genevieve leaned forward and whispered as William returned to the galley and closed the pocket door.

"Absolutely darling," Philip mimicked her, and in return she blew him a raspberry.

"Changing the subject, have we gotten any leads on a new falconer? I still can't believe Andrew Frasier left us. I thought he was really happy at Wilmingrove Hall."

"Genevieve." Philip covered her hand with his. "Don't take it personally. He's young and wants to travel, so good for him."

"All true, but I hate that Alex and Ella were so sad."

"They'll be fine. It's you, Lillie, and Becca I'm worried about. I guarantee our next falconer will not look like Andrew Frasier. Even I thought he was a hunk."

"Oh my god!" Genevieve flapped her hand in front of her face as if she were going to faint and they shared a laugh.

"Lord and Lady Crosswick, please make certain your seatbelts are fastened. We are pushing back and ready to taxi to the runway."

"Now there's another looker," Genevieve whispered to Philip. She always enjoyed hearing Captain Bruni's low voice laced with a sensual Italian accent.

"Young lady, you need to stop behaving like a hormonal teen." Philip popped two hors d'oeuvres into his mouth, one after the other, before William came to take away the plate. He held out the last canapé for Genevieve.

"Generous of you to give me the last of the shrimp puffs," she said, her sarcasm hard to miss.

"Always thinking of you, cute girl."

As if on cue, William swept in, snatched the empty platter and was gone as the engines revved for takeoff.

As they accelerated down the runway, Genevieve leaned toward Philip. "Let's hope this is worth all the effort," she said.

He reached out, took her hand and said, "If we can't get the deal done before we leave Lech, that's it. We move on. Freddie's been stringing us along for over a year, since he heard we wanted to do a Berlin museum. Remember, *he* approached us. It's time for him to put up or shut up. Don't you agree?"

"I do. I absolutely do." Genevieve looked into her flute, mesmerized by the bubbles streaming from the stem straight up to the surface. "We know the elder baron, as chairman of the von Bassewitz Foundation, has to sign off on the project, but we don't know if Freddie's done a good job selling him on the concept. At last we'll be face to face with both of them and we can put the financial thumbscrews on them—with great charm and finesse, of course."

With his palm open, Philip tapped his wedding ring several times on the side of his glass, then stopped. "I don't blame the old man for clutching the purse strings with an iron fist. I wouldn't trust Freddie with the family fortune for a second, would you?"

Genevieve's forehead wrinkled. "What do you think?"

"And the more I learn about Karl Friedrich von Bassewitz, the elder baron, the more interesting he seems. Did you know that in addition to being a falconer, he flies drones? That would be fun. I'm looking forward to meeting him."

Genevieve put her flute to her lips, slowly draining her glass again. "I predict this ski trip will be full of more than just skiing," she said as William walked through the cabin door with more Champagne. "William, thank goodness you're telepathic."

"My lady, that's a critical skill when you work for the House of Crosswick." He raised the bottle, poured and the Champagne frothed to the rim of the glass. He waited until it receded, then, with small sterling tongs, he plopped a small, succulent strawberry into the glass and the wine fizzed again.

CHAPTER 12

Two of Genevieve's favorite things about becoming outrageously wealthy were their private jet and the car that was always waiting for them when they landed. And today was no exception. Through the porthole, Genevieve could see a vehicle at the ready.

The moment William opened the cabin door, winter air filled the plane. Though she wore a hooded loden coat, a muffler and leather gloves, she shivered as she walked through the cabin toward the door. Philip stood in the doorway chatting with Captain Bruni, the two of them waiting while the stairs were rolled into place.

"Thank you for the smooth ride, Captain." The corners of Genevieve's eyes crinkled as her lips turned up. "It's always appreciated."

"It's my pleasure, my lady. And I wish you a glorious time

on the slopes. Today was a perfect flying day. Innsbruck is a tricky airport because of the mountains and wind patterns, so we pilots appreciate a day when the landing is easy. According to the forecasts, we were lucky."

"I haven't even looked at the weather report. What are they saying?" Genevieve's brows drew together. "Should we be concerned?"

"There seems to be a front moving in and there may be substantial snow." His brown eyes flashed. "That will be good for the ski slopes."

"Let's hope it snows at night and stops in time for them to groom the mountain. That would be perfect." Philip stuck out his hand and shook Captain Bruni's. "See you on Sunday, Francesco. Have fun in Innsbruck."

Bruni gave Philip a sly grin. "Lord Crosswick, you know I have fun wherever I am." He nodded at Genevieve, then put his captain's hat on, tilting it to a rakish angle.

"And behave yourself," Genevieve said over her shoulder as she started down the stairs, clutching the collar of her coat against the wind's biting chill. With Philip's arm around her, they strode the short distance to where Freddie's driver Gustov was waiting.

When they were tucked into the luxurious warmth of the Mercedes-Maybach SUV, Genevieve looked back at their Bombardier and watched Captain Bruni, tall and as handsome as a Michelangelo statue, descend the stairs with a bounce in his step. There was no question. Captain Francesco Bruni would definitely have a good time until they returned from Lech.

An hour and a half later, the SUV slowed to a stop in front of tall, wrought-iron gates flanked by fortress-like stone walls. Philip and Genevieve exchanged glances, Philip's eyes wide with awe, Genevieve's jaw dropped in disbelief. The driver punched a code into the pad outside his window and the gates rumbled open. For several minutes, they crawled along cobbled switchbacks. They drove back and forth at a snail's pace, periodically passing ancient watch towers until they arrived at Schloss Friedrichstein on top of the hill just as the sun descended behind the severe stone walls of the Tyrolean castle. Here and there, grey clouds gathered along the mountain ridges.

"Wow. This is quite a movie set," Philip said and craned his neck to see the tops of the towers guarding the entrance to the imposing winter palace.

As the driver jumped from his seat to open the doors, Genevieve leaned toward Philip and whispered, "This place looks spooky." She drew her mouth down at the corners and chattered her teeth as if she were terrified. "And look over there." She pointed to the clouds on the horizon. "Just as predicted, snow's coming."

Philip raised his eyebrows. "Yeah, right. Fifty-fifty chance."

"Very funny. Do you want to put money on whether or not it will snow overnight?"

"Genevieve, we're in the Tyrolean Alps in December. I think there's a pretty good chance it might snow tonight. Do I look like a patsy?"

She squeezed his cheeks until his lips puckered. "If you're a patsy, you're my patsy," she said, and kissed him.

Embarrassed because Gustov had been holding the door

for him the entire time he and Genevieve had been talking, Philip hopped out of the back seat. "Vielen dank," he said to the chauffeur, and walked toward what he assumed was the front entrance, where he waited for Genevieve while the driver opened her car door.

She shoved herself from the deep bucket seat, grateful for the chauffeur's helping hand. Before she could thank him for the courtesy, the massive, ancient oak doors of the schloss opened and Freddie bellowed, "Mein Gott! Get in here. It's freezing!" He dashed to Philip and gave him a bear hug, then gathered Genevieve into an embrace and kissed each cheek. "Gustov, bring the cases. Elsa will tell you where they go," he directed the driver as he threw his arm around Genevieve's shoulders, crushing her into his side, and ushered her toward the building.

She glanced back over her shoulder at Philip, giving him a look that said, "Help!"

He only smiled back and fell into step with their host.

As they walked into the entrance hall, the temperature crawled from frigid to chilly. Though a fierce blaze crackled on the hearth of a fireplace large enough to accommodate several people standing, the vast hall remained chilly despite the fire's efforts. Tapestries depicting family hunts and domestic scenes hung from brass rods thirty feet above them, where the curved walls of the oval room met the royal-blue vaulted ceiling. The centuries-old hangings whispered that there were many stories to tell about the von Bassewitz dynasty. As she imagined the history of the old schloss, Genevieve envisioned that, hundreds of years ago, torches jutted from sconces clinging to the walls and lit the space, projecting eerie shadows on the stone walls.

"Oh my, Freddie. What an extraordinary… I'm not sure what to call it?" She looked at the Baron, eyes wide with wonder.

"Oh, Genevieve." Freddie threw his head back and filled the hall with a jolly laugh. "It's just our little ski chalet."

"Of course. Silly me." Genevieve struggled to stifle her awe. "How long has this schloss been in the von Bassewitz care?"

"It's been in our family since the 16TH century; 1574 to be exact."

"Wow, Freddie. You make the House of Crosswick look like newcomers to this aristocracy thing," Philip said, straight-faced.

"Well, mein Freund, there are advantages to being a newish old family." Freddie chuckled at his joke. "Unlike your wonderful Wilmingrove Hall—which is the perfect stately home, warm, inviting, highly functional—Schloss Friedrichstein is too big, too drafty, doesn't have enough bathrooms, is crumbling, and terrifies most children." He shrugged his shoulders. "But it's ours. The wine cellar is particularly fine and we make the most of the chalet by filling it with delightful people like you." He brought Genevieve's hand to his lips and kissed it; Philip tossed her a wink as if to say, "Told you so!"

Looking like a model advertising a five-star Alpine resort, Heidi stood at the top of the wide staircase leading to the second floor. From across the chamber, her rich voice rang out. "Willkommen! Willkommen," she said as she swept down the stairs and across the hall to where Philip, Genevieve, and Freddie stood. Pulled back into a loose knot, her blonde hair snuggled against the nape of her neck. Sleek in a camel cashmere jumpsuit topped with a long chocolate-wool vest, heavily embroidered with exquisite Tyrolean needlework, she was perfection. "You're here and it's going to be the most marvelous few days."

Genevieve thought the perfect word for the atmosphere of the room and the company was a German word she'd always loved—gemütlich: warm, friendly. Between Freddie's lusty greeting and Heidi's congenial welcome, it was hard not to be charmed despite the frosty temperature of the hall.

Seemingly from nowhere, a young woman appeared, standing with military posture and waiting for direction. She waited in slim black pants and a black sweater with a Schloss Friedrichstein crest embroidered on the left, and Genevieve assumed she must be part of the household staff.

"Ah, Elsa." Heidi turned to introduce everyone. "Lord and Lady Crosswick, I'd like you to meet our house manager, Elsa Schmidt. Anything you need during your stay, just ask Elsa."

She was severely elegant from the top of her blonde, blunt-cut hair to her chiseled cheekbones, from her long, lean frame to her black knee-high leather boots, but though her smile was beautiful, Genevieve noticed it stopped at her lips, never reaching her eyes.

"Elsa, take Lord and Lady Crosswick's coats. Gustov is bringing their bags. Please show him where their rooms are. And we're ready for drinks in the Wohnzimmer."

Heidi slipped her arm through Philip's, Freddie put his hand in the small of Genevieve's back, and the four proceeded through a doorway into a cozier living room with a dark-beamed, coffered ceiling, each inset painted with a coat of arms, the colors bright and energetic.

"What a glorious room, Heidi." Genevieve delighted in the warmth and energy of the salon filled with bold, contemporary paintings and objet d'art dotted here and there, sitting on pedestals and protected by plexiglass casing. "And your art is wonderful."

"Thank you, Genevieve." Heidi beamed a grateful smile. "Every nook and cranny at Wilmingrove Hall is perfection so I was a bit nervous that you would see… I think you say, 'all the warts', here at our little ski lodge."

Genevieve couldn't help but laugh. "Oh my, Heidi. I assure you, I'm duly impressed."

"Please, sit by the fire." Freddie escorted Genevieve across the room to an overstuffed chair on one side of another enormous fireplace raging with flames. In a recess to the right, perfectly split logs waited to be sacrificed on the hearth.

"When are we expecting Lillie, Finn and Gabriel?" Philip asked.

"Gabe comes tomorrow from London. Lillie and Finn are already here." Heidi's cheeks glowed. She sat on a down-covered dark-green sofa and patted the cushion next to her, indicating for Philip to sit, which he did. "They arrived about an hour ago and have been upstairs getting settled. My goodness," she said, her smile melting away. "We should have let you do that." She brightened again. "But it's too late now. Freddie, could you let Lillie and Finn know everyone is here in the salon and we have started the party?"

"Of course, my love." He pulled out his cellphone and sent a text. Immediately, a ping announced a response. He glanced at his screen and read the message aloud, "Don't start without us. We'll be right down."

"Too late." Heidi laughed.

Elsa pushed a fruitwood serving cart laden with appetizers through the door to a spot near the seated guests. Each of the three shelves was filled with bite-sized pastry shells crammed with something Genevieve feared might be liverwurst, a cheese hedgehog consisting of cubed German cheeses on toothpicks stuck through a piece of venison and into a melon, small meatballs—probably boar—on Mestemacher bread, and all kinds of heavy, gamey hors d'oeuvres that made Genevieve's stomach quiver.

"Are you all right, Genevieve?" the Baron asked, flashing a look of concern.

Not realizing she had groaned aloud, Genevieve flushed with embarrassment. "Quite all right, Freddie. I was just clearing my throat," she said, quite proud of her quick recovery. "I have a little tickle."

"Genevieve, my beautiful guest." He winked at her and she cringed. "What would you like to drink? Would you like spirits or better yet…" He pushed himself from the depths of his chair's deep cushion, walked to the sideboard, grabbed a bottle of wine by the neck and held it up, flashing the yellow-orange label. "Tada," he said with pride. "Of course you may drink whatever you wish but I would love for all of you to try this lovely Grüner Veltliner Orange. It's very special and I want to show you that we Austrians can make wines, too. They may not rival your spectacular Chateau Beaulieu grand cru wines but they are excellent nonetheless."

Philip shook his head. "Freddie, Austrian wines are wonderful. This is not a competition."

"Ach! Mein Freund. Everything is a competition." He narrowed his eyes. "You are an American. No one is more competitive than you Americans." He cut the foil from the top of the bottle, buried the corkscrew in three expert turns and pulled it out with a satisfying pop.

"So what have I missed?" Through the door like a spring breeze, Lillie burst into the toasty room, an azure scarf draped around her neck, the ends fluttering behind her. Tendrils that had escaped her curly topknot bounced around her angelic face. "Philip, Genevieve, you're here!" she squealed. She floated to Genevieve, bent over and kissed both her cheeks then made a beeline for Philip, squeezed him around the neck and then plopped down between Heidi and him.

"Where's Finn?" Heidi asked.

A broad grin lit Lillie's delicate features. "He's on the phone… he's always on the phone." Her laugh was deep and robust, a surprising sound coming from someone so sprite-like. "Until I met Finn, I thought I was the only person in the world who would someday have to have my phone surgically removed from my hand and my ear. But he's even worse than I am." She spoke at such a rapid pace that everyone listening leaned forward so they wouldn't miss a word. Her posh English accent had the two Austrians straining to understand what she was saying.

"So Philip, Genevieve, what do you think of Schloss Friedrichstein?" Lilie leaned into Philip and turned her head so she was nearly nose to nose with him. "Isn't it like something out of a Gothic movie?"

Wishing Lillie hadn't been quite so candid, discomfort flushed Genevieve's cheeks. "I hadn't thought about that particular description. It's very authentic, isn't it?" she said.

The Baron and Baroness von Bassewitz looked around the room at their guests for a moment, feigning insult, then broke into hearty laughter.

"Lillie, that's a perfect description," Heidi chortled. "Sometimes this lodge is absolutely terrifying, isn't it, Freddie?"

"You have no idea," he said, bouncing his head up and down with enthusiasm. "Tomorrow when Papa and Gabe are here, we'll regale you with stories about how Papa used to make us behave by telling us he'd put us in the dungeons if we were naughty."

Walking into the middle of the conversation, Finn said, "Are there really dungeons?" He rubbed his hands at the idea that Schloss Friedrichstein had dark, spooky cells in its bowels.

"Finn, darling boy." Genevieve blew him a kiss and he grinned at her in return.

"I shall ask again," Finn pressed. "Are there really dungeons?"

Freddie chuckled at Finn and looked to his wife for confirmation. "Not really dungeons, right, Heidi?"

"Oh, Schatzie." Heidi gave her husband a mollifying squeeze on his forearm as he handed her a glass of orange wine. "I'd say what you refer to as cellars could easily be called dungeons."

Eager to hear more, Lillie leaned forward on the sofa. "Freddie, are there cells with locks on them where centuries ago people were held prisoner?" She watched as Freddie gave each person a crystal goblet and waited for his answer.

When everyone had a glass in hand, he raised his own. "Lillie, dear Lillie. I will happily give you a personal tour of the labyrinth below and you may judge for yourself: dungeon or cellar. That is, of course, after you see my automobile collection and show that you are suitably impressed with how stupendous it is." A deep laugh rolled from his throat. "I know you Warwicks have some extraordinary cars but wait until you see mine." Freddie glowed with pride. "In the meantime, I propose a toast to the coming days of great snow and superb skiing. Prost!"

"Prost!" everyone responded.

Genevieve took a polite sip, then drank again. "Freddie, this is fabulous," she said, lowering her glass and licking the residue of the orange wine from her lips.

"Thank you, Genevieve." Thrilled with her praise, his mouth pulled into a wide grin.

"This Grüner Veltliner is delicious." Philip arched his eyebrow and nodded in Freddie's direction.

"I couldn't agree more," Finn said . "But, if I may, I'd like to change the subject to the weather. Has anyone heard the latest forecast?"

No one looked concerned. Some people shook their heads, some mumbled, "No."

He pushed on. "I was just on the phone with the EUMETSAT." He focused on Philip and Genevieve, whose blank looks he expected. "You know, the European weather service. They're a client of ours and are having an issue with one of their satellites that requires some handholding. When I told the head of technology I'm in Lech for some skiing, he said that within the last couple of hours, a model has predicted a whopper of a storm moving into this area." When he looked at the blank faces around the room, he was certain he was the first in the group to know about the impending weather event. "So I guess this is a surprise to one and all."

"Not everyone," Philip said. "G predicted this earlier today." Glancing across the room, he smirked at Genevieve. In return, she gave him a sharp upward jerk of her head and a knowing smile.

"Aren't you the clever one?" Lillie hunched her shoulders up to her ears and grinned. It was obvious that she was more excited than concerned about a big weather event coming their way.

Because it had happened before, Heidi knew what it would be like to be marooned at the top of this berg in a raging storm and her brow wrinkled into a frown. "This is awfully early in the season to get a heavy snowstorm," she said, uneasy at the idea of a blizzard descending on them.

"You know these weather people are only right about half the time. Did your client say when it would start?" Freddie seemed less anxious than his wife.

"He said it will start slowly tomorrow, late afternoon or early evening, so if we want to get any runs in, we should hit the slopes in the morning."

Heidi rose from the sofa and walked to the sideboard where the wine chilled in a sterling silver cooler. With bottle in hand, she began to move from person to person, refilling glasses as she spoke. "Freddie and I have so been looking forward to having you all here for this lovely ski retreat. Nothing is more spectacular than shushing down our challenging slopes, but I'm afraid we need to consider the wisdom of staying here with a major winter storm on its way. Freddie, what do you think?"

He took the near-empty bottle from her slender hand and poured what was left into Philip's goblet. "I think we'll be fine. If nothing is expected before late tomorrow, I think we should enjoy a spectacular day on the slopes and then make the most of whatever comes next." He walked back to the heavily carved mahogany buffet and pulled the cork on another bottle of wine. "We have plenty of provisions, don't we, Heidi?"

"Elsa?" Heidi raised her eyebrows at the woman who had been waiting all this time to serve hors d'oeuvres.

"Ja, Baroness. We have much food and plenty of wine." The house manager didn't seem to care whether the guests stayed or left.

"Und so?" Freddie queried his guests. "What do you think?"

Heidi was as tense as Freddie was relaxed and convivial.

"We'll have a wonderful time. And my father would be extremely unhappy if he arrives tomorrow morning and finds all of you have gone home!" Freddie's eyes darted to Heidi. "Is that not true, Liebling?" His speech picked up pace as he continued trying to sell his guests on the idea of staying. "Philip, he wants to discuss many things. You know, the contribution to the museum. And he's anxious to show you his drones and his falcons and maybe do a little hunting with them." He walked to the fireplace and tossed two large logs into the massive firebox. The dry wood caught instantly; flames danced up into the chimney and wood smoke puffed into the room. "Of course that might be difficult if it's snowing like mad."

Genevieve overheard Freddie mumble under his breath as he walked by her on his way back to his chair. Though her German was not perfect, she was quite sure he had said to himself that his father would be very angry if things didn't go to plan.

"He would be very disappointed, indeed," Heidi agreed, her eyes sweeping from guest to guest. "But your father's feelings aside, Freddie, I think everyone should do what they believe is best. What does everyone think?"

Inside Genevieve was jumping up and down with the idea they could dash back to Wilmingrove Hall and she could jump into the thick of holiday preparations. But the thought of having Big Daddy Baron here to possibly commit to the Berlin museum was an overwhelming draw.

Not put off in the least by the impending storm, Lillie was game for anything. "I for one vote to stay. I have a new silver Bogner ski suit and I intend to give it a workout tomorrow on some treacherous black runs."

Not to be outdone, Finn weighed in. "Obviously I don't want to miss that," he was quick to say. "I'm in."

As she sensed no one was going to flee, Heidi's enthusiasm began to build. "There's only one black run in Lech but I promise you won't be disappointed. I think most of the pistes are underrated and some start out intermediate in the morning and by the afternoon they've turned into some of the most advanced runs I've ever skied."

After being married to her for so many years, Philip knew Genevieve well enough to read her mind, and sensed she was waiting for him to answer for both of them. "I can think of much worse things than having a great day of skiing then being snowbound for a couple of days with interesting company, plenty to eat and plenty to drink. I say two votes for staying."

"Wunderbar!" Freddie raised his glass again, a broad smile stretching from ear to ear. "To a memorable stay at Schloss Friedrichstein!"

And everyone drank. "To Schloss Friedrichstein!"

CHAPTER 13

THE MORNING DAWNED with the sky as blue and cloudless as a perfect sapphire. The deep blue color warned of something to come, but for the moment the sun ruled the sky, glancing off snowbanks, shimmering off icicles that had yet to melt, and did its best to warm the early skiers on the first chairlift, anxious to be the ones to put their marks on the virgin runs before anyone else. Hearing nothing but the swish of your own skis and the sound of your own exhilarated "whoop" was worth the price of rising early and being first down the mountain.

Among the initial clutch of mad slope riders, Philip and Genevieve shivered their way up the mountain on a double chairlift and second guessed their decision to get up and out so early. Though the plexiglass enclosure blocked the wind, at nine o'clock it was still frigid.

"Whose bright idea was this?" Genevieve said, her voice

muffled by the crimson gaiter covering her mouth and nose.

"I believe I suggested snuggling in bed, having a leisurely breakfast *then* coming out," Philip said.

"So no sympathy?"

"None whatsoever." Philip put his arm around Genevieve's shoulders and pulled her closer. "But maybe this will help."

"Much better," she said, smiling into her red scarf.

They traveled above a treeless field of groomed trails—or pistes, as the Europeans called their ski runs—with the wind blasting them sideways, swinging their chair. Genevieve grabbed Philip's gloved hand and squeezed. She loved a good lift ride, but swinging in a blustery wind high above snow-covered slopes was not her favorite thing. When they entered a funnel of evergreens, the wind died and she eased her grip on Philip's hand. She pulled her gaiter off her nose and mouth and turned to him. "I have a question for you," she said. "What did you think about Freddie's behavior last night?"

Philip took off his Vaurnet sunglasses and gave her a look that registered nothing. "Should I know what you're talking about?"

"Well, yes," she said.

His stare remained blank.

A cough of disbelief caught in the back of her throat. "Seriously, Philip! You didn't notice anything?"

He stared at her for several long seconds before saying, "I honestly have no idea what you're talking about, G. Just tell me." The sun glanced off the metal safety bar and into his eyes, so he put his glasses back on.

"You don't think he was hard-selling us to stay? He really

didn't want us to leave this morning to avoid the storm. I mean, I didn't understand why Heidi thought it would be a problem to begin with, but—"

"That," Philip interrupted her. He punched his finger in the air. "What Heidi said. I thought *that* was odd," He pulled his glasses down his nose and looked over the top rim. "I thought she was pushing us to leave. What's the big deal about getting stuck in a luxurious ski chalet in a snowstorm with plenty to eat and drink, even if the lodge is, as Lillie said, a gothic movie set complete with dungeons, apparently? If we can get the old Baron's commitment for Berlin, I don't care how snowed in we are."

"I certainly don't want to be here forever, but I can put up with a couple of days of being unbearably charming, doing jigsaw puzzles and playing charades if it means Baron-the-Elder is our captive. But Philip, I'm talking about how nervous Freddie seemed at the prospect of us leaving. It was as if he were afraid of what his father would do or say if we all left."

"I'm sorry, G. I didn't even notice. Are you sure you didn't misread him?"

"I'm positive. In fact, I heard him mutter that his father would be very angry if things didn't go to plan."

"You're sure?" Philip took his arm from around Genevieve, pointed ahead and she saw they were about to come to the drop-off area. She clutched her poles in her right hand and tilted her ski tips up. The moment they hovered over the snowy off-ramp, the two of them stood up, slid down the incline and over to an open area, out of the way of those coming off the lift.

"I'm positive," Genevieve continued. "He said it under his

breath in German, and though my German's a little rusty I'm pretty sure I got the gist of it. You really didn't notice how uneasy Freddie seemed?"

"No matter how many times you ask me, I'm pretty sure I'm not going to change my answer." His lips curled. "I thought he was just excited at the prospect of all of us being there and didn't want the party—which was just getting started—to break up. I didn't pick up any of the vibe you're talking about."

"All right." She decided the conversation wasn't worth the effort and scanned the breathtaking view. She could see miles in each direction and it was hard to believe that by tomorrow blizzard conditions would probably engulf the area. "Where are we meeting Finn and Lillie?" she asked.

"We're meeting them right here at Rud-Alp at eleven o'clock. Isn't that what we agreed?"

"I think you're right. We have time for at least a couple of runs before then, don't we?" She bent over to dislodge a clump of snow off her bindings.

"We'll enjoy as many we can. And might I say," Philip reached out with his ski pole and patted Genevieve's bottom with the basket, "you look exceptional in that black ski suit. You are really something, Genevieve Warwick."

She felt the heat rise in her cheeks and stood up. "And you, Lord Crosswick, look mighty fine in your sleek togs. Aren't we quite the pair?"

"Love is blind, right?"

"I'm afraid you're right!" She laughed and gave him a good-natured shove on the shoulder. Caught completely off-guard, Philip listed to the left and dropped into a snow bank.

Surprised at what she had just done, Genevieve blubbered an apology and extended her pole to help him up. Instead of taking the pole and easing himself out of the drift, he gave it a sharp tug and pulled her down on top of him.

"Touché," he said, rubbing a handful of snow into her face.

She gasped for air, grabbed as much snow as she could clutch in her gloved hand, and was about to stuff it down Philip's turtleneck when she heard a voice she hadn't heard for nearly two years: "Lord and Lady Crosswick?"

Philip and Genevieve squinted up into the sun but all they could see was the silhouette of a tall, angular man. The voice, however, was distinct and they knew it instantly. Almost two years ago they had spent days with this man talking, listening and helping tosolve the frightening mystery of who had disrupted their lives, threatened their new positions as the Earl and Countess of Crosswick, and tried to destroy their family. That man was Francis Darlington, Chief Superintendent of the Metropolitan Police, or as many know it, Scotland Yard.

"Chief Superintendent Darlington?" Philip said.

Genevieve brought her hand to her brow and slitted her eyes, trying to make out the face looming above her. She took the hand he offered and he pulled her to her feet as easily as a rag doll. He repeated the gesture and Philip popped up.

"What in the world?" Still holding Darlington's hand, Philip pumped it twice before letting it go. "What a surprise and a coincidence."

"It may be a surprise for you, but it isn't for me," the chief said, a lop-sided grin pulling at his lips.

"What do you mean, Francis? I'm assuming I can call you Francis since we're not meeting on official business?"

"You may certainly call me Francis, Lady Crosswick, but I think you'll be surprised when I tell you I *am* on official business. Finding you here is not a coincidence."

Philip raised an eyebrow; his head cocked to one side. Genevieve leaned on her ski poles, confused by everything Francis Darlington had just said.

"I… I… um." Philip shook his head as if to clear his mind. He started again. "I don't understand," he said, speaking slowly.

"Shall we go into Rud-Alp? They're not serving meals yet, but we can get something hot—coffee, chocolate—and I can fill you in." The officer pointed to the two-hundred-fifty-year-old alpine lodge and led the way. The three skied to the terrace overlooking the entire valley, released their bindings and stepped out of them. In silence they cradled their skis against a wooden rack and filed into the hut, nodding as they passed a burly skier standing just inside the door.

"Why don't you two sit here by the fire and I'll see what I can find to drink." He snatched his ski cap from his head and tossed it on the table next to his gloves. He shrugged out of his ski jacket, hung it on the back of a chair, and headed across the restaurant, cozy with beamed ceilings low in some spots, pitched and soaring in others.

Philip and Genevieve peeled off their jackets and sat. They looked at each other, perplexed, then looked back at Darlington and watched him walk through the swinging doors into the kitchen. Geneieve had forgotten how attractive the Met officer was. Longer than she remembered, his hair curled over his navy-blue turtleneck and was more salt and pepper than two years ago.

For a long minute, they said nothing to each other. The smell of wood smoke from the fireplace and meat cooking in the kitchen hung in the air and Genevieve noticed saliva flooding her mouth in response.

Philip sat rigid, not taking his eyes off the door across the room.

With her hands on the table, Genevieve fidgeted, lacing and unlacing her fingers until Philip covered her hands with his.

"Please stop," he whispered.

They locked eyes and he saw confusion, fear, and maybe panic in Genevieve's face. Still cradling her hands in his, he leaned close. "What is it, G? Why do you look so worried?"

"None of this can be good, do you think? Why would Darlington track us all the way to an Austrian ski village?"

Philip relaxed back into his chair and patted her hands. "Let's not jump to conclusions. Let's just give Francis a chance to tell us why he's here."

They watched as he pushed back through the swing doors into the dining room, carrying a tray filled with three cups of steaming coffee and a plate of cookies. As he approached the table, Philip jumped up and pulled out a chair for him.

"Here we are. I knew they'd have something for us." He put the tray down, distributed the mugs and set the plate of Linzer cookies in the middle, while Philip and Genevieve watched his every move. He sat, splashed cream in his coffee, stirred it, then took a drink.

Already tense with curiosity, the Warwicks were anxious to hear what he had to say. They rested their elbows on the table, Genevieve with her hands wrapped around her cup. Philip took a gulp of his black coffee and winced as it burned his throat on the way down.

Darlington stared at the spoon and stirred his coffee. He seemed unsure of how to start the conversation but at last he said, "I shan't keep you in suspense any longer."

"At last," Genevieve mumbled under her breath then said aloud, "We appreciate that. This is all very cloak and dagger."

"You have no idea." A low chuckle rolled from Darlington's throat. "Ah, where to begin?"

"At the beginning, I suppose," Philip said, matter of fact.

Darlington put up his hands in defense. "All right, all right. Let me start with the murder of Angelina von Bassewitz at Wilmingrove Hall."

Startled, Genevieve's brows flew up. "Why would you start there? What does Angelina's death have to do with you? Why are you…" She stopped herself midsentence as a light dawned, and she thought she understood. "Aha," she said. "Angelina was a foreign aristocrat and the Met deals with such things, right?"

Philip squeezed her arm. "G, why don't we let Chief Superintendent Darlington explain. I bet we don't have to guess. I'm sure he'll tell us everything, right, Francis?" He glanced at the officer, who offered a grateful nod.

"Lord and Lady Crosswick, I have changed positions within the Met."

"Really?" Genevieve said with feigned interest.

"G, let Francis speak."

She shot Philip an annoyed glance then looked back at Darlington. "Go on," she said.

"Shortly after the business at Wilmingrove Hall, the Met asked if I would be interested in heading up the Arts and Antiques unit. It's a group that has existed in fits and starts since 1969. I decided it would be an exciting new challenge so I am no longer Chief Superintendent Darlington of the Met. For the last year, I have been Detective Chief Inspector of the Metropolitan Police Services' Arts and Antiquities Unit."

"That's quite a mouthful," Philip was already thinking of how useful it would be to have a contact in the art crimes world, if such a need ever arose again.

"You're the head of the entire department?" Genevieve said, her curiosity piqued. "Are you like Gabriel Allon in Daniel Silva's novels?"

"No, my lady. I am not. I am very much a copper chasing art thieves with one of the smallest units in the world—six, counting me. But if you'd prefer to think of me as a romantic fictional character, I'm delighted." His eyes danced at Genevieve.

"Francis," Philip shook his head. "Would you please call us by our first names?"

"I would be honored, my lord. I mean, Philip." He leaned back and pulled his mug toward him.

Anxious to hear why Darlington had tracked them down in Austria, Philip asked the question. "Obviously, you have more to tell us. Where do we fit into all this?"

"The Baroness's murder is an interesting case, but only a piece of the bigger issue we've been following for the last year. What I'm about to share with you is considered confidential information."

"Well, you certainly have our attention." Philip plucked a cookie from the plate and took a bite. Genevieve pointed to the crumbs that had dropped on his sweater and he brushed them off onto the floor.

"But is it secure to have this conversation here?" Genevieve scooted her bottom to the edge of her chair and leaned as close as she could to Darlington. "What if there are bugs?" she whispered.

Philip exploded with a laugh. "Are you kidding, G? This isn't international intrigue. I doubt if Francis would press us into becoming agents of Scotland Yard, right here on our ski holiday at the von Bassewitzes' schloss."

He caught Darlington's sober expression and stopped chuckling.

"That's remarkably close to the bone, Philip. Clearly, we're not asking you to be covert agents, but do you remember seeing a man at the door when we came into Rud-Alp?"

They both nodded.

"He swept the restaurant for bugs earlier and he and two other officers are making certain that no one comes into the dining room until we're finished."

Bewildered at what she was hearing, Genevieve had no idea what questions to ask so she was grateful when Philip said, "This sounds serious. What does this have to do with us?"

"That's the perfect question, Philip, and the answer is, the Met, or Scotland Yard if you'd prefer, needs your help."

CHAPTER 14

"I s this a prank?" Philip needed more than coffee. He would welcome a shot of schnaps.

"No, Philip. This is not a prank. This is quite a serious mission, if I may use that word without frightening you. It's not dangerous but it would mean a great deal to the art world if you agree to help and that's something I know is important to your family. When I explain, you'll see why you and Genevieve are critical to this task." As if he were reading Philip's mind, Darlington said, "Why don't I see if I can get the owner to open a bottle of schnaps? Do you have a preference?"

"Pear," was the first thing Genevieve had said in several minutes.

"Pear, it is." Darlington left the table in search of strong drink that would help him deliver his message.

The moment Francis was out of earshot, Genevieve elbowed Philip in the ribs. "What the hell?" she whisper-screamed. "Can you believe Scotland Yard wants us to go on a mission for them?"

"Whoa, Genevieve. Calm down. And stop calling it Scotland Yard." Philip blew a puff of air from his cheeks. "You are not Dr. Watson and I am not Sherlock Holmes." He cocked his head to the side. "Though I have to say I have occasionally been mistaken for Benedict Cumberbatch."

Genevieve snorted a laugh. "I think of you more as a Moriarty than a Sherlock. But, either one…" She gave him a flirty smile. "All I'm saying is, wouldn't that be exciting if we really could be of help to Scotland Yard—the Met… whatever-you-want-to-call-it?"

"By all means, be your usual enthusiastic self, but let's be realistic. We're not British agents. Say that with me. We're not British agents."

She rolled her eyes and refocused her attention on Francis heading back to their table with a bottle of Kammer-Kirsch pear brandy in one hand and three shot glasses in the other.

"Success," she said as he put the glasses on the table and stripped the seal off the crystal cork. "Don't you love the whole pear-in-the-bottle thing? It's amazing how they put the bottles on the branches and grow the pears inside."

Darlington poured the liquid into the waiting shot glasses. Crystal clear, it looked as benign as water, but at forty percent ABV it wouldn't take much to bring on a buzz.

"Zum vohl," Darlington said, raising his glass.

"Cheers." Philip and Genevieve followed suit.

They threw the shots back, emptying their glasses, and slapped them down on the table in true schnaps-drinking fashion. "Now," Darlington said. "Let me tell you a story."

CHAPTER 15

Tʜᴇ Cʜɪᴇꜰ Iɴꜱᴘᴇᴄᴛᴏʀ poured another round of schnaps, set the bottle down and was ready. "I have no doubt," he began, "that you know the story of the Isabella Stewart Gardner Museum in Boston."

"Wasn't it the biggest art theft in history? And, as I recall, none of the art was ever returned." Genevieve leaned forward, her elbows on the table. "It was in the early 1990's, right?

"March 18, 1990, the day of Boston's St. Patrick's Day parade," Darlington said. "The thieves took thirteen items: paintings, etchings, a finial from a French flag and a Chinese gu, a vessel for serving wine dating from the 12ᵀᴴ century."

As Darlington spoke, Genevieve barely breathed, hanging on his every word. The more he shared, the more engrossed she became.

The lines on his forehead deepened as he spoke. "As you

mentioned, none of the works was ever retrieved." He shook his head slowly. "For several years, the FBI speculated that some of Boston's organized crime families were involved. They thought maybe the works were sent to the Middle East, Europe, or the Far East. There was even conjecture that the works were smuggled to Northern Ireland to help fund the IRA. Though hundreds of leads were followed and periodically things looked hopeful, to this day nothing has developed into anything other than speculation."

"As I recall, there was a huge reward for any information leading to the recovery of the works?" Philip's glass was empty again, but he put his hand over the rim as Darlington offered to fill it.

A smile played around Darlington's full lips. "If you call ten million dollars a huge reward, then, yes. And it's still there for the taking. That makes it even more amazing that the works remain missing." He filled his own shot glass and emptied it immediately.

Genevieve stood, put her hands on the table and leaned on them, looming toward the Detective Chief Inspector. "Francis, I love puzzles and the entire time we've been talking, I've been trying to piece together how Angelina's murder, the Gardner heist over thirty years ago, and Philip and I could possibly be connected and I have come up with zip, zero, nada." She pushed off the table, walked to the fire and stared at the dancing flames.

She felt Darlington and Philip watching her in silence and turned at last.

Francis started to speak but she held up her hand. "Unless Angelina's death has something to do with the Gardner Museum robbery, which seems unlikely since she was a toddler in 1990."

She saw a flicker in Darlington's eyes and knew she was on to something. "Are you going to tell us what's going on or do I need to keep guessing?"

"Very clever of you, Genevieve." Darlington's gold-flecked hazel eyes sparkled and he was ready for the big reveal. "Genevieve, please come back, sit down, and I'll cut to the chase."

Having no idea what time it was, Philip looked at his watch and saw that it was already 10:37 a.m. "Francis, we're meeting friends here at eleven o'clock. Should I text them and cancel?"

Darlington didn't seem terribly surprised. He shook his head. "No, you needn't cancel."

Philip checked his watch again. "But it's nearly 10:40."

Darlington held up his hand. "You've been extremely patient so let me just get on."

"I think that would be a good idea," Genevieve said.

He began again. "Since the Gardner robbery in 1990, the FBI has reached out to the Met numerous times when they had a new lead and they thought we could help them with some aspect of their investigation. About a year ago, just as I came on board as head of the unit, we got a call from them. The fact that they called was not a surprise. But what they told us was."

Philip relaxed, his elbows on the arms of his chair, his hands tented.

Genevieve leaned forward, holding her lower lip between her teeth.

"For several years after the heist, everyone—the museum director, the FBI agents, the *Boston Globe*—constantly received calls: calls with crazy tips about where the works had been hidden, who had been involved with the robbery, how the works were smuggled out of the country. Some people said they had seen the major work taken in the heist, Rembrandt's *The Storm on the Sea of Galilee,* hanging on the wall of a home during a real estate open house they had attended."

Genevieve shook her head as if trying to dislodge that absurd idea from her mind. "Are you serious?" she said.

Philip noticed his schnaps glass was full again and couldn't help but bring it to his lips at such an absurd idea.

"But that's not the best one," Francis continued. "This is my favorite. Fairly recently an elderly woman called to claim the ten-million-dollar reward. She said she wanted to turn in her grandson for masterminding the robbery. Her grandson is six years old."

Genevieve exploded, her full-throated laugh filling the restaurant.

Philip nearly choked on the schnaps he had just drunk, almost spraying it out of his nose.

"Funny, right?" Darlington said, delighting in their response. "Poor kid. "As I was saying, tips poured in for the first few years—thousands. As time went by, they tapered off but to this day, the FBI still gets a couple of hundred tips a year, almost none of which are useful."

Darlington rolled his shoulders and pressed on. "No matter how barmy the tips are, they are catalogued. About a month ago, the Boston FBI received an anonymous call. It was a Sunday and the agent on the phone was young, and doing what all new hires do, putting in time on the call desk. They consider the work boring, mundane and unimportant."

Philip looked at his watch again. 10:59.

He glanced at the entryway, expecting Lillie and Finn to appear at any moment.

The Chief Inspector followed Philip's gaze to the door just as it banged open, echoing through the empty restaurant.

"Oh, shit," Philip said, his head spinning to Darlington. "Our friends!"

"The cavalry has arrived!" Finn said as he and Lillie came through the door. Side by side they strode to the table.

Lillie extended her hand. "Chief Inspector, it's good to see you."

"Francis, old man. You made it!" Finn greeted Darlington like an old friend.

"What in the... um, er, what the blazes is going on here?" Confused, Philip stumbled over his words.

Genevieve sat wide-eyed and mystified, swiveling her head from this person to that as each spoke, trying all the while to figure out what was happening.

"How far have you gotten, Francis?" Finn cut straight to the quick. "Are Philip and Genevieve up to speed?"

Philip didn't wait for Darlington to respond. "We are not," he said, louder than he intended. "Sorry," he said raising both palms in apology. "The Chief Inspector gave us the background on the Gardner Museum robbery, which we vaguely remember, but that's as far as we've gotten."

Finn narrowed his eyes at Darlington. "So, Francis, Philip and Genevieve are still in the dark about what's to be done?" he said, then noted the bottle of pear brandy and the three empty glasses on the table, as well as a plate holding a few crumbs.

"We are," Genevieve spoke up. "Even more so now. How do you two fit into all of, whatever this is?"

"It all makes sense when you hear the plan." Lillie pulled out a chair next to Genevieve and sat.

"Alles Gut?" A man pushed the kitchen door open, stuck his head out, and yelled across the room.

"Ja, ja," Finn said, "aber Sie Zwei mehr Schnapsgläser mitbringing, bitte." The Rud-Alp manager gave a thumbs up, came into the room and headed to the bar to retrieve more glasses. "If we have all this yet to reveal, Lillie and I are going to need glasses and lots of schnaps."

Finn intercepted the manager halfway across the room, took the glasses, returned to the table and sat.

"Okay, let's get this done." Finn clapped his hands, ready to wrap things up.

Everyone saw relief wash over Darlington. "You're the seasoned security person on this team, Finn. You take over, please."

Finn poured his and Lillie's glasses. He held up the bottle but the other three shook their heads. "So you know all about the Gardener Museum heist. Did Francis tell you my company, Mountbatten International Security, has worked on virtually every lead they've had for the last twenty years? Before I took over the firm, my father worked with the Gardner, the FBI, the

Met, and Interpol so the firm is pretty deep into the case. But that's just the preface to why we five are here." He looked around the table to confirm he had everyone's attention. He did.

"Did you tell them about the most recent tip?"

"I was just starting to when you and Lillie came in and here we are."

"Okay. I'll recap because this is important. You know about the call the Boston FBI received last month?"

Philip and Genevieve nodded.

"Unfortunately, this call was possibly the piece of thread that, if pulled just right, could unravel the Gardner Museum tapestry." Finn huffed out a disappointed breath.

Genevieve shifted in her chair. "What did the caller say?"

"According to the agent's notes, she said she had information that would lead to the recovery of at least one of the pieces taken during the Isabella Stewart Gardner Museum heist. She had a European accent, or maybe Russian, the agent wasn't sure. She asked how the woman knew where the painting was, and the woman said she had been in its presence." Darlington paused for effect. "I understand why the agent got pretty excited. It was probably the first time she'd had a call other than someone with a tip on where Jimmy Hoffa is buried or someone asking when they'd be doing a Sopranos sequel. Unfortunately, she put the woman on hold while she got in touch with her supervisor and when the agent came back to the line, the woman was gone."

"That's all very interesting but I still don't understand why the five of us are sitting here talking about it." Fatigue slumped Philip's shoulders. "I keep asking the same question and I keep getting the same answer, which is no answer at all. What does all of this have to do with us?"

Genevieve tilted her head and flashed Philip a sympathetic smile. "Maybe that's what Finn's going to tell us next, darling."

Finn threw back his schnaps, gestured to Darlington and said, "Francis, do you want to pick up the story here?"

"Certainly." Darlington sat a little straighter in his chair. "About a week later, my office got a similar call. A woman with a European accent wanted to share information about an item taken in the Gardner heist. She said she had seen the item. Our agent asked for her name, where she was calling from, that sort of thing, but she said she wasn't comfortable giving that information… yet. She wanted to talk to someone who could ensure her safety. So the agent called me in." Darlington ran the back of his hand over his jaw, feeling the stubble on his chin. "It took me at least half an hour to convince her she was talking to the right person. At one point, I said that obviously we would have to have her details in order for her to receive the ten-million-dollar reward. She said the reward was not important." He and Finn exchanged a look across the table. "Significant, right, Finn?"

"Indeed. But go on, Francis. What happened next?"

"She said she had photographs of the artworks on her phone." The Chief Inspector paused and swept his gaze around the table. "If that were true, it would validate she's been in the presence of the pieces."

"And the fact that she didn't care about the substantial reward would mean that she's probably wealthy, right?" Genevieve's eyes darted between Darlington and Finn.

"One could assume," Finn said.

"So, do you know the identity of this tipster?" Philip leaned forward.

"Patience, Philip. Patience." Finn smiled at Lillie, enjoying the slow reveal.

"Eventually, I convinced her that she was in the right place and talking to the right person. I assured her the FBI, the Met, Interpol—all of us work together and all of us work with a private security firm that has been involved with this case since the beginning." Darlington pointed to Finn. "Mountbatten International Security. Finally she said she felt comfortable working with us but she wanted to come to the office rather than continue our conversation over the phone. The earliest she could do that was Monday because she had to go away for the weekend. She made an appointment to come to the Met Monday morning at 10:30. Until then, she wanted to remain anonymous."

"You couldn't trace her identity from her phone?" Philip had some sense of how technology worked and he was quite certain you could get a lot of information if you kept a person on the phone for long enough.

"Burner phone." Finn made a zero with his fingers and thumb.

"What about her location?"

"She called from the Connaught in London," Darlington said.

"So I was right. She has a few pennies." Genevieve kept her eyes on Darlington.

"What happened when she came in? Did she have the photos? Who is she?" Genevieve pressed.

"First of all, she did not come in. She did not keep her appointment. So the rest of that Monday we followed up as much as we could, then filed the hot tip, with the gazillions of other hot tips we've received over the last thirty-five years. Then Tuesday morning we got a call from a man you two know only too well." Darlington could hardly control the corners of his mouth that were trying to stretch into a broad smile.

Philip and Genevieve glanced at each other then at Darlington. "I can't imagine who that might be." Two furrows bloomed between Genevieve's eyebrows as she tried to figure out who Francis could be talking about. "I give up," she said. "Who called and what did they have to say?"

Darlington looked at Finn, ready to give him the floor. "Oh, no, Francis. This is your big scene."

"The phone call came from your good friend DCI Cecil Fields."

Genevieve's frown deepened. "Cecil? He called you, Francis? Why?"

"That clever boy found a day planner in a car and that planner had some entries and an appointment with SY penned on the calendar. When he connected all the dots, he decided SY was Scotland Yard. The owner of the planner and the person who was supposed to have an appointment at SY was none other than— drumroll, please." On his cue, Finn and Lillie rapidly beat their palms on the table. Darlington made a cutting sign across his throat and they stopped. "The person who did not keep her appointment with the Met was Angelina Hauffman, the former Baroness von Bassewitz. She did not keep her appointment on Monday because she was murdered on Friday."

CHAPTER 16

Though the sun still glared in a bright azure sky, clouds were beginning to gather over the Alpine peaks and the first flakes of the storm marching toward Lech wafted through the air. Karl Friedrich, the senior Baron von Bassewitz, tapped his foot and belted the words to Beethoven's Ninth Symphony, the glorious strains of the final choral movement, "Ode to Joy," pouring from the Bang and Olufsen speakers. His driver, Max, smiled, enjoying his employer's full baritone. The black Audi Q7 embraced the steep hill and eased around the corners of the switchbacks, the Baron hardly listing from side to side. Karl enjoyed this drive. He loved that over many decades, little had changed to alter the view, its soaring snow-covered peaks and swooping valleys breathtaking in the winter and filled with wildflowers, grassy meadows, red deer and bunnies all spring and summer.

Max slowed the car as they rounded the last turn onto the cobblestone driveway that circled in front of the schloss. The moment he turned off the engine, he jumped from the driver's seat, loped around the car and opened the door for the Baron. At ninety-one, the Baron was fit as a robust seventy-year-old, as energetic as his two sons, and he pushed out of the back seat with ease. "Danke, Max." Looking into the sun, he shaded his eyes and watched three golden eagles soar above them. "They're gathering before the storm. Not a bad idea, eh, Max?"

"Ja, Baron. A good idea indeed." Just as Max put his hand on the front door's iron handle, it swung open and Freddie burst through, an uneasy grin plastered from ear to ear.

"Papa! You are here," he said, trying to sound pleased though his stomach churned with unease.

"You are surprised? You were not expecting me?" Karl said, his gruff tone slapping Freddie.

"Of course, Papa. We just didn't expect you so early." He offered his arm. "Come, Papa. Let's get you some coffee and I'm sure there are pastries coming out of the oven."

Karl shoved his son's arm away. "I'm not a feeble old man." With the posture of a soldier, he marched ahead of Freddie through the front door into the outer hall. "Is everyone here?" he said, turning so abruptly that he and Freddie were nose to nose.

"Sorry, Papa," he said, taking a step backwards. "No, Lord and Lady Crosswick are on the mountain as well as Lillie Langdon and Finnegan Mountbatten. I'm certain they'll be back any time."

"They'd better be. They say the snow will start by noon. That's just half an hour from now. We already saw some flakes as we were coming up the drive. I don't want any of our guests getting stuck on the mountain. We have things to discuss. I'd suggest you try to get them on their mobile and tell them to head back."

"Yes, sir." Freddie pulled his phone from his pocket and dialed Philip's number. The phone rang through to voicemail. "Philip, it looks like the snow is going to start within the hour so you might want to head back to the schloss. My father just arrived and is anxious for everyone to be here safe and sound under his roof. Please call me back when you get this."

"Voicemail?"

"Yes, sir. I would imagine they're skiing back here so Philip won't even hear his phone."

Karl pulled his arms out of the blue leather jacket that perfectly matched his eyes, still clear and icy even though his crepey lids sagged into crow's feet at the corners. "When will Gabriel be here?"

Freddie steeled himself to deliver news his father would not like. "He called this morning and unfortunately his flight has been cancelled because of the storm." He held his breath, bracing for his father's tirade.

Instead, the elder Baron threw his jacket on an upholstered bench next to the front door without glancing at Freddie or saying a word. He headed into the living room and walked to the fire. "Gabriel should be here. I shall not forget this slight to the family. Freddie, you realize how important this Berlin museum is to me, don't you?" he said with the intensity of a man thirty years his junior. "With our name on a Laney Musée des Beaux Arts, I will become revered in the world of art, something

I have wanted for decades. Jonathon Laney will turn in his grave to know I have stolen some of his precious prestige and have become one of the most renowned patrons in the art world," he said, holding his palms toward the blaze to warm his hands. "What we do here over the next two days will secure this family's position in a rarified world."

Freddie stared out the fourteen-foot windows, their beveled edges distorting the view of the mountains beyond the terrace, across the valley. He had looked at this panorama for as long as he could remember. This schloss and this valley had belonged to the von Bassewitz family since the end of the Thirty Years' War when Ferdinand III awarded the property to one of his most loyal military advisors, Kaspar von Bassewitz, and the family began to claw its way to power and wealth. Since he was old enough to understand what his family name meant in the long history of Austria, his father had never missed an opportunity to impress on his elder son that the family's next and final rung on society's ladder was what his father longed for most: the admiration and validation of his peers as a man of extraordinary discernment. And he intended to do that through art.

There had been few days in his life that Freddie had not been terrified that he would disappoint his father. He certainly didn't intend to do it over the next two days.

CHAPTER 17

W HEN PHILIP HEARD his phone ring deep in his jacket pocket, he let it go to voicemail. He and Genevieve were so stunned by the revelation that Angelina had been the woman reaching out to the Met about the Gardner Museum pieces, they were speechless.

"Are you surprised?" Lillie's eyes were bright with excitement.

"And we two are the last to know, is that correct?" Genevieve poked an accusing finger at Lillie and Finn.

Lillie's embarrassed smile offered an apology.

"Obviously, there's more to this than you've explained, Francis." Philip pulled out his phone and perused the voicemail list. "Ah, that call was from Freddie." He smiled at Genevieve as he listened to the message, then pressed speaker and played the call for the table, everyone listening as the Baron advised they return to the schloss before the weather deteriorated." Philip grinned at Darlington. "I don't think he means you, Francis, since he doesn't know you exist."

Darlington smiled back.

Finn glanced at his watch and saw it was almost 11:30. "Ok, team. We need to wrap this up so you two," he said, nodding at Philip and Genevieve, "understand what's at stake and exactly how you can help."

"That sounds quite serious." Philip reached over and took Genevieve's hand, interlacing his fingers with hers. "Go on, Finn."

"In addition to her planner, DCI Fields' people recovered Angelina's phone. The Met was able to access everything: email, texts and photos. When they went through the photographs, they discovered the pictures she was going to show the Met. From the background, the analysts were able to match bits on the edges of the photos to surroundings—slivers of wallpaper, paint colors, a bit of fabric—that appeared in a photo spread from a *Vogue* article. Just after Heidi and Freddie got married, the magazine did quite an article on the couple, the schloss, how they entertain; you know, the kind of thing magazines do on you and Philip all the time," he said to Genevieve. "AI gathered all the fabrics, paint colors, stone, plaster, windows, in any database anywhere and matched them to the background in Angelina's photographs, and it identified Schloss Friedrichstein as the match."

"Are you suggesting that there is a piece stolen from the Isabella Stewart Gardner Museum at Schloss Friedrichstein?" Genevieve shook her head slowly. "That sounds crazy to me."

"I think what's crazier," Philip said, blinking in disbelief, "is that it sounds like you're asking us to confirm that the von

Bassewitz have stolen goods. Is that what's happening here?"

"Not really. Well, maybe… sort of," Darlington mumbled. "Finn?"

"Let's take a step back. When DCI Fields—"

"Finn," Lillie interrupted, "let *me* explain."

Finn relaxed back into his chair. "By all means, Lillie. Go for it." He smiled broadly, eager to watch this beguiling bundle of energy in action.

She met his smile with her own and jumped in. "When Fields and Darlington decided there was a good chance that Angelina had bona-fide information, they hatched a plan. They knew that not only were you two invited to Schloss Friedrichstein, but Finnegan Mountbatten—" she jerked a thumb at Finn, "—one of the foremost specialists on the museum heist, *and* Lillie Langdon—" she turned both thumbs toward herself, "—a renowned Isabella Stewart Gardner Museum scholar, had been invited as well. What an opportunity to have eyes on the inside and people who know what they're looking for, looking."

Genevieve narrowed her eyes at Lillie. "Did you plan all of this with DCI Fields before you left the disastrous grouse shoot?"

"We did not," Finn said. "DCI Fields didn't know about the connection until several days after Angelina was murdered."

"Oh, of course he didn't." Genevieve slapped her forehead then leaned forward, waiting to hear more.

Darlington took over. "What we're asking you to do is simply observe. While you're at the schloss, just be sensitive to the artwork on display and if you see this piece, text me, with confirming photos if possible. Then delete the photos immediately after you send them." He held up his phone and showed a picture of *The Concert* by Vermeer.

"Are you going to send those to us?" Philip said.

Francis shook his head. "If somehow one of the von Bassewitzes saw these photos on your phone, that would be a colossal tipoff."

"Ah, good point," Philip agreed. "That's it? That's all you want us to do?"

"It is. In fact I would go so far as to order you to do nothing else, if I had any authority to order you to do anything," Darlington said with a laugh.

"I'm glad you said that, Francis, because, if, at any point I think I can flirt any information out of Freddie or his father, I won't hesitate to do it. It works on donors, why wouldn't it work on art thieves?"

"Lillie, if anyone can use vamping to her advantage, you are the one. And, if you find any indication this work is on the premises, text us these words: 'The von Bassewitz collection is extraordinary.' Then leave it to us to sort it out from there. Any questions?"

Genevieve turned to Philip. "I think that's perfectly clear, don't you, darling? We walk around the schloss peeking under sofas and in drawers for a stolen art treasure while we're trying to extract millions of euros for a new museum from the people we're trying to send to prison. Is that pretty much it?"

"Exactly," Darlington said, just as the chef pushed through the kitchen door.

"Francis," he hollered across the restaurant. "We just got a call from the base of the mountain. They will be closing the lift in fifteen minutes so we are shutting everything down. Does that work for you?"

"Thanks so very much, mate. We really appreciate having the restaurant to ourselves." Darlington gave him a thumbs up, shoved his chair back, and stood. Through the window he saw a wall of fat flakes. "Perfect timing," he said, tugging on his ski jacket. "Is anyone taking the lift or are we all skiing down?"

"Just as promised, here comes the blizzard," Lillie said, shoving her arms into her jacket. "I think this is exciting. This is going to be very Agatha Christie." She assumed the voice of a 1940s radio announcer. "Four guests at a house party, snowbound in a gothic castle in the Austrian Alps. Will they find the long-lost art treasure or will their evil host discover their plan and put them in the dungeon? Will they find more treasures there or will it all end in tragedy...?"

"Ooooh. What a great idea, Lillie. We should go into the dungeons and search. Actually, Freddie said last night he'd give me a tour. I doubt he'd show us any stolen art or artifacts, but you never know." Genevieve zipped her parka, tugged her hat on and snapped its flaps under her chin. She pulled her gaiter up over her mouth and nose and was ready to put on her gloves.

From across the room, Finn yelled, "Are you two going to join us or shall we leave you here by the fire, daydreaming about being Monuments Men?" Francis was already outside, stepping into his bindings. Finn and Philip waited in the doorway, impatient to head down the mountain while there was still enough visibility to make their way safely.

"We're coming, we're coming." Genevieve and Lillie clomped their way to the door and out into the thickening snow.

With few skiers left on the mountain and the snow thickening, the summit felt more treacherous by the moment. Poised at the top of the run, the five agreed to stay together. In his red ski suit, Philip was the easiest to see so he would lead the way, and Francis would bring up the rear, making certain no one was left behind.

As they headed over the top of the run, sweeping down onto the main part of the trail, everyone's nerves jangled. As dangerous as this seemed, skiing down the mountain in nearly whiteout conditions would be the safest the team would be for the next two days.

CHAPTER 18

After forty-five minutes of traversing through a whiteout, deep powder and gusty winds, Philip led the band of skiers down an offshoot run marked 'Privat Nur Schloss Friedrichstein Bewohner: Private Schloss Friedrichstein Residents Only,' which led to a mountain-side entrance to the schloss.

"That was both exhilarating and terrifying," Genevieve said as she released her bindings and stepped off her skis. "I can't imagine we'll ever have such an exciting skiing experience again."

"Wasn't it absolutely brilliant?" Lillie shoved her goggles up to her forehead and shook like a dog; snow flew in all directions.

"You two are seriously mad." Though Philip's voice was sober, his smile stretched from ear to ear. "You may have thought you heard me whooping, but you didn't!"

"I trust Francis made it the rest of the way to the bottom." Finn grabbed his right glove fingers in his teeth and pulled. He stuck his glove under his arm and pulled off the other. "I'm ready for a huge bowl of knödelsuppe and a beer."

"I want hot chocolate and a piece of warm apple strudel." Genevieve salivated as she picked up her skis, clapped the bases together, and balanced them on her shoulder. She grabbed her poles and stomped through the door Philip had left open for her. The warm air of the ski room blasted her in the face, immediately fogging her ski goggles, and she felt as if she were back in the blizzard. "Help! I can't see a thing," she laughed.

"Well, that was predictable." Philip lifted the skis from her shoulder and snatched her poles. "Maybe next time take off your goggles before coming inside."

"Thanks for the tip, oh wise one." Genevieve kissed him on the tip of his red nose. "This setup is pretty perfect. I never want to ski again anyplace I have to carry my skis from the base lodge to the car, drive back to the lodge or condo or wherever we're staying, carry my stuff into the… yada, yada, yada. You get my point." She sat on the upholstered bench in the middle of the square room where she had left her after-ski boots just three hours ago and loosened the buckles of her ski boots. Philip straddled her leg with his bottom toward her face and pulled her boots off, then slipped them onto the arms of the wall-mounted dryer.

"I had no idea I was so exhausted." Lillie pushed herself off the bench and trudged toward the door to the hallway that led to the main staircase. "I'm just going to grab a coffee and cookie, take a hot shower, and have a little nap. I'll see you all later."

"I'm right behind you, Lillie. I think I'll pass on the soup and follow you right into the shower."

Lillie turned and raised both brows, her eyes wide and her smile mischievous. "Really, Finn? I don't remember inviting you."

Pink flooded his cheeks and he cleared his throat. "That's not exactly what I meant to say." He slipped his arm around Lillie's waist. "But I can think of worse ways to get warm." He wiggled his eyebrows at Lillie then looked back over his shoulder at Philip and Genevieve. "We'll see you two later," he said and ushered Lillie out the door.

"Those two seem to be getting along well. They're serious, aren't they?"

"I'd say so. Since we invited them last year for Christmas they've been, as my great-grandmother would say, as tight as two cheeks in a girdle." Genevieve gathered her gloves, hat and goggles, and laid them on a shelf in an open wooden locker. "This really is the epitome of luxury, isn't it?"

"I'd say that's an understatement. If you have a centuries-old chalet on the side of one of the world's best mountains, this is exactly what it should be. Spare no expense. Everything should be perfect." He held the door open for Genevieve and appreciated when she stopped and tilted her head up to him, her eyes smoldering into his. He leaned over and nipped at her warm lips, tugging on her lower lip with his teeth before covering her mouth with his.

She breathed deeply and leaned into him. When he heard her take another deep breath, Philip wondered if she had fallen asleep. "Psst, G. Your Prince Charming is supposed to wake you, not put you to sleep."

"Hmmm?" she said, dragging her lids half-open. "Sorry, darling. I think I'm about to doze off."

"Not flattering but understandable. Come on. Let's get you to bed for a nap or you won't be very sterling company tonight." He shoved her into the corridor and tugged the door to the ski room closed. "Remember, tonight is all about our charm offensive regarding the museum."

"And don't forget our other task." Genevieve shuffled down the hall ahead of Philip, struggling to put one foot in front of the other.

As they turned the corner and passed a thick wooden door, it creaked open and a Nordic specimen of a man filled the doorway, one hand on the doorknob and one hand holding a crate the size of a small painting.

"Whoa!" Startled by the man's unexpected appearance, Genevieve's hand flew to her heart and blood raced to her head. "Sorry," she said, waiting for the man to respond.

"I'm Philip Warwick and this is my wife, Genevieve." Philip extended his hand.

Max snapped to attention and gave Philip a sharp nod. "Lord and Lady Crosswick, ich bin Max Klein, Baron von Bassewitz's valet."

"The elder baron?" Genevieve said.

"Ja und his driver, and a few other things," he said as he held up the crate.

Philip pointed to the box Max held. "Is that something interesting?" he said, not expecting much of a response.

"I would imagine it is. The Baron asked me to bring up number 247 from the art vault before dinner this evening." He tipped the box up to show the stamped number. "I believe he wants to show it to his dinner guests." Max stood a bit straighter and his eyes shone with pride. "The von Bassewitz family has an extraordinary collection, as I am certain you know."

"We do." Genevieve glanced at Philip then focused back on Max. "We hope the senior Baron will give us a tour of his collection while we're here." She captivated the Baron's man with a dazzling smile. "Max, you mentioned the art vault. I bet you know all about it. Do you have a large depository downstairs?"

Unable to resist Genevieve's charm, Max was anxious to share information. "We do, my lady. It is, of course, temperature and humidity controlled. The Baron mentioned that one of the guests is a security expert and I know he is anxious to talk to him about how the vault security should be upgraded. It is not the best." He leaned toward Genevieve and lowered his voice. The Baron has much, um, Arroganz? Is this a word in English?"

"Arrogance?" Philip confirmed. "Great pride?"

"Ach, ja." Max bobbed his head. "Ja, that is the word. Stolz. Proud. The Baron is extremely proud of his art. He will love to show you the collection. Now, before I go, is there anything I can do for you?"

"Thank you for the chat. I don't think there's anything we need. Right, G?"

"Wrong, Philip. Max, would it be possible for someone to

bring sandwiches to our room? I'm starving but too tired to go in search of food. Is there any chance you could help us with that?"

"Consider it done, madame."

Genevieve put her hand on his arm. "You're my hero." She squeezed his bicep. "Thank you." She slid her hand into Philip's, and together they trudged toward the staircase while Max pulled the door closed, locked it, then punched numbers into the keypad next to the door jam. Down the hall, Philip and Genevieve could hear a thunk then a beep and knew the door was locked and the alarm armed.

CHAPTER 19

THOUGH THE CURTAINS were drawn wide, at 6 p.m. the room was as dark as midnight. Wind rattled the wooden windows and whistled through tiny spaces between frames and jambs. Genevieve pulled the duvet over her head and wiggled further into her cocoon. As she was about to drift back into a lovely doze, the fragrance of Rose Otto filled her nostrils and her eyes flew open.

"Charlotte," she whispered. She breathed deeply, inhaling the intense fragrance. "Charlotte," she said again, this time aloud.

She peeled the covers down over her forehead, blinked several times trying to adjust to the darkness, then swept the room looking for signs of her ghostly friend. She squeezed her eyes tight, then, just as she flickered them open, the lamps flashed on and her hand flew to her mouth, stifling a scream. Nowhere did she see Charlotte's beautiful spirit but there, in the doorway with his hand on the light switch, Philip lounged against the doorjamb.

"Holy macaroni! You scared the bejesus out of me." Genevieve still felt the blood rushing through her veins and her pulse thundering in her ears. "I smelled Rose Otto, stuck my head out from under the duvet and the lamps came on."

"Perfect timing on my part, I'd say."

As Philip ambled toward the bed, Genevieve pushed herself to a sitting position. "What do you have there?" she asked, spying the glass he was holding.

"I thought you might like a glass of Champagne while you're getting ready for dinner." He walked around the bed, handed her the flute, and gestured for her to scootch over. She wiggled her way to the middle of the bed, creating a ledge where he could sit. "Now, what did you say about Rose Otto? Tell me again."

She cleared her throat then cleared it again. "I had come out of a deep sleep and just as I was drifting back, the smell of Rose Otto hit me."

"Really?" Philip's brow arched.

"Yes, really." She took a gulp of bubbles. "First I whispered her name, then I called out to her. Just as I stuck my head from out of the covers, the lights flashed on and I nearly had a heart attack. But it was you and the fragrance was gone." She took another drink. "Thank you for this."

Philip stood and pulled off his navy cashmere crewneck. "You don't think you were dreaming?" he said, sitting back down on the bed.

"I do not."

"Do you think there's any correlation between my rather aggressive interaction with her at Wilmingrove Hall and her being here?" Philip was still delighted that Charlotte had visited him at Wilmingrove Hall while Genevieve was away.

"You mean, is she trying to send us a message about family von Bassewitz? Maybe. I guess we'll just have to wait and see."

He looked at his watch, took the Champagne glass from Genevieve and drained the little bit that was left. "You, my darling, need to get your very attractive butt in gear. It's almost 6:30 and we're due downstairs in zee Wohnzimmer at exactly seiben Uhr. Dat's seven o'clock to you, Schatzie."

"Yikes!" With her foot, Genevieve shoved Philip off the bed, threw the covers wide, and leapt to the floor before Philip realized he was sitting on his bottom on the carpet.

"What the…?" was all he could say.

"Needs must, babe. Needs must," she said, already in the bathroom working her magic.

With the blizzard fully raging, the massive grandfather clock in the great hall struck the seventh of seven bongs just as Philip and Genevieve strode into the living room arm in arm. In thirty minutes Genevieve had tamed her bedhead into a glossy, chestnut mane, swinging just above her shoulders with her every step. Her black, floor-length sweater dress accentuated her long, lean muscles and was cinched in at the waist by her favorite wide leather belt with a gold lion's head buckle. The only other accessory she needed was chunky gold earbobs and her wedding ring.

Looking equally dazzling, Philip escorted Genevieve across

the room to where Freddie and Heidi stood in front of the fireplace. On the hearth, flames lapped at fat birch logs, their sweet, wintergreen aroma wafting into the room.

In her crisp white shirt, her black, well-cut blazer, and narrow trousers, Elsa offered a tray of flutes filled with Champagne. Philip plucked two from the tray, offered one to Genevieve and kept the other.

As always, Heidi looked stunning: her loden green jumper was a perfect Tyrolean masterpiece and she the perfect model. Genevieve could only imagine how long it had taken a needleworker to embroider the intricate design of the Austrian eagle, laurel, and edelweiss around the neck, arm holes and waist of the jumper that billowed to the floor. Her thick blonde hair was caught in a braided bun at the nape of her neck and she could have been on the cover of "Vogue Austria".

That woman would look fabulous in a trash bag, Genevieve thought to herself with a laugh. *Ah, to be forty-five again.*

"Genevieve." Heidi jolted Genevieve from her thoughts. "I love your belt." The hostess brushed her fingertips across the lion's head buckle. "And, Philip, how handsome you are." She ran the back of her hand up and down his lapel. "Mmm. Cashmere, yummy. You look zehr Ralph Lauren. Very to the manor born." She leaned into him and kissed his cheek.

And what's all that flirting with Philip about? I didn't notice that when they were at Wilmingrove Hall. Genevieve felt jealousy knit her brows and tried to relax her forehead.

The heat of a blush crept up Philip's neck. "And you, Heidi, are stunning," he countered. "In fact—" He took Genevieve's hand and twirled her from his side so she stood next to Heidi. "—Freddie, can you imagine two luckier men on the planet than we are?"

"Perhaps I am the luckiest man on the planet." The four at the fireplace turned toward the booming voice. Standing in the entrance to the room, with Lillie draped on his arm and Finn standing behind him, Baron Karl Friedrich von Bassewitz's athletic physique filled the doorway. At ninety-one, his thick shock of white hair was magnificent and even at such a distance, one could see the Baron's steel-blue eyes sparkled with fierce intelligence. He moved briskly toward the group across the room, his noble bearing evident with every step. A charmed smile played on Lillie's lips as she floated at his side, the wide legs of her velvet jumpsuit fluttering as she tried to keep up with him. And on the Baron's other side, Finn widened his stride to keep pace.

When they arrived at the group, the Baron extended his hand to Philip. "Lord Crosswick. It is such a pleasure to finally meet you." He turned to Genevieve. Taking her hand in his, he said, "And Lady Crosswick. You are stunning. I would tell you in German but it does not sound romantic at all and I am trying to charm you. I should speak to you in French but my French is terrible so we shall settle for English." He brought her hand to his lips and held it there for several seconds. He looked up at her with his crystal eyes and his mouth pulled into a sultry smile.

Genevieve raised her other hand to her face and fanned it back and forth. "And, Baron," she said, "if I were a southern woman, I would say, 'Be still my beating heart.'"

Everyone broke into laughter and the party began.

The Champagne flowed and Genevieve had to stop herself from taking hors d'oeuvres every time Elsa offered. She wanted to save herself for what was to come. By the time dinner was announced, the group glowed from the sparkling wine and was as easy with each other as old friends.

With Genevieve on one arm and Lillie on the other, Karl Friedrich led a procession from the warmth of the Wohnzimmer, through the chill of the great hall and into the dining room, where a mighty blaze in the fireplace made a valiant effort to warm the cavernous salon. Heavy drapes were drawn against the blizzard's howling winds that seeped around the window frames. An enormous Persian carpet did its best to absorb the cold from the stone floor, its vibrant burgundy background visually warming the room. As a cautionary measure, cashmere lap robes hung over the back of each upholstered chair, waiting for diners to drape them over a lap or a shoulder.

Torches and candelabras blazed everywhere, their candlelight splashing the room with romance, making the vast space almost cozy. Delighted by her grand surroundings, Genevieve glanced from one stunning tableau to the next, smiling as her eyes paused on a pair of twenty-taper candelabras polished to a high, brass sheen, each flanking an enormous bowl filled with apples, pears, oranges, grapes, and nuts, with pheasant feathers tucked in among all the fruit and a sparkling gold braid woven throughout. As she was about to turn her head and thank the Baron for holding her chair, her eyes fell on a small wooden crate leaning against the wall just behind one of the candelabras. *Aha.*

The crate Max was bringing from the vault when we saw him in the hall, she thought, and felt her pulse race. She took a deep breath and released it slowly, then sat.

"Baron," she said, keeping her voice light. "Everything is atemberaubend. I believe that is German for stunning, is it not?"

His booming laugh bounced around the room. "You see what a terrible word this is for such a magnificent quality? I could not possibly use that word for you." He turned to Lillie, who was seated on his other side. "Or you, lovely Lillie. German is so harsh. We Austrians do our best to soften it but often people from other countries cannot understand our German. Rather like what the Kiwis do to the English language. They soften everything, change random vowels and all of sudden no one can understand their English. They turn deck into dick. Six into sex. Mein Gott in Himmel! What are they thinking?"

Chuckles rippled around the table as Karl Fredrich monologued as if he were a standup comedian.

"Bitte, everyone be seated," he said, but remained standing. "I am so pleased that my dear Freddie arranged this weekend. It is wonderful to finally meet the extraordinary Lord and Lady Crosswick, their smashing foundation director, Lillie Langdon, and the infamous Finnegan Mountbatten. Elsa—" He smiled at the house manager. "—thank you for pouring this lovely Riesling, the king of German wines. Please raise your glasses and let us toast to an atemberaubend few days together." His face exploded into a grin and he looked directly at Genevieve. "To a stunning house party!"

"To this atemberaubend wine and our atemberaubend host," Genevieve responded, her eyes flashing with purpose and her spirit determined to pry information from the Baron.

Silence reigned as everyone took the first drink of the aromatic, fruit-forward wine, its honey color glowing in the candlelight.

Genevieve leaned close to the Baron and covered his hand with hers. "Karl, this is delicious."

When he offered Genevieve a proud smile she could see the handsome man of decades ago: the sparkle in his eyes, the mischief twitching his lips.

She leaned a little closer, pressing into his shoulder. "Karl, I'm so curious. Tell me what's in the box behind the candelabra?" As she looked at it again, it occurred to her that the box was smaller than the one she had seen earlier, but she could be wrong.

"Oh, you clever girl," he said with a grin. "You saw my little surprise. I have something simply extraordinary to show all of you, my new partners. This will make our Berlin musée the most talked-about art museum in the world. Everyone will come. No one will believe what they see."

Just as Genevieve was about to ask the Baron when he would reveal the contents of the box, Frieda, one of the servers, arrived to place a steaming bowl of Kartoffelsuppe in front of her. She sat back in her chair so the young woman could leave the soup, then turned immediately back to Karl, but he was already deep in conversation with Lillie. She heard her stomach grumble as the aroma of the potato soup hit her nostrils and realized she was ravenous.

"Guten Appetit," Heidi said, when everyone was served. She sat at the opposite end of the table from Karl, lifted her spoon and surveyed the guests, her smile caressing each person, making everyone feel lucky to be a part of the evening.

Conversations that had started in the living room before dinner flowed again and new subjects gathered steam. Topics ranging from politics to food, to wine popped up, then dwindled until finally art took center stage, with everyone chattering about the exhibition at the Laney Musée des Beaux Arts in Paris that had recently opened. All the while, Genevieve kept glancing at the small carton on the sideboard and she struggled to keep track of the conversation.

Servers—Frieda and Christina—collected soup bowls and replaced them with plates of artfully arranged Rinderrouladen: thin beef slices wrapped around a savory filling. Braised red cabbage added vivid color and a sweet and tangy flavor contrast.

All of a sudden, Karl interrupted his chat with Lillie, snapped his fingers at Christina, and all conversation stopped. "You, there. You girl, tell Elsa we are ready for the Spätburgunder," he barked, then turned back to Lillie. "Tell me about the new exposition you've just mounted at the Musée des Beaux Arts, Madame Executive Director," he said, his charm oozing again.

Confused by Karl's abrupt change of behavior, Genevieve shot Philip a questioning look and he shrugged his shoulders almost imperceptibly.

Before the server was out the door, Elsa entered the dining room, a bottle of red wine in each hand.

"Gut, the pinot noir. Elsa, we've been waiting. What is

Rinderrouladen without our excellent pinot?" Though the Baron had resumed his jocular demeanor, annoyance clenched his jaw. Elsa splashed a taste of the ruby red wine into his Zalto glass with the wide bowl and narrow neck. He swirled the pinot noir, admiring its lovely color, then closed his eyes and slurped it into his mouth, the lip of the glass so thin it was as if there was nothing between his palate and the wine. His inhale could be heard around the table while the dinner guests waited in silence. They watched his Adam's apple rise and fall as he swallowed.

"Ah," he said at last. "Perfekt." He looked up at Elsa, who stood at his side and snapped his chin up. "Pour," he commanded.

Genevieve wondered if anyone else had noticed the daggered glance Elsa flashed at the Baron and tucked that observation into her pillow-talk-file for Philip later.

With all the glasses filled, Karl raised his. "Zum Wohl," he said. "To your health." He drank several gulps before he thwacked his delicate goblet down on the table. "Und so, Lillie," he said, turning back to her. "Where were we?"

With her elbow on the arm of her chair, she leaned toward the Baron so her shoulder was only inches away from his. With a coquettish tilt to her head and a husky note in her voice, she said, "I know exactly where we were." Her lips lifted in a flirty smile. "You had just asked me to tell you about the newest exhibition at the Laney Musée des Beaux Arts."

"Ah ja," he said, unable to take his eyes off of Lillie's Botticelli face. "Do tell me everything, bitte, meine kleine Maus."

My little mouse; really? Lillie mused and eased back to the center of her chair. She took a sip of wine without breaking eye contact with the Baron. "You have not seen the show yet, is that right, Karl?"

"Nein. I have not. If I come to Paris to see it, will you give me a personal tour?" the Baron said, playing with his knife, turning it over and over.

Lillie laid her hand on top of the Baron's. "I can't think of anything I'd rather do." She almost batted her eyelashes at him but decided that would be too much and stopped after one blink.

The Baron took Lillie's delicate hand in his large palm and interlaced his fingers with hers. "I have some secrets to tell you about some of the artwork in our collection," he mumbled, staring into Lillie's eyes. His lids sagged halfway over his eyes, his breathing went deep and rhythmic, and for a moment, Lillie thought he might have fallen asleep with his eyes open. She stared at him for several seconds until he licked his lips, startling her.

"Oh," she said, wiggling her hand from his grip. "We should eat this lovely meal, don't you think?"

"I'd rather eat you," he said, but stabbed a bite of beef and put it in his mouth.

Lillie's eyes darted around the table to see if anyone had overheard the conversation and landed on Genevieve, who sat on Karl's other side and had heard everything. Her wide eyes and tight lips sent Lillie a cautionary warning.

Lillie responded with a slow nod of her head, sending Genevieve the message, "I've got this under control."

"Baron." Genevieve squeezed his arm to get his attention. "When you come to Paris for the 'Vermeer: the Impressionists' Hero' show, Philip and I would love for you to stay with us at our

Avenue Foch house. We could have a little dinner party so you could meet some of our board members."

Karl stared at Genevieve for several seconds then turned to look at Lillie. "Mein Gott im Himmel," he said, slurring his words a bit. "You two are simply atemberaubend."

The women exchanged an amused glance.

"And you, Baron, are stunning as well," Geneveve said and nodded at Lillie to go on.

"Karl, we were talking about the new show at the Laney Musée des Beaux Arts."

The Baron frowned at the glass Elsa had refilled only seconds ago. He held it aloft, staring at it as if he had no idea how it had come to be full again. He took a drink then plunked the glass on the table, sloshing wine onto the crisp white tablecloth and watched as dark red crept across the linen.

"Karl?" Lillie shook his arm that rested beside her on the table. "Karl, are you all right?"

When he looked at her, his face was contorted with pain. "My head is splitting. You must excuse me," he gasped. "Elsa, get Max. Bed," he whispered, and Lillie could barely hear him.

She looked up at the stern house manager. Thinking Elsa had not heard him, she said, "The Baron would like Max to help him to bed."

"I heard," Elsa slapped Lillie with her reply.

The Baron tried to push out of his chair but was too weak and he plopped back onto the seat. Philip had been keeping a watchful eye on Genevieve, Lillie and the Baron during their conversation and was at his side in a dash. He held the chair as

Elsa helped him to his feet, holding his elbow by one hand and clutching the bottle of wine she had just poured in the other.

"Papa, what is the matter?" Freddie looked across the table, confused about what was happening.

"Baron?" Max was through the door and at his side, putting his arm around Karl's waist. "Baron, was ist los? What is happening?" Max's brows drew together, fear flashing in his eyes.

"I'll get him some water," Elsa said, and dashed from the room.

"Nussing isamatter," Karl slurred his insistence, but clutched Max's arm, trying to steady himself. "Maybe jus, uh, too, much wine." But as Max withdrew his arm from around the Baron's waist, Karl staggered and fell into Philip, who caught him, wrapped his arms around the Baron's shoulders and eased him to the floor.

"Something is seriously wrong," Philip bellowed. "Max, call 911 or whatever the emergency services are here."

Max pulled his phone from his pocket and looked at the blank screen. "Scheiße! My phone is dead. I'll go to the kitchen and use the landline."

"Hurry."

Hearing panic in Philip's voice, Genevieve dashed around the table and squatted next to Karl. As she put two fingers on his carotid artery, his ice-blue eyes stared vacantly up at her. She felt nothing on the left side of his neck so repositioned her fingers on the right. Still no rhythm. She leaned down and put her cheek next to his nostril. No breath. When she pulled back, a gasp caught in her throat. The Baron's lips were parted and a bloody froth bubbled from his mouth.

CHAPTER 20

"I**S SHE DEAD?**" Heidi screamed and flew into Freddie's arms.

"I'm afraid so." Genevieve put her fingers on his carotid once more to confirm what she believed. She leaned forward until her nose was almost touching his mouth and breathed deeply, smelling for an almond scent. Instead, the strong smell of Rose Otto assaulted her senses. Her head whipped up to see a circle of faces staring down at her and she wondered if anyone else had smelled Charlotte's scent, which had already vanished. *Charlotte,* her mind screamed. *What are you doing?*

"Genevieve, you look like you've seen a ghost!" Lillie's words almost made her laugh.

Philip took her by the shoulders and pulled her to stand. "Are you okay?" he asked, then wrapped her in a comforting embrace.

"Yes." Her voice muffled into his chest. "Unnerved but okay."

"Of course you're unnerved, G. You just watched a man die."

Pulling Genevieve into his side, he turned to Freddie, with Heidi sobbing in his arms. "Freddie, Heidi, I'm so sorry." He put his hand on Heidi's back and squeezed her shoulder. "I'm so very sorry."

Heidi took a tissue from the pocket of her jumper and dabbed her eyes. She inhaled a ragged breath and much to his surprise, Philip saw relief flood her face.

"Oh, thank god," she whispered, her breath still hitching.

Seeing surprise and confusion in Philip's wide eyes, Freddie hastened to explain. "What Heidi means is that, over the last year, Papa has grown more and more difficult. You saw this evening how erratic and rude he was with the staff." He held Heidi a little tighter at his side. "For the last ten years, Elsa has been more of a friend to Papa than a servant, but recently he has treated her very badly. He has treated her like a scullery maid, an indentured servant. We are very lucky she has not left us, though many times she has threatened to do just that." Heidi put her head on her husband's shoulder. "But the worst part is how he has begun to treat Heidi."

Philip's lips tugged into an affectionate smile. "I can't imagine how the Baron could have been unkind to you, Heidi."

"It is hard to believe, isn't it. After Angelina, who was so very unpleasant the two years before we divorced, he thought Heidi was perfect—until he didn't. At first he adored her, then lately it has become worse, more erratic with each passing day. One day he rages at her for hoarding gummy bears under our mattress, which would be comical if it were not so deranged. The next day he verbally attacks her for stealing his favorite Vermeer painting, which, of course, he does not own. The next day he again thinks Heidi is the most wonderful person in the world and wants to rewrite his will and leave everything to her—excluding Gabriel and me completely. Every day is a new nightmare."

"Surely you have taken him to his physician. What has his doctor said?" Finn asked.

"For the last two years he has refused to see his doctors. His philosophy has been that he has lived a long life. As he's been saying, 'What will they tell me? "Baron, you don't have long to live." Who can argue with that? I am ninety-one years old.' He has a point, no?"

Though the guests were still stunned by the Baron's abrupt death, uncomfortable laughter rippled through the room.

"I have spoken to Herr Doktor Schmidt, his physician, many times over the last year, but of course he couldn't diagnose my father over the phone. Our plan was to have a dinner party next week when we were back in Vienna and include Doktor Schmidt so he could see Papa's behavior for himself. I guess next week will be too late." Tears swam in his eyes, Heidi tilted her head up and Freddie kissed her on her forehead.

As if to add its sorrow to the gathering, the blizzard winds moaned through the room and the heavy drapes wafted ever so slightly. When Genevieve saw the curtains move, she couldn't help but sniff for Charlotte's fragrance. She smelled nothing.

"Freddie," Finn put his hand on the younger baron's shoulder. "I hate to state the obvious, but we should call someone to report your father's death. Who would that be here in Austria?"

"If we were in Vienna, I would call his doctor. I suppose I should call the hospital. Or perhaps I shall simply call 133, the police station, and they can direct me what to do next."

Finn raised his hand. "I'll take care of that. Don't you need to go call Gabriel and let him know what's happened?"

Freddie slapped his forehead. "Mein Gott! Gabriel. I must call Gabriel. He will be devastated that he wasn't here."

"Freddie, mein Schatz. We shall call Gabriel together?" Heidi's tears were gone and strength stiffened her spine.

Freddie swept the back of his hand across his eyes. "Let's go to the living room." Hand in hand, they walked out of the dining room, Heidi's shoulders back and head high, Freddie's shoulders slumped and head hanging.

With the room to themselves, Genevieve motioned for Philip, Finn and Lillie to gather around her. "G, what is it?" After more than forty years of marriage, Philip knew when she had something more to say. Instinctively he expected something explosive.

Finn and Lillie waited with no idea what was to come.

"Okay, guys," she said. In spite of the chill in the room, Genevieve felt sweat dampen her armpits. "I'm quite certain, though Baron von Bassewitz the elder was ninety-one years old, he did not die of natural causes."

"What? What do you mean?" Holding her breath, Lillie stared at Genevieve, waiting for more information.

Genevieve glanced over at the dead Baron, lying on his back, staring vacantly at the ceiling. The froth she had seen on his lips was no longer visible. She squatted beside him again and squinted at his mouth. The bubbles were gone but the lips were still damp with a red tinge.

"What are you looking for, G?" Philip was on one knee beside her.

"When I was checking for a pulse, I saw bloody froth on the Baron's mouth." She glanced up at Finn and Lillie standing over her. "I've seen enough *Midsomer Murders* episodes to immediately think of cyanide poisoning. I expected to smell almonds, because that's what detectives always smell."

"Did you?" Though he contained his smile, Philip chuckled unable to hide his amusement.

"I did not," Genevieve said. "But guess what I smelled instead." Three blank faces returned her question.

"For an instant, I smelled Rose Otto. Charlotte was here." Both Finn and Lillie had heard the stories of Charlotte Chaubert's ghost and how she had chosen to befriend Genevieve, but they viewed her legend more as family lore than reality.

Lillie pulled out a dining room chair and plopped onto it. A single curl slipped from a silver clip holding her hair in a cluster on top of her head, fell onto her forehead and bounced in front of her left eye. She huffed at it. It wafted up, then back to where it started and, annoyed, she tucked it behind her ear. Unsure how to respond to the news of Charlotte's presence, Lillie measured her words. "What… um… do you think… uh, that might mean, Genevieve?"

Still on her knees by Karl, Genevieve eased his eyelids closed then sat on her bottom next to him. "I really don't have any idea but this is not the first time Charlotte has let me know that she's here at Schloss Friedrichstein."

"Really?" Lillie slid her eyes sideways at Philip, who gave her a tiny shrug. "When have you felt Charlotte's presence other than just a few minutes ago?"

A whisper of a smile crossed Genevieve's face. "I know you think Charlotte is nonsense, Lillie, but I assure you her spirit is real. She was in our room this afternoon when I was taking a nap. I don't know why she's here, but I'm sure her appearance at Schloss Friedrichstein is significant."

"As fascinating as this is, I need to call 133 and find out what to do next." Finn walked across the room to the inglenook fireplace and sat on one of the benches. "I hope their English is better than my German," he mumbled as he glanced back at Lillie sagging in the dining chair. Still kneeling on one side of Karl, Philip grabbed the back of Lillie's chair and heaved himself to stand. On Karl's other side, Genevieve still sat cross-legged, her sweater dress pulled above her knees.

As he looked at his screen to dial, Finn saw his hand trembling, felt his stomach fluttering and realized he was nervous about the gravity of his mission. He was about to call the Austrian police about a dead nobleman and his German was absolute crap. "Hey, what happened to Max? And where is Elsa? If this copper doesn't speak English, I could use them to translate." He took a calming breath and dialed 133, putting his phone on speaker. Immediately the busy signal bleated through the speaker and he exhaled, relieved. He punched "end", waited several seconds then retried. The busy tone sounded again. "You don't suppose this is going to go on for a long time, do you?"

"Oh no. Of course not." Philip's sarcasm was not lost on Finn. "There's a raging blizzard out there and we're in dire need of emergency services. Of course you're going to continue to get a busy signal, probably for the rest of the night." Philip extended his hand to Genevieve and pulled her to her feet. "Keep trying. I'm going to go find Max and ask him where we can find a tarp." He headed toward the far door that led to the kitchen.

"A tarp? Whatever for?" Lillie's cupid mouth puckered the question.

Philip stopped and turned around. "If we can't get any emergency people to come for Karl, we're going to need to store him somewhere cool and I think it would be a good idea to put him in a tarp. Don't you? If we have to put him outside, we don't want any critters nibbling on him, do we?"

"Oh, Philip!" Genevieve rolled her eyes. "You could have put that more delicately."

He exploded with a laugh. "Darling, what about any of this situation is delicate? We're here in a raging Alpine storm, in the dining room with a dead man who according to you was possibly poisoned. There's nothing delicate about any of that, is there?"

Finn—who continued to dial, hang up, and dial again—lowered his voice, whispering from across the room. "Don't forget Scotland Yard is relying on us to feed them information when we find some evidence about the stolen art."

"Good point, Finn. I can't believe what a mess we've gotten ourselves into. And we have a long way to go before we get to the other side. And Lillie—" He pointed to her. "—I'd say our partnership with the von Bassewitz family on a museum in Berlin is shot to hell."

With her elbows on the table and her head in her hands, Lillie was quiet for several seconds before she raised her head and said, "Philip, one way or another, the von Basswitzes are going to help build the Berlin museum."

"Oh, Lillie." Philip shook his head, feigning deep sorrow. "Oh, poor, naïve Lillie. There is no way you're going to pull this fiasco from the jaws of disaster and turn it into a success for the Laney Musée des Beaux Arts, Berlin. The ex-wife of one of our major donors was murdered on our estate and now the head of that same family is dead, maybe poisoned. I think Freddie is going to be rather preoccupied for the foreseeable future."

"Are you up for a wager on that, oh ye of little faith?" Lillie's flagging energy began to simmer. She loved a challenge and Philip throwing down the gauntlet was just what she needed to revive her.

"I'm always happy to take a lady's money." Out of the corner of his eye, Philip saw Genevieve smirking as he questioned Lillie's ability to extract enormous donations from the most challenging prospects.

"So how much is this wager going to be?" Genevieve could hardly wait to hear how much each challenger was willing to ante.

"I'd say a hundred pounds," Lillie challenged.

Philip affected a sense of ennui. He patted his mouth as he fake-yawned. "Hardly worth the effort, I'd say. I'm thinking at least a thousand pounds."

Genevieve caught Lillie's eye and winked.

"I'll be happy to take your thousand pounds, Philip. To be clear, by the time we leave Schloss Friedrichstein, we shall have a commitment from the von Bassewitz foundation for the Berlin museum." She crossed to him with her hand extended and they shook on their bet.

"This is all so unseemly: making bets while we have a corpse in the room. Honestly." Genevieve scoffed a breath of disgust, emphasizing how unsavory she thought the entire situation. She pulled a cashmere lap robe from the back of one of the chairs and draped it over Karl with grave reverence, covering his six-foot frame from his head to his toes. Then she waved her hands at Philip, shooing him out of the room. "Now go find Max so we can tarp up this dead Baron," she said, shocking everyone into laughter.

From the time he started many minutes ago, Finn had been continuously dialing, trying to get through to the police. "I'm going to call five more times," he said, "and if they haven't picked up by then, I'm going to stop and we can just stick Karl outside until the blizzard's over."

Heading out in search of Max, Philip stopped in the doorway, waiting to see if Finn would have any luck in the next five tries.

"One," he said, thrusting one finger in the air. With the phone in his right hand, he pressed the green "call" button with his thumb. There was a beat of silence before the flat ring of the call going through filled the room and a cheer rang out from the four listening.

"Polizeiinspektion Lech. Wie kann ich Ihnen helfen?" a tired voice growled.

"Bitte, sprechen Sie English?" Finn held his breath, hoping for the right answer.

"Ja, of course I speak English," the officer snapped. "What do you need?"

"Uh." So surprised was Finn that he'd finally gotten through, that for a second he forgot why he was calling. Then he caught sight of the big lump on the floor under the coverlet and blurted, "We have a dead body here in the house and we don't know what to do with it."

"Who is this?" the voice at the other end of the line demanded.

Finn's wide, panicked eyes begged his friends for help. In two long strides, Philip was at his side. "Officer, this is Philip Warwick, the Earl of Crosswick," he said, directing his voice toward the phone, which was still on speaker. "My wife, Lady Crosswick and I are at a house party at Schloss Friedrichstein and I'm sorry to report that Karl Friedrich von Bassewitz, the Baron von Bassewitz died this evening during dinner. We are calling to notify the police. We have no idea what we should do next."

Silence filled the room. Philip waited then said, "Hello, bitte?

At the other end, they heard someone say, "Moment," then over the speaker, they could hear a muffled conversation in rapid German. For several long seconds Philip, Genevieve, Finn, and Lillie stared at the phone as if the officer might jump through it.

"Hallo," a commanding voice finally burst through the phone and all four people in the dining room jumped. "Hallo," he said again. "Is there someone there?"

All eyes were on Philip, and Genevieve gave him a gentle shove in the shoulder.

TANA L.H. BOERGER

"Sorry, officer," Philip said.

"Chief Inspector," the man at the other end corrected.

"Forgive me," Philip made a comic face and the other three tittered. "Chief Inspector. This is Philip Warwick, Earl of Crosswick from the UK," he repeated. "We have a situation here at Schloss Friedrichstein." He explained again what had happened but added, "We aren't quite certain about the cause of death. And we need your counsel on what to do with the body."

"What do you mean you're not quite certain about the cause of death?" the Chief Inspector snarled. "We are talking about the elder Baron, correct?"

"Yes, sir. We are."

"Isn't he almost a hundred years old?"

"He's ninety-one." Annoyance was creeping into Philip's voice and he told himself to keep his tone under control. He could only imagine what the police had been dealing with all day.

"Why would you think a ninety-one-year-old's death was not from natural causes?"

"Chief Inspector," Genevieve broke in. "This is Genevieve Warwick, Lord Crosswick's wife. It may be nothing, but I saw a bloody froth on the Baron's lips shortly after he stopped breathing. It could have been a completely natural result of dying. I haven't seen that many people die." She thought a moment. "Actually, I've never seen a person die before. Regardless, I thought it should be noted."

"Consider it noted." They heard the Chief take several gulps of something before he said, "As you can imagine, no one from our office can come to you until this storm is over. They are predicting another thirty-six hours so it could be two days before we can reach you. I would suggest you keep the Baron's body in a cold spot, which shouldn't be difficult in these weather conditions. If anything unusual occurs, call us."

"You mean more unusual than a man dying in the middle of a dinner party and his guests putting him out in the snow? That might be difficult, Chief," Genevieve snapped at the policeman, not at all concerned about her tone.

Philip's eyebrows shot up and his lopsided smile applauded her retort. "Thank you, Chief, for your help," he said, wrapping up the conversation. "We'll preserve the Baron as well as we can and we'll follow up with your office as soon as the blizzard is over. Auf Wiedersehen."

"Ja. Goodbye, Lord Crosswick," the Chief Inspector said and the line went dead.

CHAPTER 21

"I GUESS WE HAVE our marching orders. We really do need to go in search of a tarp, don't we?" Lillie grabbed one of the lap robes and snugged it around her shoulders. "Isn't it getting cold in here?"

Finn pulled a large log from the copper wood bin, and rather than settle it on the waning fire with care, he tossed it into the firebox. Sparks flew everywhere, crackling and snapping, and the flames jumped back to life.

Philip swung his gaze from one end of the dining room to the other and from door to door. "This is absurd," he said, his earlier simmering annoyance bubbling into irritation. "Where the hell are the people responsible for this man? Why are we taking care of this dead Baron who doesn't belong to any of us?"

Genevieve put a soothing hand on Philip's cheek. "Darling," she calmed, "we did tell Freddie we'd help. Finn assured him he would make the call to the police and so he did. And I covered Karl with a blanket. I hardly think we've provided extraordinary services, do you?" She saw his brow relax and felt the stress of responsibility soothed as he laid his hands on her waist.

"You're right, of course. It's just that this is all so bizarre."

At the same time, Max came through the door from the kitchen, and Freddie and Heidi returned from making the difficult call to Gabriel.

"Freddie," Philip said. Relieved to see his host, he felt the tension that had been gripping his neck melt. "How did that go?"

"Remarkably well," the younger Baron said. "He was surprised at the news but certainly not shocked. As he said, it wasn't exactly unexpected at his age. It is unfortunate that Michael is in New York and not with him in London."

Heidi slipped her hand into Freddie's and gave it a squeeze. "Gabriel said to thank you all for everything you are doing to help Freddie through this. He is very sorry he cannot be here with us." Her eyes were red-rimmed and her body sagged with fatigue.

"Freddie, after many attempts, I finally got through to 133," Finn said. "With everyone's help explaining what had happened, the police now understand the circumstances of your father's death."

"Ach, gut." Max whooshed out a breath. "I've been in the kitchen on the landline dialing and redialing all this time. As you found, Herr Mountbatten, it was always busy. Und what did they say we should do?"

Philip gave a synopsis of their conversation then turned to

the elder Baron's valet. "Max, we need a tarp. Do you know if there's one in the schloss?"

"Of course, Lord Crosswick. I know exactly where a tarp is. It will take me a bit of time. That sort of thing is in the garage, which are at the far side of the schloss."

"Max, I'd like to go with you," Genevieve said, jumping at the chance to explore other parts of the castle. Perhaps she could get Max to tell her something he shouldn't. Maybe she would even see something that might lead to clues about stolen art, if such clues existed.

Max opened his mouth to speak but wasn't sure what to say. "Are you certain you want to go through the cellars to the garage?" was all he could think of.

"Absolutely," she said, thrilled at the idea of traipsing through the dungeons. "Do I need a coat?"

"Ja, ja, my lady. You need a coat. And I would put on warmer clothes."

She was already at the dining room door when she stopped and turned around. "Does anyone else want to go with us?" she said. Then, as an afterthought she asked, "Max, where is Elsa? I haven't seen her since she rushed to the kitchen to get Karl some water."

"That is a very good question. I have no idea. When I went into the kitchen to use the landline, she was not there and I have not seen her. Strange."

"Hmm," Genevieve said. "Strange indeed. Well, we'll sort that out when we get back with the tarp. I'll meet you in the great hall in ten minutes," she said and was off and running.

Still confused about Genevieve accompanying him, Max turned to Philip. "Lord Crosswick, is it quite all right if Lady Crosswick comes with me?"

Stifling a smile, Philip asked, "Is there a reason she shouldn't?"

Max's face clouded as he floundered, looking for a reason Genevieve shouldn't go with him. Finally he shook his head. "Nein. No. I suppose not. It will be cold and not at all pretty and the Countess seems like someone who likes to be warm and in beautiful places."

"I see your point, Max, but Lady Crosswick also loves an adventure and I believe she thinks a trip through the dungeons will be quite exciting." Philip was having a great time watching Max's discomfort with the idea of Genevieve accompanying him and he wasn't about to make it easier for him.

Max's tone softened. "We won't exactly be going through the dungeons, but at least she will have a chance to see all the autos." He raised a brow at Philip. "And that is certainly worth seeing."

Ten minutes later, when Max walked into the great hall, Genevieve was bouncing to a tune in her head while she waited for him. Warm in navy suede pants and a tweed cable-knit sweater, one of her favorites for early-morning, winter horseback rides at Wilmingrove Hall, she was ready to start their trek deep into the dungeons, or—as Max insisted on calling them—the cellars. High color flooded her cheeks and her heavy wool coat rested across the arm of a wooden bench next to the door to the descending staircase, waiting.

"Are we ready?" Her excitement bubbled.

Max tugged on his green duffle coat. "I believe we are, my

lady," he said, fidgeting with his toggle buttons, apparently still uncomfortable with Genevieve's company.

She grabbed her coat, shoved her arms into the sleeves and buttoned up.

As he opened the thick oak door, its three panels held together by forged iron cleats, the ancient hinges groaned an eerie moan and a shiver ran up Genevieve's spine. "Ooo," she said with an excited giggle.

Max tapped a rocker switch and the stone stairs were bathed in a soft yellow glow. He stood to the side, said, "Lady Crosswick, please," and gestured for her to precede him.

She put her hand lightly on the iron handrail cleated to the stone wall and stepped on the first tread, worn smooth by hundreds of years of use, and began the descent. She turned her head to ask Max a question, stumbled, and pitched forward.

"My lady," Max shouted and grabbed her by her coat collar, nearly lifting her off her feet.

"Oh my goodness, Max! Thank you. I guess I'd better keep my eyes on the stairs!" The adrenaline that pulsed in her ears subsided as she felt Max's grip relax on the back of her coat.

"Yes, do keep your eye on the stairs, please," he said, "and perhaps I should go first." He squeezed by and stopped two stairs in front of her, his broad shoulders and athletic physique making it impossible for her to tumble far if she tripped again. "I think that is a better arrangement. Shall we carry on?" He turned and proceeded—too slowly, Genevieve thought. At the landing, they turned a corner and Max flipped on another light. This stairwell was narrower, the lights dimmer, and the air colder and musty.

"How deep will we go, Max?" With each step, Genevieve calculated how far underground they were.

"This is the last flight. There is nothing convenient about where the garage is. When automobiles came into fashion, it was a challenge to find a place where they could be accommodated here at the schloss. After considering and rejecting many options, it was determined there was only one place with enough space to create a large garage. Naturally, that would be the furthest point from the working part of the schloss: the kitchen, the staff quarters. But when you are built on the side of a mountain, you must work with what the terrain offers you."

Genevieve stepped off the last tread. She could only see a few feet into a low-ceilinged stone hall. Max reached over and punched a button on an old brass switch plate and the long corridor came to life. Every ten or twelve feet a low-watt, wrought-iron and glass light hung from the ceiling, casting shadows on the walls and floor.

"Are you warm enough, Lady Crosswick?"

"I'm fine, thank you, Max," Genevieve said, buttoning the top button on her coat and sticking her cold hands deep into her pockets. Though her legs were long and she always walked at a fast clip, she had to extend her stride to keep up with Max's quick pace.

About twenty feet down the hall, a wide arch opened on the left, and though it was inky dark beyond the light from the corridor washing a few feet into the cavern, Genevieve sensed a vast space. "The dungeons?" she said, stopping to squint into its shadowy depths.

Max hunched his six-foot-two body over like Quasimodo from *The Hunchback of Notre-Dame*. "The dungeons, my lady," he said in a monstery voice.

Genevieve shivered a chuckle and they moved on.

"So what's in there?" she asked as they passed a small metal door set into the stone wall. "It looks new."

Max continued his quick pace and said nothing.

"Max? Did you hear me?"

"My lady?" He kept walking.

"I asked you what's behind that little door?"

"Oh. It is, uh, just mechanicals," he said without looking at her.

"Ah, yes. It must require a massive boiler to heat Schloss Friedrichstein. We had to replace ours at Wilmingrove Hall last year. It took several days and cost a fortune."

"Hmm," was all he said.

When they reached the far end of the corridor, they reversed the beginning of their trip and trudged up two flights of ancient stone stairs, Max still leading the way.

"You weren't kidding when you said it was quite a hike to the garage."

He grinned at Genevieve and a spark lit his beautiful eyes.

They hit the top landing, Max slipped the key into the lock, and it clicked. He turned to Genevieve, a grin of absolute joy tugging the corners of his mouth. "Are you ready for this, Lady Crosswick?"

She had no idea what he was about to share. *No matter how special the tarp is, it can't be that wonderful,* she thought.

He threw the door open, hit a panel of switches and there

before her were at least fifty automobiles, shined to a fine luster and glittering under perfect lighting.

"Whoa!" Genevieve said. "I thought *we* had a lot of cars."

The magnificent machines were angled with precision in four long rows, two on the left facing the center of the garage and two on the right. The glossy, acid-stained floor reflected each lustrous image and the cars were displayed by color, starting with reds and flowing into purples, blues and greens before shifting through deep golden yellows to palest cornsilk and whites. Finally there was a row of breathtaking black machines; some elegant, some terrifyingly brutish.

"This is a passion of the younger Baron," Max said.

Genevieve chuckled at the obvious statement. "He mentioned his car collection at dinner and appeared to be quite proud of it, but I had no idea it would be worthy of a museum on its own." She wandered up the first aisle starting with the red group, the first car being a 1957 Ferrari Testa Rossa with its long, elegant hood surging forward, ready to grab the road and hug the corners. The classic Ferrari-red car sat next to Genevieve's favorite car in the world: a 1970 signal-red Jaguar XKE convertible with biscuit interior. She felt her heart race and envy clutch at her soul and for a fraction of a second, she caught a whiff of Rose Otto, then it was gone. When Philip inherited his late cousin's estate and title, much to their excitement, they became the owners of many spectacular cars. Though there was a Cotswold-blue XKE coupe among their many cars, sadly there was no signal-red E-type convertible. As yet, finding and purchasing her dream car hadn't been at the top of Genevieve's list. *Maybe I should reorganize my priorities*, she thought. *Even better, maybe Freddie would sell me this car.* "Do all the cars belong to the younger Baron or do any belong to the elder or Gabriel?" she said. If she were going to go after the car, she'd better know whom to charm.

Engrossed in looking at the Jag's dashboard, it was several seconds before Genevieve realized Max hadn't responded. Just as she glanced at him to see if he had heard her question, he said, "No. All the automobiles belong to the younger Baron."

She opened her mouth to ask him if Freddie had ever sold any of the cars but before she could speak, Max continued.

"The elder Baron does not approve of the collection. In fact, he and the younger have had vigorous, um… perhaps one could say *discussions* about the collections and the excessive expense."

Waiting for Max to continue, Genevieve said nothing but after a few beats, she decided he had finished sharing. Feeling uncomfortable at Max's confession, she said the most innocuous thing she could think of. "That's unfortunate. It's always difficult when parents and adult children have different views on what's good for the family."

"Ja. Das Stimmt. That is very true." As if he'd just remembered why they came to the garage, he said, "Und so, we must get a tarp for Baron von Bassewitz, the elder." He strode to a cabinet on the far wall of the vast showroom, opened the door and pulled out a neatly folded dark blue package. "This will do nicely for you, Baron," Genevieve thought she heard him say.

As she watched Max walk the distance back to her, his head

down, his energy gone, she wondered, for the first time, if they had been close. When he arrived at her side, he raised his head and a tear oozed from the corner of his eye.

"Max," Genevieve said, squeezing his forearm. "I'm so sorry. You must be terribly sad."

He shrugged and said, "Lady Crosswick, I am sad but I am more relieved, and the fact that I am relieved makes me sad."

"Oh," was all Genevieve could think of to say.

He headed for the door and Genevieve followed. "Do you understand?" he asked.

"I think I do." The corners of her mouth hovered in a sympathetic smile. "How long did you work for the Baron?"

"Nineteen years. I was just twenty when I began to drive for him." Max opened the door to the stairwell, hit the garage light switch and the room plunged into darkness. As they began to retrace their long walk back to the main house, he continued. "For so many years he was wonderful to work for. He was seventy then, but as vigorous as a fifty-year-old. He traveled the world buying and selling art to increase the family's collection and doing business with fascinating people. Some maybe not the best people." A laugh gurgled in his throat as if a memory had wafted into his mind. "It didn't take me long to become more than his driver. Soon I was traveling with him and making certain that all the details of his life were taken care of. He trusted Elsa and me with everything. Then, in the last year, he became impossible: mean, angry, suspicious. It was difficult for me, but I realized that something was happening to him that was making him act badly. As time went on, it was not possible for Elsa to tolerate his behavior. She threatened to leave several times but I always managed to persuade her to stay."

As Genevieve listened to his story, she heard concern creeping into his voice.

"Lately, I have wondered if that was the right thing to do."

"What do you mean, Max?"

He hesitated, then said, "I've been wondering if it has been too much of a strain for Elsa. Perhaps it would have been better for both Elsa and the Baron if she had left his employment."

"Has she said anything to you to make you worry?"

They stood at the base of the stairs, the last bit of their trek before they would be back in the relative warmth of the schloss. Max nodded for Genevieve to go first and switched off the lights to the long corridor they had just traversed.

"She did say something that concerned me when I talked to her about a week ago."

Halfway up the first set of stairs, Genevieve stopped and turned around. "What did she say, Max?"

His tanned, chiseled features softened in the yellow light from the iron light fixtures hanging on the walls. "I called from Vienna to see if she needed me to do anything for this—" He stopped and snickered. "—this ski party, or what was supposed to be a ski party."

"And?" Genevieve urged him on.

"And she said the best thing I could do was to keep the Baron under control when he got here. If I didn't, she was not going to be responsible for what happened to him."

CHAPTER 22

Genevieve's head swam with what Max had just said to her. Then out of the blue she heard herself say, "You know, Angelina—Freddie's ex-wife—was murdered on our estate in England in September." She peered at Max, watching for any signs he might have significant information about her death. What she saw was sadness. His eyebrows drew down at the ends, mirroring the corners of his mouth. He held the folded tarp tight against his chest with one hand and covered his eyes with the other.

"Oh, poor Baroness." He gulped back a sob. "She did not deserve such a fate." He dropped his hand to his side and Genevieve saw pain had replaced the sadness.

Surprised to see such emotion, Genevieve proceeded with care. "Max, were you close to the Baroness?" she asked, her voice quiet and comforting.

"I liked the Baroness very much and I told her many times to be careful." His voice was barely audible.

Genevieve wasn't sure she had heard him correctly and stepped down one tread so they were eye to eye. "Did you say you warned her to be careful?"

"I did. I told her to be careful and look what happened to her," he said in one great sob. "Please tell no one what I've shared with you. I don't know what is happening in the von Bassewitz family and I don't know who I can trust but I had to tell someone. For some reason, I felt I could trust you and Lord Crosswick. Please tell me I didn't make a mistake."

Genevieve threw her arms around Max's neck and hugged him to her. She squeezed him and whispered in his ear, "You did not make a mistake, Max. You can tell Lord Crosswick and me anything. In fact…" She was on the verge of telling him they were working with the Met then stopped herself. "In fact, I hope you feel much better," she said instead. "As the Brits say, 'A problem shared is a problem halved.' We haven't solved any problems yet, but I'm sure with the three of us working together we can figure out a few things, if there is anything to figure out." She pulled away, held Max by his shoulders, and gave him a kind smile. "I guess we'd better get this tarp to the dining room so we can roll up the Baron and put him on ice." She turned around and started back up the last few stairs, taking them two at a time.

As she pushed open the door to the great hall, Genevieve was reminded there was still a blizzard raging. Below ground, they had heard nothing, and she had almost forgotten there was a monster storm burying them in mountains of snow. The wind buffeted the schloss more vigorously than half an hour earlier when she and Max had started their trek to the garage. It moaned its way into the building through crevasses and between mortar, rattling windowpanes until Genevieve imagined a giant was shaking the castle in his fist.

When she and Max walked into the dining room, it was a sullen, solemn place. Four weary people sat around a table that was still laden with half-eaten dinners. Freddie and Finn leaned back in their chairs, Freddie staring at the fire, Finn staring at the weather app on his phone, watching the blizzard that covered his screen. Heidi and Lillie talked quietly, a bottle between them, their wine glasses half-full. Philip stood by the fireplace, his chin resting on his chest and his arm draped along the mantle. She knew her husband well enough that she could almost read his mind. She would bet good money that he was trying to figure out if she, Lillie, Finn and Philip were in any danger, and if so, what to do about it. And Karl Friedrich von Bassewitz still maintained pride of place, exactly where Philip had eased him to the floor little more than an hour ago, now a cashmere-covered mound on the carpet. At the sight of the Baron, Genevieve's eye flew to the sideboard. The small wooden crate was gone. Thinking perhaps someone had moved the package, her eyes darted to every corner of the room. She saw nothing. She surveyed the sad scene and, almost whispering, announced, "We're back."

Philip raised his head and threw an exhausted smile to her. "That must have been quite a journey," he said, walking toward her. "Any luck?"

Max held up the tarp then glanced at Karl's body.

"Success," Genevieve said, sweeping her arm toward Max. "And, Philip, you won't believe the cars! Freddie, oh my god! I desperately want your red Jag—" She caught herself. "But we'll talk about that later. Did Elsa come back?"

Her companions exchanged puzzled glances, and then they all looked back at Genevieve.

"Uh—apparently not." Finn pulled his lips into a sheepish grin. "I guess you didn't see her on the way to the garage, did you?"

Lillie pushed out of her chair and walked to Genevieve, her wine glass in her hand. "We absolutely forgot about her," she said. "I don't know how you made it all the way to the garage and back. We barely had enough energy to pour wine." Lillie handed Genevieve her glass and she took a deep gulp.

"Thank you," she said and handed the goblet back to Lillie. "We need to find her. She couldn't have left the schloss." She licked a drop of wine from the corner of her mouth. "Something is wrong with this picture."

"You're right, darling," Philip said. "Now that you're back with the tarp, let's take care of the Baron, then we'll find Elsa. My guess is she's in her room crying. Freddie, she and your father were close, right?"

"As I said, they were until recently, when Papa became such an unpleasant person."

"Regardless of how their relationship has soured in the last few months, I am certain his death is very difficult for her," Heidi said, swirling her wine, mesmerized by the golden liquid in the bowl. "More difficult than it is for me," she mumbled as she raised her glass to her lips and drank.

Recalling the conversation she had just had with Max about Elsa, Genevieve raised one eyebrow at him and he nodded.

He unfurled the tarp and a long piece of twine fell out. He flapped the coated canvas again and let it float to the floor next to the Baron. He breathed out a heavy sigh. "I guess we must do this," he said, pulling his lower lip between his teeth.

Freddie squatted next to his father and slowly pulled the lap robe from the body. "The sooner the better, I'd say. His muscle control is disappearing," he said, pointing to the damp patch on the front of the Baron's wool trousers. He choked back a sob then gazed up at the six sympathetic faces looking down at him. "Shall we get on with it?"

"How can we help?" Lillie asked on behalf of the three women.

"We may need all of us to carry Karl outside, but I think we can manage getting him on the tarp," Philip said. He bent over and lifted the Baron's hand from his chest. "Finn, do you want to take his other hand? You and I can lift him by his arms."

Freddie moved to his father's feet and stood next to Max, who already held Karl's foot, shod in fine Italian short boots. He picked up his father's other leg by the ankle and the four men held the two arms and two legs straight up. Rigor mortis was already distorting Karl's face, twisting his jaw open and into a lop-sided smile

As the four stared down at Karl, each made a gallant effort to maintain decorum but a snicker caught in Freddie's throat.

Trying to control a laugh desperate to escape, Philip bit the inside of his cheek, Finn coughed a chuckle, and Max squeaked a giggle, an odd sound coming from such a big man.

"Shall we lift him onto the tarp on three?" Philip said.

"On three," the others confirmed.

"One, two, three," Philip said and they all tugged. Barely raising him off the floor, they shuffled sideways and lowered him onto the tarp.

"Wow," Philip said. "He's heavy."

"Like a ton of bricks." Finn let out the breath he'd been holding.

"Before Philip inherited his cousin's estate, we hadn't been around many dead people," Genevieve said leaving the table and walking toward the men. "Since then we've made up for lost time, haven't we, darling." She had come from the table and stood next to Philip, ready to help.

"What's next?" Heidi said.

"Let's gift wrap him," Genevieve said. "You know, fold the top and bottom of the tarp in, then the sides."

"I think we should scooch him over to the edge and roll him up like a cigar, then flap the ends over," was Finn's suggestion.

"Could we just get him wrapped in the tarp and outside?" Anxious to get his father to a cooler place, Freddie's patience was wearing thin.

Philip slapped Max on the back. "Come on, Max. Let's move Karl to the side and roll him up." The two of them slid Karl to the edge and began turning him over and over until they got to the other side of the canvas. They folded each end of the tarp in and secured everything with twine.

"There we go." Philip stood and rubbed his hands. "Now, Freddie, where do you want us to put your father?"

"There is a little alcove with a bench just outside the kitchen door. I think that would be a good place. It's very close and somewhat protected."

"Let's get our winter gear on and get this done." Philip headed to the great hall with everyone close on his heels. There was a flurry of coats, boots, gloves and hats, and within minutes everyone was back in the dining room ready to carry the precious package of Karl Friedrich von Bassewitz out into the blizzard.

"Let's get him on our shoulders," Philip said, continuing to direct the effort. "If we have three people on each side, that should do it. Lillie, you be our spotter and door opener."

"What you're saying is I'm too short to be a carrier." Her mouth lifted at the corners. "I'm not offended. The door opener is critical. If the door isn't opened, you can't get out."

"Exactly," Philip said. "Is everyone ready? Max, you do the countdown again. You're very good at that."

On one side Max, Heidi, and Freddie bent down and grabbed the tarp in their gloved hands. On the other side, Philip, Genevieve, and Finn did the same. On three, the six of them heaved the shrouded body onto their shoulders.

"Everyone okay?" Philip asked and received grunts of acknowledgement. "All right, let's go. Lillie, you're our guide."

She opened the door to the kitchen and held it while the procession squeezed through the opening, staggering their passage as best they could so they could get through. Once in the kitchen, they turned toward the outside door. Lillie scooted around the group and into the small anteroom. She put her hand on the knob and felt the wind rattle the heavy wooden door. Assuming it turned on an outside light she hit the switch next to her on the wall but the window in the door was plastered with snow, making it impossible to see if a light had come on. She turned to her friends, "Are you ready?" she said.

Everyone nodded.

The moment she turned the knob, the door blasted open and snow swirled into the kitchen. "Come on," she yelled, trying to be heard above the howl of the wind.

The cortege leaned into the gale and pressed out into the storm. Lillie tugged the kitchen door closed, dashed back to the front of the parade and turned on her flashlight.

"Over there," Freddie shouted above the wind, pointing to a mound of snow only a few feet away.

When they trudged the last few feet and arrived at the spot, Lillie held up her hand. "Wait just a minute," she said, handed the flashlight to Finn, and began brushing the snow from the bench in the alcove. She worked furiously, moving snow as fast as she could until her hand hit either stone or ice. Not wanting to break a finger, she slowed her pace and carefully brushed a few more flakes, then she stopped, a scream stuck in her throat as Elsa's frozen eyes stared back at her.

CHAPTER 23

Finn swept the flashlight beam across Elsa's frozen face just as a searing scream ripped from Lillie's throat. She staggered backwards, away from Elsa's ghostly countenance and stumbled into Freddie, who lost hold of his father's tarped body and wobbled into Heidi, then everyone but Finn dominoed to the frozen ground.

"Bloody hell! What is that?" Finn gasped, focusing the light on the corpse who was rapidly being reclaimed by the snow.

"What the hell, indeed. I'd say we found Elsa." Genevieve struggled to believe what she was seeing. She pushed herself out of a wet pile and gave Philip a hand up.

"Sitting there on the bench, she looks like she came out for a smoke and froze to death before she could go back into the kitchen." Lillie grabbed the flashlight from Finn and crept toward Elsa, keeping her in the beam. She brushed snow off her shoulders and chest. "She's not even wearing a coat."

"That's crackers." Finn retrieved the flashlight and leaned in to gaze into the corpse's cloudy corneas. He turned to Freddie, who still sat on the ground, his head in his hands. "Freddie, do you have any idea what's going on here?"

His shoulders shook and above the moan of the wind, they heard his sobs.

"Freddie." Heidi put her arms around her husband's neck and soothed. "Liebling. Come. Come, Freddie." She tugged, trying to get him to stand, but he didn't move.

Before she could ask for help, Max lifted Freddie under his arms and pulled him to his feet. "Everybody," Max raised his voice so everyone could hear. "You need to get back inside. There is nothing we can do for Elsa until the storm is over. Lord Crosswick, Mr. Mountbatten, help me put the Baron over there." He pointed to the alcove where Elsa sat. "The rest of you get back in the schloss."

Finn, Philip and Max dragged the tarp the few yards to their goal, leaving a path through the snow that would soon disappear.

"Out of respect, should we put something over Elsa?" Finn couldn't feel his nose and desperately wanted to be inside but felt uncomfortable leaving Elsa sitting in the blizzard without even a jacket.

Max squatted and tucked the edge of the tarp under the twine holding the Baron's bundle then put his hand on Elsa's cheek and shook his head. "No, Herr Mountbatten. Covering her won't help her now." He stood and began dusting the snow from his shoulders as he slogged toward the kitchen. He pushed the door open and held the knob to keep the wind from slapping the thick oak slab against the anteroom's tiled wall. When Philip and Finn were safely inside, Max pushed the door closed against the bluster and locked it.

"My god, Max. What is going on here?" Philip unwound his muffler from around his neck and undid the toggles on his coat. "Do you have any idea what's happening?"

When Max pulled his knit cap from his head, his thick blond hair sprang everywhere. He threw the beanie on the pine kitchen table, peeled off his heavy jacket and draped it over a ladderback chair. He laid his palms flat on the scrubbed wood and leaned his full weight on them, his head hanging heavy.

With only the ticking of a charming cuckoo clock breaking the silence, Philip and Finn exchanged a questioning glance as they waited for Max to respond.

Alone in his thoughts, the sweet aroma of warm pastry wafted into Philip's nostrils. Just as he was about to check the raspberry-colored AGA to see if it was on, Max shoved off the table, his eyes bright with unshed tears, and Philip refocused his attention on the tall, fair man.

Max rose to his full six feet two inches and his voice was strong when he said, "Lord Crosswick, Mr. Mountbatten, within the last few weeks, three people connected with the von Bassewitz family have died, two within the last few hours." He lasered his focus on Philip. "Lord Crosswick, you asked me if I know what is happening here. My answer is no. I don't know who is killing people in this family or why. But if you asked me to look into the future, I would say the killing is not over."

CHAPTER 24

SHE WAS SO tired she couldn't sleep. She squinted at the dark ceiling, then closed her eyes and listened to the moaning, groaning winds outside and to Philip's steady breath. *How in the world could he sleep? Men,* she thought. Men were remarkable. Sometimes that was a good thing, but not always. After everything that had happened today, how could Philip be asleep, much less sleeping soundly? By the time she had crawled into bed, he was already gently snoring while she was bubbling over with nervous energy, ready to hash over everything that had happened from their encounter with Darlington to Elsa's death. And she needed to tell him about the wooden crate and what the Baron had said to her about it. She turned onto her side and pushed up to see the clock. 3:27. She put her hand on Philip's chest and felt it rise and fall with his gentle inhale and exhale.

"Are you awake?" she whispered, knowing the answer. "Philip, wake up. We need to talk." Instead of flickering his eyes open, he grunted, rolled away from her and pulled the duvet up to his ears.

"I guess I'll go down and see if I can find a cup of tea," she said, loudly enough to rouse Philip if he were close to waking, but he didn't move.

Her feet slid into her Frette slippers, grateful for their cozy fit. She patted the end of the bed looking for her robe and finally found it between the end of the bed and the footboard. By the time she slipped her arms into the robe's wooly warmth, wrapped it around her and cinched the belt tight, she was shivering. "I wonder what the temperature is in here." The fire that was crackling on the hearth when she climbed into bed showed no signs of ever having existed. No flames warmed the room. No embers glowed.

She grabbed her phone off the side table, turned on the flashlight and headed for the door. Not particularly concerned about being quiet, she opened the door and closed it with a louder bang than she had intended. The hall was like a tomb—pitch dark and dead silent. *How fitting,* she thought.

Though the light on her phone gave her confidence that she could move about without running into anything, she still kept her hand on the wall as she crept down the corridor until she got to the stairs, where she paused to get her bearings. As she stepped onto the first tread, Rose Otto surrounded her. She pulled her foot back up to the landing and sucked in a sharp breath.

"Charlotte?" She bit her lips. "Charlotte?" she said again. When she inhaled, she expected the fragrance to be gone but it was still strong. "What are you telling me?"

Then Charlotte's icy hand touched the back of Genevieve's neck and like a rag doll, she plopped onto her bottom on the thick hall runner. "It's something about the stairs, isn't it?" She peered through the corridor's wrought iron spindles down onto the stone floor below and shivered, recalling the story of Charlotte's demise. She knew instantly what the beautiful ghost was telling her.

Desperate to return to Philip and the safety of their room, Genevieve had to wait several minutes until her limbs stopped shaking and the jelly left her bones before she could pull herself to stand. She stepped as far away from the overlook of the lower floor as she could and hugged the wall all the way back to their guestroom. By the time she reached their door, she was sweating and shivering, so terrified was she about what had just happened.

She pressed the levered knob, pushed to open the door and stopped the moment the hinges gave a painful whine, lashing through the silence of the middle of the night. She squeezed through the narrow opening and cringed as the hinges squealed the door closed. In the dark, she sped toward the bed, walking out of her slippers on the way. She raised the duvet and scooted under it without removing her robe, then wiggled her way to Philip's side of the bed. Finding he was still lying on his side, she molded her body to his, trying to steal some of his heat. She eased her arm under his and put her palm on his chest. He took her hand in his and pulled her closer to him so her hot breath was on the back of his neck.

At last she stopped shaking and began to relax into the snug warmth of the bed and her husband's sturdy body. Just as she tumbled over the edge of sleep, Genevieve heard Philip murmur, "Are you wearing Rose Otto?" but she had fallen too far to answer.

CHAPTER 25

IT HADN'T EVEN been twenty-four hours since the blizzard started but Genevieve was ready for it to be over. She wanted to be back in the safety and comfort of Wilmingrove Hall, where they were surrounded by people they trusted and people who trusted them. Two dead bodies and maybe a killer among the guests didn't make for a very jolly house-party vibe.

She struggled to claw her way to consciousness but kept falling back into a doze. She needed to wake up and gather Philip, Lillie and Finn. They needed to make a plan and get on with their art discovery before anyone else was eliminated. Finally she worked her eyes open and kept them open. She stared at the ceiling, thinking, thinking, thinking, then realized Philip wasn't in bed. When she brought her wrist close to her eyes, it took several seconds before she could focus and see, much to her surprise, it was ten o'clock. She had no idea when Philip had opened the curtains but appreciated that he had. The flakes frozen to the windows made kaleidoscope patterns on the panes.

"Bless you, Philip," she said to the empty room as she heard the fire crackle. She rolled over to see flames lapping at fat logs recently added to the blaze. Just as a coffee wish floated into her mind, the door opened and there he was, his green eyes dancing at her, making her heart flutter. Philip carried a tray filled with a carafe, mugs, pastries, jelly, butter and a bottle of seltzer, set it on her bedside table, and sat on the edge of the bed next to her.

"Good morning, darling girl." He kissed her on her forehead, then on her nose.

A shy smile played on her lips and she grabbed the front of his sweater and pulled him to her. Still smiling, she brought him close until they were nose to nose. "I have so much to tell you," she said, surprising him.

"Okay," he said. "That wasn't what I was expecting. I thought you were going to give me a kiss."

"I can do that, too, but I really do have a lot to tell you, Lillie and Finn. We need to get them alone somewhere. Any ideas where or how?"

"I was downstairs for a while getting all this stuff and Max was the only person up. Why don't you text Lillie and Finn to come to our room and I'll go get more provisions?"

"Good plan," Genevieve said, already pushing the covers off and throwing her feet to the ground and reaching for her phone on the side table.

"You're quite a sight." Philip smiled at Genevieve, her hair sticking out like a troll doll, her robe twisted, and the belt nearly up to her armpits.

The moment she saw her reflection in the cheval glass, she coughed a laugh. "I look like Michael Keaton in *Beetlejuice*, minus the horrifying makeup. Thank goodness I washed my face last night before coming to bed." She twisted her robe so the front was in the front and wiggled her belt down to a more comfortable spot around her waist, then shoved her phone into her robe pocket. "Before I gather the troops, I think I'd better do something about this," she said, sweeping a graceful hand from the top of her head, down her torso. "It won't take me a minute."

Philip's eyes widened in disbelief.

"Trust me," she said and headed for the bathroom to do her magic.

Twenty minutes later, Philip returned with more pastries, more coffee, and a bowl of plump, dark-red cherries meant to top last night's Black Forest torte.

He set the tray on the table in front of the fireplace—burning hot with the logs Genevieve had tossed on the pile just moments ago—and smiled an appreciative smile as Genevieve walked out of the bathroom. "Why would I ever doubt you?" he said, admiring the casual elegance of the woman before him.

She shook her head. "I can't imagine," she said. "Even after all these years, you still doubt my ability to make a silk purse out of a sow's ear." She kissed him on the cheek as she walked past him on her way to the coffee, hardly missing a beat. "Did you see anyone downstairs?"

"Only Max. He was in the kitchen. He'd been outside making certain that Elsa and the Baron were still there."

"And?" Genevieve asked.

"According to him, they're fine—as fine as they can be, I guess. He hasn't seen Freddie or Heidi."

To Genevieve's surprise, he wrapped her in a hug and held her tightly. "This is a pretty damn serious situation we find ourselves in. I think we need to get Darlington on the phone." When he finally released her, Genevieve startled at the concern in his bright green eyes. "We have a few too many dead bodies for my money. I think we should call him as soon as Finn and Lillie get here."

"I think that's an excellent idea. They should be here anytime." No sooner had the words popped out of her mouth than a cautious tap sounded at the door and it creaked open several inches.

"Come in. Come in." Genevieve dashed to pull the door wide, grabbed Lillie by her hand and pulled her into the room. Finn followed and Genevieve stuck her head into the corridor. She looked both ways and, seeing nothing, stepped back into the room. She quietly closed the door and turned the lock, which sounded to her like a thunderous click.

"Oh my gosh, Genevieve. I was so glad to see your text." She rushed to the fireplace and held out her hands, more to comfort herself than to get warm, Genevieve thought. "Finn and I have been under the covers whispering all night about how serious this is. What are we going to do?" Hanging free, her curls corkscrewed long and thick, framing her romantic Botticelli face. Because they rarely appeared, the frown lines between her eyebrows looked deeply out of place. "Philip, what do you think we should do?"

Having just topped off his coffee, he sat next to Genevieve on the wool-covered loveseat next to the fireplace. One hand holding his mug, he draped the other over Genevieve's knee.

"G and I were just talking about that and, now that you two are here, we're going to call Francis."

Hovering over the tray of pastries, Finn put two on a small plate, then poured coffee into a mug. He walked to a wing chair next to the love seat and before sitting, offered Lillie the pastry plate. Rather than take one, she took the plate and he was left with nothing but coffee. Immediately she realized his intention and a laugh gurgled in her throat.

"I'm so sorry, Finn," she said but didn't return the two flakey tarts. Instead, she sat across from Philip and Genevieve. "I'm absolutely starving, aren't all of you?" She swept her gaze to the other three. "I realized in the middle of the night that we had only eaten the potato soup when the Baron died, not that anyone felt like eating after that… and then Elsa." She shook her head, thinking about the tragedies barely twelve hours ago.

"If everyone has everything they need, I'll dial Darlington." The number was ringing before anyone could object.

On the second ring, Francis' deep voice came through the speaker. "Hello. Philip?"

"Yes, Francis. This is Philip. And I have Genevieve, Lillie, and Finn here as well."

"So the whole gang is there. How is everything going? Anything on the stolen art yet?"

"Oh, Francis, where to begin." Philip let loose a lengthy sigh.

"Ah. This is either remarkably promising for the Met or something else is going on."

"I'm sorry to say it's the latter and—"

"—And," Genevieve broke in, "Philip, Lillie, and Finn don't know the half of it."

CHAPTER 26

Watching the three faces staring at her, Genevieve launched into the review of the hours since they left Darlington. "First we have to tell you that last night, Karl, the elder Baron, died during dinner. I think it was poison of some sort, probably arsenic but I'm—"

"Hang on a minute, Genevieve," Darlington's shock rang through the speaker. "Karl Friedrich von Bassewitz is dead?"

"Yes, that's right."

"And you think someone killed him with poison?"

"I do."

While he listened to Genevieve give her version of last night's events, Philip watched her every movement: her hands gesturing, emphasizing every point; her eyes dancing and darting between the three other people in the room, looking for confirmation of what she was saying; her legs crossed and her foot bouncing with nervous energy.

"But let me go on, Francis. When we took Karl outside in the blizzard to preserve him, we found Elsa, the von Bassewitz's house manager, frozen to death."

"Bloody hell," Darlington murmured.

"But before that—"

"Just a minute, G. Francis, earlier in the day—actually, just after we left you and before all the dead people started appearing—we ran into Max, the elder Baron's valet and chauffeur, coming out of the cellars."

"I was getting to that, Philip." Genevieve flashed her annoyance and narrowed her eyes at him as she said, "Max was coming out of the cellars with a wooden carton the size of a small canvas. He told us the Baron wanted to show his dinner guests the painting inside."

"You didn't tell us about that," Lillie accused.

"And when did I have time?" Genevieve didn't like losing steam. "When we went into dinner," she continued, "I noticed the carton on the sideboard and plucked up the courage to ask Karl about it. You won't believe what he said." She paused and regarded each person then looked at the phone screen as if Francis were there.

"Well?" everyone said in unison.

"He said something like—" She tapped her pursed lips with her index finger. "—something like, 'The painting in that carton will make our Berlin museum the most famous in the world.' How about that?"

She could almost hear everyone's mind racing.

Finally, Darlington asked, "Did he say anything else?"

"Sadly, no. The second course came and he started talking to you, Lillie. Then shortly after that, he died."

"And the carton. Where is the carton?" Philip leaned forward, his elbows on his knees, his hands clenched between his legs.

"When Max and I came back from getting the tarp, I noticed it was gone. Gone, as in not on the sideboard any longer."

Finn shook his head like a dog shaking off water. "Wait, wait, wait. You're telling us all this happened during dinner and you haven't said a word until now? What the bloody blazes, Genevieve?"

"Take it easy, Finn." Philip leaned back in his chair and crossed his long legs. "Genevieve certainly didn't want to share any of this information in the presence of Freddie, Heidi, and Max. Right, G?"

"Exactly. We have no idea who's responsible for what's going on here. We need to keep it among the four of us… well, the five of us, assuming none of us is the culprit."

"I think that's a pretty safe assumption." Lillie's curls bounced and she laughed as she shook the thought of being a suspect out of her imagination.

"I must say my head is in a bit of a spin. Are you suggesting whatever was in the crate was a piece from the Gardner Museum heist?"

Genevieve scoffed. "So I just told you about two dead bodies, maybe murders, and you focus on a wooden crate. I say, Francis, rather callous of you."

"I'll get to the bodies in a minute, but before we go there, do you have any idea who took the painting away?"

"Absolutely not. It was there when we sat down to dinner. It was gone when Max and I came back from the garage with the tarp."

A loud rap on the bedroom door made the four people in the room jump, then they heard Freddie say, "Philip, Genevieve, are you awake?"

Philip pushed from his chair, scooped up the phone in one quick move and pressed the speaker off. "Francis," he whispered. "We'll have to call you back. Freddie's knocking on the door."

"Right, I'll be here, waiting," he said and clicked off.

Genevieve unbolted the door as quietly as possible but the distinct click of the lock gave her away. Drawing her lips into a welcoming smile, she pulled the door open and there stood Baron von Bassewitz the younger, holding a wooden crate.

Genevieve was speechless at the sight of box. Oblivious to her surprise, Freddie leaned forward, the box between them, and kissed her on both cheeks. "Good morning. Oh, good. Everyone is here," he said, his forced smile doing nothing to belie his weary voice. "Did anyone sleep?"

There were mumbled replies then Philip said, "What do you have there, Freddie?"

The Baron looked down as if he'd forgotten that he had a wooden box in his hands. "Oh, this. Heidi reminded me that Papa wanted all of you to see this piece. I am taking it downstairs. If you are ready for breakfast, I shall meet you in the dining room and we can do the unveiling."

"We'll be right down," Genevieve said, almost before he

finished speaking. "Lillie, Finn, let's go." She ushered them out of the bedroom and looked back at Philip who was picking up his phone to let Darlington know what was going on. As she closed the door, she showed him her crossed fingers and he nodded.

CHAPTER 27

Someone had stoked the dying embers of last night's dining room fire. It was roaring again but it would be a while before it could chase away the overnight chill and warm the room enough to make it comfortable. For the time being, a sweater—maybe two—was the order of the morning.

From the moment Genevieve entered the room, her eyes roamed high and low in search of the crate. Casually she walked around the salon looking behind chairs and in the inglenook. She pulled a tissue from her pants pocket and dropped it on the floor so when she bent over to pick it up, she could look under the dining room table. Nowhere. It was nowhere to be seen. It had disappeared again.

"Has anyone seen a weather forecast?" Heidi seemed no worse the wear from the prior night's events. Pert and pretty in a deep purple wool sweater and trousers, she pulsed energy. Coffee pot in hand, she moved from person to person pouring the steaming black nectar into each cup.

Finn looked up from his phone. "About an hour ago, I talked to my guy at the weather service and all the models look as if the storm will taper off by tomorrow around noon."

A cheer filled the room. High fives and knuckle bumps rippled from person to person.

The two servers from the previous evening had created a brunch feast worthy of devouring. Rolls fresh from the oven and still warm, shared baskets filled with cherry-filled pastries and warm apple strudel. Platters overflowed with thinly sliced ham, rounds and slabs of cheese, sliced cucumbers and tomatoes, rich, unsalted butter and marmalades to suit every palate.

"Come, everyone. Sit, please." Heidi motioned to Philip to sit on her right and everyone else to fill in around the table. He held her chair then pulled his out and there, lying in the seat, was the crate.

"Well, well." Philip tried his best to keep his voice from quivering and maintain a relaxed air. "What do we have here?" he said as casually as he could.

About to take a sip of coffee, Genevieve looked up just as Philip held the crate high. Their eyes locked and she paused a fraction of a second before her cup fell from her grasp and shattered on the edge of the table. Coffee splattered everywhere—over the white, starched tablecloth, over her camel sweater, onto the front of Freddie's white turtleneck—everywhere.

She jumped up, knocking her chair over, her head swiveling

between Heidi and Freddie. "Oh, my goodness, I'm so sorry. I don't know what happened." She dabbed at the coffee spots on the tablecloth with her napkin then looked at Freddie. "Freddie, look what I've done to you." When she swung back to Philip, his eyes were laughing and he was struggling to keep his mouth from following suit. "Philip this isn't funny. Look what I've done."

"Genevieve," Heidi soothed. "This is nothing. I'm just sorry about *your* lovely sweater but I'm sure we can soak the coffee out. Why don't you go change and we'll give it to one of the girls. They are very clever with stains." Her glance swept to her husband. "And you, Freddie. Go change and bring your sweater down and give it to Frieda."

Hating to leave the dining room lest she miss the reveal of what was in the crate, Genevieve raced out the door and through the great hall. As she jogged up the stairs, it struck her that the crate she had just seen in the dining room was smaller than the crate she had seen last night—maybe. Within five minutes, she was back in the dining room in a black zipper-neck pullover with the fresh, young Frieda waiting to take her coffee-stained sweater.

"What happened while I was gone?" she asked, her fingers mentally crossed, hoping she had missed nothing. Philip stood where she left him, the crate still on the seat of his chair.

"You missed absolutely nothing," Lillie assured her.

"We're all waiting for you to return, and here you are." Heidi gestured to Philip. "Lord Crosswick, before you do the honors, let me tell you what you are about to see. Before he died, Papa was about to show you the painting he believed would make the Musée des Beaux Arts Berlin the most famous museum in the world."

Genevieve's stomach began to flutter. She wanted to look at Philip but couldn't for fear she would say something crazy like, "That can't be the stolen Vermeer we're looking for! It's too small." Instead, she kept her eyes on Heidi and said, "That's exactly what he told me just before he died."

She squinted at the box and assessed the size again. It looked about sixteen by twenty inches. As she recalled from looking at the list of pieces from the Gardner Museum heist, the *Chez Tortoni* by Manet was ten inches by thirteen, a tiny size for such an important piece. That precious canvas would fit perfectly in the crate Philip was holding.

"…Papa was so excited about donating this tiny jewel to our new museum, wasn't he, Freddie?" With her heart pounding in her ears, Genevieve could barely hear what Heidi was saying.

"He was." A smile curved his lips as Freddie watched his wife weave a fascinating story.

"The exquisite gem Philip is about to reveal hasn't been seen for decades. It only became available when a French apple farmer found it in one of his outbuildings in Giverny, about twenty kilometers from Monet's home. He was converting the building to a house for his son and when he cleaned it out, he found what is in here." She tapped the box with her long, red nail. "The painting was wrapped in toile de jute—I think you say burlap in English— and hidden in one of the storage bins, probably during the Nazi occupation. When he found it, he really didn't know what it was. But people who live in Giverny are not stupid about art. He got in touch with an art dealer in Paris. The dealer called Papa and voilà!" She tossed her graceful hands in the air with a flourish. "Philip, will you please do the honors?"

Philip and Genevieve locked eyes, the electricity between them almost palpable. Heidi held out a screwdriver and Philip took it as Lillie and Finn watched with mounting anticipation. He began to pry up the cleats that held the two sides of the crate together. The wood was soft enough that he could wedge the flat screwdriver under the fasteners and pop them up. He released the two cleats on each side then carefully turned the carton clockwise to the next edge. When he reached the last side, he looked at Genevieve again, a nervous smile playing at the corners of his mouth. He pried the last two cleats from the wood and laid the screwdriver on the table. "Well, what next?" he said to Heidi.

"Open it!" Heidi commanded.

"If you insist." Philip laid the small wooden box flat and wiggled the top until it was ready to come off. He scanned the table. Everyone except Freddie was sitting forward, waiting for the big reveal. "Here we go," he said, carefully lifting the top.

Genevieve was out of her chair and dashing around the table to Philip's side, sure she was about to see *Chez Tortoni* from the Gardner Museum robbery. "Let's see it. I can't wait to see wh..." The words caught in her throat and her eyes widened to saucers.

"What is it?" Lillie could wait no longer and joined Philip and Genevieve in a flash. The moment she saw the canvas, she gasped and her hand flew to her mouth.

Finn leaned on Philip's back and peered over his shoulder. "What is it?" he whispered into Philip's ear, having no idea what he was looking at, and felt Philip shrug.

"Well, what do you think?" Two lines popped between Heidi's brows as she waited for a response from the four.

Genevieve was the first to stutter a response. "I, um, I, I'm not sure what I'm looking at, Heidi."

Lillie took her hand from her mouth and reached with both hands to pull the canvas from the crate. "I know exactly what I'm looking at." She gently lifted the painting from its wooden nest. "Heidi, is this genuine?"

"Of course it is," Heidi said, sounding insulted. "You don't think Baron von Bassewitz would have a *copy* of such a work, do you?"

"No, no. Of course not," Lillie soothed.

"Sadly, there are three people here who don't realize we should be impressed," Philip jumped in. "Could someone please enlighten us?"

Careful to hold the canvas by the stretchers in the back, Lillie set the small painting on the sideboard and propped it against the bowl filled with fruit and pheasant feathers. "Heidi, may I tell everyone about this treasure or would you prefer to do it?"

The Baroness relaxed back into her chair and nodded. "By all means, Lillie. It is only fitting for an art expert of your caliber to share the history and importance of this treasure." She glanced to the other end of the table where Freddie kept a watchful eye.

"I can't believe that I am in the presence of a study Monet did for his wisteria paintings." Lillie beamed, her cheeks pink with excitement.

Looking slightly embarrassed, Finn said, "I clearly am the least clever person in this room when it comes to art." He rolled his eyes and twisted his lips into a crooked smile. "So in the interest of educating this uninformed boy, could you please tell me more? I thought Monet was all about water lilies, Rouen Cathedral, and a few haystacks. He painted wisteria?" He bent to analyze the canvas more closely. "And this doesn't look like Monet at all, does it?"

Lillie patted him on the head like a good puppy. "In his later years at his garden in Giverny, Monet painted several works featuring wisteria. In the end, there were a total of eight paintings. You have a good eye, Finn." She smiled at him and kissed him on the cheek. "Rather than impressionistic, the wisteria paintings are leaning more to an expressionistic, abstract style. His intention was to have them displayed at the Musée de l'Orangerie in Paris as a crown to his *Water Lilies,* but the Orangerie didn't have room for the wisteria paintings so they remained at Giverny." She glanced around at her companions. "What a bunch of fools, right? I dare say each one of us would have found room for them?"

"I don't understand what we have here." Philip still was unsure what he was looking at. Though the colors were vibrant and the brushstrokes energetic, it was so small that he needed more context to fully appreciate what he was seeing. "The water lily exhibition at the Orangerie is huge. This is tiny."

"What you're looking at is a small study of the wisteria blossom itself. It's quite possible that Monet gave this oil sketch to the man who supplied him with cider or brought wood for his fire. Unless we talked to the farmer himself, which of course is impossible, it would be hard to say. Once our museum owns the work—" She gave Heidi and Freddie a broad smile. "—we will do thorough research on the provenance. But for now, suffice it to say, this is a thrilling find and a spectacular first acquisition, indeed."

Lillie put her hand over Heidi's. "I am so sorry Karl didn't have a chance to present this to Philip and Genevieve himself."

Heidi turned her palm up and grasped Lillie's hand. "Thank you, Lillie. He could hardly wait to share this with all of you." She looked to the other end of the table. "Freddie, don't you think this calls for Champagne?"

He picked up his phone, ready to text. "I believe Papa would agree. Let me ask El—" He stopped, startled that he was about to call for the house manager. "Let me get Max to bring up some bottles from the cellar."

Putting the top and the bottom of the crate together, Genevieve picked up the box. "Where shall I put the crate?"

Freddie jumped to his feet. "Let me take it, Genevieve."

"Don't be silly, Freddie. I'll find a place in the kitchen to leave it until we're ready to re-crate the painting." Genevieve pushed through the kitchen door and saw the perfect spot for the box to wait until it was again needed for its precious cargo: a window seat at the far end of the room. In spite of the warmth of the ovens that had been baking wonderful treats all morning, the room was chilly from the blizzard's winds and the snow splatted against the windows. She put the box on the window seat cushion and turned the top around so she could align it with the bottom. There she noticed a black number stamped on the edge: 176.

"Hmm," she said and bit her lip as she searched her memory.

As she recalled, the crate Max brought up last night from the art vault for Baron von Bassewitz the elder had the number 247 stamped on the bottom. The painting they had just been fawning over was 176. What the…? Her mind raced. Heidi had made every effort to pass the Monet off as the painting the senior Baron had wanted them to see. The blood drained from her head and the room swirled; she plopped down on the seat next to the crate.

"Oh my god," she said under her breath. "What are Heidi and Freddie playing at?"

CHAPTER 28

Genevieve pulled her phone from her trouser pocket and brought up the camera. She squatted in front of the crate and focused on the black, stamped number. She played with the size, getting the 176 as large as she could while keeping it in focus, then she hit the round white button on the screen.

"Everything okay in here?" Max called out as he pushed through the door, startling Genevieve. Her phone flew out of her hand and across the tiled floor. She fell back onto her bottom, a deer-in-the-headlights expression on her face.

"Oh my goodness, Max." Her hand slapped her heart. "You surprised me."

"What are you doing?" He looked down at her sitting on the floor in front of the window seat.

Her mind raced for a plausible explanation before she said,

"I took a photo of the crate number so we would be certain to replace the painting in the same box." *Quick thinking*, she congratulated herself.

"But we only have one painting up here. How could we put it in the wrong box?"

"Good point," she said, not making a move to get off the floor. "I just thought in case you brought any more paintings up, it would be a good idea to keep them straight." She felt her palms sweating as her mind raced with lies she could tell if she needed to.

"I see." He pulled a ring of keys off a pegboard. "I'm going to the cellar to get Champagne. Unless, of course, you'd rather do it." He grinned an impish grin. "I know how much fun you had in the cellars last night."

Relieved he had changed subjects, she said, "It was great. Except for the reason we went, I loved seeing the bowels of the schloss. And the cars, of course."

He held out his hand and she slipped hers into his. With one tug, she was back on her feet. "Thank you, Max." A smile rounded her cheeks and wrinkled the corners of her eyes. She liked this man. "Don't let me hold you up. The sooner you go, the sooner you'll return with Champagne. Right?"

"Lady Crosswick, no truer words have ever been spoken." He held the door to the dining room open for her.

"Thank you, sir," she said, flashing him another smile.

"I am always at your service, my lady."

Philip and Lillie lingered by the fireplace, deep in discussion with Freddie about the Monet and how they would best use it at the launch of the still-hypothetical museum. Finn listened, trying to learn as much as possible about the world of art museums, their acquisitions and what it was going to take to get the Berlin museum from dream to reality. And Heidi was trying to herd everyone across the great hall and into the living room, with little success.

"Max, when you return we shall be in das Wohnzimmer, so bring the Champagne to the living room, please. That is, of course, if I can get these people to move."

"Ja, Baroness. I shall do that. Shall I bring glasses in as well?"

"Ask Frieda to do that, please."

"Of course, meine Baroness."

Desperate to tell Philip about the discrepancy in the paintings, she crafted an excuse to get him alone. "Philip," she said. "Will you come upstairs with me before the Champagne arrives?"

He glanced up from his group and flashed her a grin. "What do you need, G?"

"I think we should call Duncan, bring him up to date. Talk to the kids." She jerked her head toward the door and hoped he wouldn't ask more questions. "Come on." She waited in the doorway.

"When I get back, let's pick up this conversation where we left off." Philip crossed the room then stopped and turned around before he walked out the door. "Freddie, I'm interested to hear more of your thoughts on how we're going to blow the socks off every other museum with our collection. We've got to think quality, we've got to think big, and we've got to think of ways we can blow people's minds with our exhibitions. It sounds as if you have some innovative ideas."

"We have Michael and his extraordinary new concept," Freddie glowed at the prospect of talking museum plans and the future.

Philip and Genevieve walked across the great hall in silence. When they were nearly at the top of the stairs, Philip said in a quiet voice, "Why did you decide we need to call Duncan right now? I was right in the thick of a conversation with Freddie that might prove quite revealing regarding our Met mission."

Genevieve slid her hand through the crook of Philip's arm. "Coincidentally, I have something to add to that very subject. I'm not sure how it fits yet, but I'm positive it's a critical piece of this puzzle."

"Really? What could you have discovered since we opened the Monet? And wasn't that painting a surprise?"

They laughed together. "I was certain you were going to take the top off the crate and there would be Manet's *Chez Tortoni.*"

"You thought it would be the *Chez Tortoni*?" The corners of Philip's mouth drew down and his brows shot up. "Why was that? I was absolutely certain it would be the Vermeer." Philip opened their bedroom door and ushered Genevieve inside. He closed the door and locked it just in case.

"Initially, I thought it was the Vermeer as well, but then I remembered the size. We know the Vermeer is about twenty-nine by twenty-six inches. The Monet crate was much smaller. It was the size of *Chez Tortoni.*" Genevieve went on to tell Philip about the different numbers stamped on the crates. She reminded him how Heidi represented today's wooden box as the same painting the elder Baron had wanted them to see yesterday. "I have no idea what all of this means but I'm damn certain it means *something* and now I'm concerned that the two dead bodies literally cooling their heels outside the kitchen have something to do with all of this. If that's the case, Philip, we are in the middle of a major danger zone."

"That almost rhymes," Philip quipped. "A major danger zone." He punched his phone, put it on speaker and waited for it to connect. On the second ring, Duncan answered.

"Dad, how's the blizzard? Still raging from all reports."

Anxious to know about her family before they talked about anything else, Genevieve commandeered the conversation. "Hi, darling boy. How are Alex and Ella?"

"They're fine. Everything here is fine." Duncan blew through the perfunctory exchange. "What I want to know is how you two are and what's the status of the blizzard."

"The European Weather Service is one of Finn's clients so the head of the service has been keeping him posted with up-to-the-minute information. I think they're talking about the storm tapering off tomorrow about midday, which won't be any too soon for us, right, G?" He patted her hand.

"To say the least." She nodded slowly.

"We have a few things to share with you about what's happened here in the last twenty-four hours. You won't believe most of it, but it's all true."

"What are you talking about, Dad? Aside from the fact that you're snowed in, what could possibly be happening? Did the boiler go out so you don't have heat? I can only imagine the sizes of the fireplaces in that schloss. Surely there's plenty of wood to keep you warm Or did the pipes freeze so you don't have water? Bring in some snow and melt it. You guys taught me to be self-reliant. You're not going to get much sympathy from me, weathering a storm, cozy in a luxury schloss in one of the fanciest ski resorts in the world. Besides, the von Bassewitzes are known for their extraordinary wine cellar. What could be so bad?"

"Try two dead bodies outside the kitchen in the snow, which may or may not have died from foul play. That means there may or may not be a murderer among us. Oh yes, and another thing. Our dear friend Francis Darlington, who helped solve our problem at Wilmingrove Hall last year, seconded us to find several pieces of stolen art the Met believes are here at the schloss." She stopped for a second to see if there was anything else. Philip started to speak but she held up one finger. "One other thing. We appear to have our first acquisition for the Berlin museum. Sadly, we don't yet have the museum but that's a detail, right?"

There was silence on the other end of the phone.

"Duncan? Are you still there?" Genevieve looked at Philip then at the phone, which was still connected. "Duncan?"

"I'm here, Mom. Just trying to figure out what to ask. I guess I'll start with who's dead?"

"Oh, sorry. I should have said. Karl Friedrich von Bassewitz, the elder Baron. He either died of old age or poison. And the other deceased is Elsa Schmidt, the house manager here at the schloss. We called the police, but obviously they can't get here. They told us to put the Baron outside so we bagged him and put him in the snow. That's when we found Elsa sitting on a bench without a coat, frozen solid. We have no idea how that happened. Weird, huh?"

"I'd say so."

Genevieve and Philip watched the screen waiting for Duncan to say more. They heard the rustle of paper and Genevieve asked, "Are you taking notes?"

"I am. You just gave me a lot of information and I don't want to forget anything. Now, what is this business about Darlington, the Met and stolen works of art?"

They raced through the story of how Darlington intercepted them on the mountain, how Finn and Lillie were involved and how Francis had pressed them into helping the Metropolitan Police Services' Arts and Antiquities Unit confirm that a stolen work was at the schloss. He finished with, "This morning we thought Freddie and Heidi were about to reveal one of the stolen paintings, perhaps the Vermeer, perhaps *Chez Tortoni* by Manet. Instead, they showed us a little Monet study of wisteria. So we don't have anything on the stolen works yet."

As she neared the end of the story, Genevieve's breath grew short and shallow with excitement. "But I have a plan." A sly smile flashed across her face.

"Of course you do." Philip let out a long sigh. "You always have a plan."

They could hear Duncan breathing over the phone and waited patiently for him to speak. Sitting cross-legged, Genevieve bounced her foot. Studying the chandelier above him, Philip tapped his fingers on the arm of the loveseat he and Genevieve shared.

At last Duncan said, "Your only plan should be to get out of there." His intensity reached through the phone. "I mean it. You need to get out of there and get someplace safe."

"Duncan, darling, it would be insane to leave the schloss. You can't imagine the intensity of the blizzard."

Before the words were out of her mouth, Duncan lambasted his parents. "Are you two insane? You just told me two people died last night and they might have been murdered. There are four people in that house you can trust: each other, Lillie and Finn. Who else is there?"

"Freddie, Heidi, Max, Frieda, and Christine," Philip said.

"Who are Frieda, Christine, and Max?"

"Frieda and Christine are two young local women who work in the kitchen."

"We're not concerned about them," Genevieve added.

"Why not?" Duncan wanted to know.

Philip and Genevieve shrugged at each other, then Philip said, "They're just young girls from one of the villages in the valley. We don't know anything about them."

"Except that they make spectacular apple strudel," Genevieve added. "And Max is a lovely man who served the elder Baron as a driver and valet, you know, someone very like our own Henri," she said, referring to their chauffeur in France who did much more than drive.

"Mother." Duncan had gone from concerned to distraught. "Do you two understand what a serious situation you're in? I don't think you do."

"Duncan, calm down." Genevieve leaned toward the phone as if the closer she got to his voice, the closer she was to her son. Tears stung her eyes and for the first time since the misadventure started, emotion overwhelmed her and she longed to gather her little family together in the safety of Wilmingrove Hall, where no doubt at this very moment Mrs. MacIntosh and Wallace were in the middle of Christmas preparation, directing the house staff to raise that bough a little higher and straighten that bow, until everything was hung, fluffed, and polished to perfection. She sniffed and swallowed the lump in her throat before she said, "Darling, we are not going to do anything to put ourselves in danger, I promise."

"As far as I can tell, Mom, you and Dad are already in danger. Does Darlington know about the deaths?"

"He does," Philip said.

"And what did he say?"

"Actually, he didn't have time to say much. Freddie interrupted us while we were talking to him." She tilted her head to Philip. "In fact, we need to call him to let him know about the Monet."

"At least he knows about the dead bodies. That's something. Mom, you said you had a plan. I'm almost afraid to ask. What is it?"

Genevieve's eyes sparkled. "Our mission…"

"Mission?" Duncan interrupted.

"Our mission," she started again, "is simply to report anything we see that might be a piece stolen in the Gardner robbery. That's all we have to do. Earlier today when I was in the kitchen, Max came in and got the keys for the wine cellar so I now know where all the keys are. So, here's my plan."

Philip watched his wife with a combination of dread and amusement.

"I'm going to say I need to lie down with a splitting headache.

Then, while I go down to the cellars and look in every nook and cranny, Lillie and Finn will keep Freddie and Heidi occupied discussing museum plans."

Without missing a beat, Duncan shot back, "I understand how you can keep Freddie and Heidi busy but how can you manage the driver. You said his name is Max?"

"Yes. Max. That's easy. While the other four are deep in museum conversation, your dad will ask Max to show him the car collection. Tada."

Philip relaxed back into his chair and nodded slowly. "That just might work. What do you think, Duncan?"

"Not bad, Mom." Duncan sounded less stressed. "At least all of the murder suspects will be under your observation. Well, except for Freida and Christine."

"Don't worry about them," Genevieve said. "Honestly, they are not involved in any of this."

"Any bets?" Duncan chuckled for the first time. "I'll hold you to that. Listen, you two." He sounded like a parent warning his children. "You call me every hour. Is that clear?"

"That's a little excessive, Duncan." Genevieve shook her head.

"How about every three hours, more or less? Considering the circumstances, that's reasonable, isn't it?"

"All right, Dad. Every three hours. I'm setting my alarm. Starting now."

CHAPTER 29

"Correct me if I'm wrong, but what I hear you saying is that, for your paltry two-hundred-million-euro contribution, you think our new Berlin museum should be called Freddie and Heidi's Place?" Lillie had a difficult time saying it without bursting into laughter.

Straight-faced Heidi said, "We think that's the least you can do. Right, Freddie?"

"Whatever you say, Schatzie." He lounged by the fire across from Finn, who was nestled into an overstuffed chair with his feet on an ottoman. Freddie raised his flute of Champagne to Finn and said, "What do you think?"

Finn acknowledged Freddie's uplifted glass with his own, then drank. "I may not know as much about art as the three of you, but as a Mountbatten, I do know a thing or two about money. The Mountbatten philosophy is always have your name front and center when you donate. None of this anonymous rubbish. I'd say Freddie and Heidi's Place is an excellent name."

With lethal aim, a decorative pillow sailed from Lillie's hand across the short distance from where she sat on the tapestry-covered sofa next to Heidi, straight into Finn's arm, sloshing his wine.

"Well, that was unnecessary." His head whipped to Lillie and his eyes rounded with surprise.

In an instant she was up and dabbing the Champagne that had spilled on the front of his sweater. "I'm so sorry. I didn't mean to knock your glass."

"As I recall, another Mountbatten rule to live by is never spill good Champagne—or maybe that's a Finnegan philosophy," Philip said with a chuckle as he and Genevieve entered, arm in arm.

"It doesn't look as if you waited for us to start the party." Genevieve swept the room with a mock scowl. "Is there any Champagne left?"

"Freddie, get Philip and Genevieve a glass of Sekt," Heidi pointed to the sideboard as if he might not know where it was.

Genevieve put up her hand. "Stay, Freddie," she said as if commanding a puppy. "Philip and I know how to pour a glass of Champagne, I assure you." She waved Philip toward a chair." Sit down, darling. I'll get yours."

"How's Duncan?" Lillie was anxious to confirm that someone outside of Schloss Friedrichstein knew about their plight.

As Philip eased into a chair next to Finn, he said, "Everything is just fine at Château Beaulieu. Needless to say, Duncan was anxious to hear how we're fairing with the blizzard and pleased when I gave him the latest report." When he turned to Freddie his eyes softened. "Freddie, Duncan was so sorry to hear about your father. He sends his warmest regards and said to tell you both—" He swiveled his head to Heidi. "—that he and Julia regret they never met the elder Baron."

"That's very kind, Philip, thank you. He would have loved your Duncan and Julia and would have adored your grandchildren."

"I must say, Duncan was a bit unnerved that we have two bodies out in the snow. And, like all of us, he'll feel much better when the snow stops and we can determine how both people died." He caught Genevieve's eye and could see her tension ease, if only a little, now that everyone was aware that someone outside this small circle knew about the deaths.

A blast of wind shook the windowpanes as if it would shatter them. "When we hear that, it seems impossible to believe it will ever subside, doesn't it?" Freddie stood and rolled his shoulders. "But by tomorrow at this time, the blizzard should be well gone and perhaps Max can start clearing the road." He hefted a log from a brass box and tossed it into the flames, which sprang up to devour it.

This is a perfect time, Genevieve thought. "I hate to be a spoiler, particularly when the Champagne is so special, but I think I'll go upstairs and lie down. I have a splitting headache." She made a pained face to add to the effect and Philip couldn't help but smile.

"Oh, Genevieve, what can I get you?" With a look of concern, Heidi started to rise.

"No, no, Heidi. I have everything I need. I'll take a couple of ibuprofen and lie down for an hour or so and I'll be fine." She walked to Philip and handed him her flute. "My loss is your gain." He tilted his head and she kissed his forehead. "Just in case I'm coming down with something, I don't want to give it to you." She thought that was a nice touch.

She tossed the room a wave and could barely control her excitement as she left the living room, tugging the door closed, pulling it until she heard it latch. She willed herself not to run, keeping her pace to a rapid stride. In seconds she was through the great hall, through the dining room and into the kitchen, where she stood in front of the board with all the keys.

"Are you kidding me?" she hissed. "How could I be so stupid?" As she stood there, it hit her like a lightning bolt. She couldn't take any keys. With Philip's request to see the garage, Max would be getting the keys to the garage. If she took anything from the board, he'd notice. "What an idiot." She rolled her eyes as she accused herself.

She surveyed the kitchen for inspiration. Not knowing what she was looking for, she eased a drawer out, hoping something would inspire her. Instead, what she saw was silverware nested in plastic organizers. She closed that drawer, pulled out the next and slapped her hand over her mouth to stifle a scream as a cockroach scurried up and over the side of the drawer. When her heart stopped racing, she realized a flashlight was lying in the drawer, waiting for her.

"Of course I need a flashlight," she said under her breath. She put it in her trouser pocket, making a bulge on her thigh. Then she noticed a small notebook and several pens on the counter in front of her.

"Okay, this is starting to make sense. Since I can't take the keys until tonight, this first trip will be a reconnaissance mission. I'll go downstairs, look around and make notes of any doors that are locked. Then tonight when everyone's asleep, Philip and I can get the keys and see what's behind the doors." Satisfied with her plan, she filled a water glass in case anyone saw her come from the kitchen and made a beeline for the stairs to the cellars. When she arrived at the door, she drained the water glass and left it behind a vase on the table next to the stairway entrance. She put her hand on the knob and remembered the door squeaked when Max had opened it yesterday. *Was that just yesterday?* She couldn't believe it.

As slowly as she could, she turned the ancient knob. Its slight grinding noise was so soft she was certain no one else had heard it. She held her breath and eased the door open. The moment the hinges groaned, she stopped then lifted the handle and tried again. This time it opened silently. When there was just enough space, Genevieve squeezed through the small opening and pulled the door closed behind her. She drew the flashlight from her pocket and switched it on, blinking at the beam's brightness. With her hand on the railing, she focused the light on the stairs. "Be careful," she said, remembering how the night before she had almost tumbled down this flight. Cautiously, she took the first step on her journey, her leather soles silent as she crept downward stair after stair until she got to the landing. Air whooshed from her lungs and she realized she had been holding her breath. "One down," she said, her voice echoing around the narrow space.

"I hope these batteries hold out," she said with a scoff. "This is a pretty stupid time to think about that, Genevieve." By the time she hit the last step, she was feeling quite confident. Swinging the flashlight back and forth in front of her, ahead she could see the wide opening Max had referred to as the dungeon. When she arrived at the arched entrance, she stood, frozen by the idea of what might lie beyond. Looking into the dark, her mind raced: spiders, rats, ghosts of dead prisoners, bats. "Bats." She shivered. "Please don't let there be bats."

Though she was cold, her armpits felt damp and sweat prickled her hairline. "Buck up, Genevieve." She pulled her lower lip between her teeth, took a step into the abyss, and swept the flashlight beam across the ceiling of the cavernous space. A huge, hairy spider sat motionless at the center of its web that stretched across several stones. "Spiders, check."

Creeping deeper into the vast space, she kept the beam focused on what lay in front of her until she was several feet into the dungeon. She stopped to survey the area, slowly swiping the light around the room, over the walls and ceiling and was relieved to see that the space appeared to be ordinary, as dungeons went— no ghosts, no rats, no bats. At the far end, an archway led to a corridor that stretched into the darkness. Keeping the beam waist high, she walked straight through the archway and into the long hall, flanked on either side by small stone cells with heavy, barred gates. She shivered at the idea that men, or maybe women, had spent long, dark days in these cold, forlorn chambers.

Tears welled and she blinked to keep them at bay. The idea that people were actually locked there, possibly for years, made her weep.

"I'm afraid there are no hidden art treasures here," she said, unhappy she had made no discoveries. Just as she was about to turn around, she noticed a grey metal door in the shadows at the end of the hall. It blended into the stone so she'd almost missed it, except for the chrome handle reflecting the light of the flashlight. She felt the corners of her mouth pull up and her pulse pick up pace. "Oh boy, maybe this is something."

Walking toward the door, she heard heavy, raspy breathing. She stopped to listen. It was close to her and getting louder. She walked a few more paces and stopped again. It was still close, and even louder. She listened intently, trying to figure out where it was, but her heart was thumping in her ears so it was hard to hear. She closed her eyes, counted to three then swung around, sweeping her flashlight from side to side. There was no one there but the breathing was on top of her, louder and raspier than before. She held her breath and it stopped. She waited, then breathed again, then croaked a laugh. "Damn, Genevieve, it's you, you fool. It's you breathing so loudly."

Shaking, she pressed on until she stood in front of the door. "You're sure you want to do this?" She shifted the flashlight into her left hand, placed her right on the round doorknob and turned, almost hoping it was locked. It rotated smoothly and she heard the latch click. She hissed in a breath between her teeth and edged the door open just enough to see that, though it was dark, it wasn't inky-dark like the rest of the cellar. And, unlike the rest of the cellar, rather than old dust and must, it smelled new and electronic, like warm plastics with a faint hint of chemicals.

She cleared her throat, warning any living thing on the other side of the door that she was about to enter. Slowly, steadily, she pushed the door wide and aimed her beam into the middle of the room. Four computers stared back at her, all showing 13:03 on the screen. Around the room LEDs blinked or held steady, indicating things were on, charging or hibernating. The flashlight beam wandered to the left where steel shelving housed three rows of what appeared to be model airplanes of all sizes. "Drones," Genevieve said out loud. "These are drones. And a lot of them. These have to be Karl's. Pretty impressive for a ninety-one-year-old to be on top of this technology."

She turned around and shone her light to the side of the door. "Aha, lights. She flipped the switch and squeezed her eyes shut against the florescent lamps which flooded the room. When she flickered her eyes open, she gasped at the high-end technology filling every shelf. In addition to the four computers and the many drones, on the other wall, Genevieve recognized night vision goggles, cameras she thought might be thermal imaging, and many other gadgets well beyond her understanding. She pulled out her phone and began to take pictures of everything, then decided videos would be better. She narrated, naming the things she could, then, with one last sweeping shot, decided it was time to go.

As she stood outside the door of the room full of technology, she ran through a checklist of what she had done since she entered the room. She had touched nothing. She had left no lights on. She had closed the door and wiped the doorknob with the hem of her sweater. Taking a cleansing breath, she turned and began to retrace her steps, her mind racing with everything she had just seen.

She was so deep in thought that she barely noticed a chubby rat scurry across the floor as she came to the end of the corridor. When she stepped into the cavernous space at the front of the dungeon, she saw light flooding several feet through the arched entry and heard Freddie's robust voice and Philip's boisterous laugh. She snapped off the flashlight and melted her body to the cave's frigid wall. Their footfall grew louder and louder and their lively banter sounded as if they had shared more than a few Champagne toasts.

"You know, Genevieve is in love with your red XKE." Genevieve heard Philip hiccup and had to stifle a giggle. They passed the opening to the cave. As they passed by her on the other side of the stone wall, she scrunched her eyes closed and held her breath.

"She told me," Freddie said.

"Would you ever sell it, ol' buddy, ol' pal?"

Freddie snorted a laugh. "You know, mein Freund, everything is for sale."

Genevieve strained to hear the rest of the conversation as they moved out of earshot. "It would make a wonderful Christmas gift," was the last thing she could make out.

The moment Genevieve felt certain Philip and Freddie were mounting the stairs at the other end of the hall, she tiptoed out of the cavern back down the hall and up the stairs.

When she opened the door into the great hall, her heart dropped to her toes.

"Lady Crosswick, what are you doing coming out of the cellar?" Max asked, holding a tray of clean glasses and two bottles of Veuve Clicquot. "Is there something I can do for you?"

"Oh, Max! What a surprise." She groped for a response. "I, um. I just wanted to tell Philip something, but I guess he's already gone to the garage. I thought you were going to show him the car collection."

"No, Lady Crosswick. The Baron wanted that pleasure. Are you able to text the Earl? Or I can take him a message."

"Never mind. It was nothing. Will you please tell the Baroness and Ms. Langdon I'm feeling much better and I'll join them shortly? Thank you."

Before Max could ask any more questions, Genevieve was halfway up the stairs. Maybe her racing heart was from charging up the staircase, but she didn't think so and was quite certain it would take a while for her to calm down.

CHAPTER 30

"I WOULD SUGGEST YOU wait to see the car, Philip. You know I would gift it to Genevieve myself, but I have a feeling you would not take kindly to that idea." Freddie's boozy smile puffed his cheeks and Philip thought how much he looked like a little boy.

"You are so very right, Baron. If you gave Genevieve your red Jaguar I'm afraid I would have to duel you for my lady's favor. So better if you just sell it to me."

Freddie patted Philip on his chest. "Just take a look at it first, my friend." He threw open the door to the garage, hit the panel of switches on the wall and light flooded row upon row of cars.

Philip's jaw dropped. His lips formed a perfect 'O' but it was several seconds before, "Oh. Wow!" whispered from his mouth. "This is impressive." His gaze ran up one aisle and down the other. "How long have you been collecting, Freddie?"

"I bought my first car with money my grandfather gave me for my eighteenth birthday. It's the 1957 Mercedes 300 SL Gullwing." He pointed to a sparkling silver Benz that Philip knew to be rare and worth millions. "That car, my friend, I would never sell you, but the XKE, of course you may buy it for our darling Genevieve. Let me go into the office and find the records on it." He started toward the garage bureau. "Take a closer look at it," he said over his shoulder. "I won't be a minute."

Smiling at the possibility of giving Genevieve such a surprise for Christmas, he walked slowly around the Jag, appreciating every angle of one of the most beautiful cars ever made. He opened the door and sank into the low-slung, biscuit-colored seat, breathing in the rich aroma of leather. "She would love this," he called across the garage to Freddie, but didn't think he heard. "It would certainly beat the raincoat I gave her last year. Granted, it was a Burberry, but still, it was a raincoat."

He reached under the dashboard and pulled the cable to release the trunk lid. With some effort, he heaved himself out of the seat and walked to the back of the car. "I bet she won't be able to get an overnight bag in here." He chuckled as he lifted the lid. He stared into the compartment, frowned, lowered the lid and stared across the garage, through the window of the office where Freddie searched on his computer. He inhaled through ridged lip and slowly raised the deck lid again. There, nestled in the small trunk's cozy compartment was another wooden crate about the size of a medium-sized suitcase. And on the bottom, in black ink, the number 247 was stamped.

CHAPTER 31

FREDDIE AND PHILIP returned to find the living room in the middle of a furious game of charades. Her shoulders scrunched up to her ears, Lillie blew out a mighty puff of air.

"It's a book," Heidi yelled to the two newcomers.

"*Gone with the Wind*," Philip said as he walked to the sideboard to pour two glasses of Champagne.

"Philip!" Lillie stamped her feet in annoyance. "How did you get that? You barely saw any of my dramatics."

"Oh, but Lillie, you're such a spectacular actress," he teased. "Your performance was Oscar-worthy. What else could it be?" He handed Freddie a glass and sat next to Genevieve on the sofa, grabbing her hand and squeezing hard, so hard that she winced and was about to ask why he was hurting her, when she realized he was sending her a message that something had happened in the garage. "How's your headache? Are you feeling better?" he said.

"Much, thank you. The ibuprofen and a little nap did the trick." She raised her brows, hoping he could whisper more information, but he shook his head almost imperceptibly, so she asked, "What did you think of the collection?"

"Magnificent. Simply magnificent. Kudos to you, Freddie. Congratulations on creating something so spectacular in spite of parental obstacles."

"Ah, yes, Freddie," Genevieve joined in. "Max told me your father was not one of your biggest supporters when it came to your automobile collection."

Sadness seemed to suck the energy from Freddie as his shoulders slumped and his head drooped.

"Poor darling Freddie." Heidi moved to sit on the arm of her husband's chair and draped her arm over the back. She tickled his ear. He swatted at her fingers. She did it again and the left side of his mouth tugged up into a crooked smile. When her fingers wafted down to his chin, he grabbed her hand and kissed her palm. "You don't have to worry about Papa anymore, do you, darling?"

He sniffed and moaned a forlorn chuckle. "Sadly, no. I don't have to worry about Papa's disapproval anymore. Until this moment, Papa's death has not seemed real. And, of course, Elsa. The blizzard and our isolation from everyone…" His voice trailed off. He shook his head. "Until just now, it had not occurred to me that I am now the senior Baron von Bassewitz." Pain distorted his handsome face and he swiped at a tear trailing slowly down his cheek.

"Freddie, old man, I think you've done a remarkable job keeping it all together. It's been very impressive." At Finn's comforting words, the corners of Freddie's mouth drew into a sad smile.

"He lived a long and amazing life. I just wish Gabe were here with me. I know it is difficult for him to be alone right now. Particularly with his darling Michael in New York."

"Tell us about Michael's patent. It has something to do with the experience one has in museums, right?" Genevieve said, trying to move the conversation to a happier subject.

Heidi left the arm of Freddie's chair and stood in front of the fireplace, her eyes sparkling with enthusiasm. "What Michael has created is extraordinary. His patent will change the way people experience art forever." As she talked, she walked around the room. "Have you been to any immersive art experiences?"

Genevieve's head bounced enthusiastically. "Philip and I have. We saw the Klimt exhibition in New York and the Van Gogh in London."

"I have to say, being the fancy-pants, artsy professional I am, I was scathingly skeptical about these 'bring it to the masses' exhibitions." Lillie's hands fluttered as she spoke. "But when I went, I was blown away and have been noodling about how we can incorporate more of this kind of experience in our museums."

Finn leaned forward, putting his elbow on his knees. "Does Michael's technology have something to do with those kinds of experiences?"

"I shouldn't tell you anything without a non-disclosure agreement, but I think he'd forgive me. Freddie and I are heavily invested in the company and have been involved since the beginning. There are potentially millions and millions of euros on the upside. Needless to say, we're quite excited about the project."

"That's another thing Papa didn't support. He thought it was a lot of rubbish. Again, we don't have to worry about him now."

Genevieve waved her hand, fanning his gloom away. "So tell us about Michael's concept."

A smile lit Heidi's face. "Imagine you are at the Tate Gallery in London, or the Belvedere in Vienna, or better yet, you are standing in front of Vincent Van Gogh's *Starry Night* at MOMA in New York. Now close your eyes." She was in complete command of the room. "You are wearing a lightweight headgear, somewhat like the women in *The Handmaid's Tale*. As you look at Van Gogh's magnificent painting, you're taken to the moment in time when, in mid-June of 1889, he painted this piece in his studio in the asylum where, only a month earlier, he had committed himself. You will hear the music that was popular in Provence at that time, hear the noises that surrounded Van Gogh in the asylum, smell the aromas of Vincent's favorite foods, hear the letters he and his brother wrote to each other. Michael's technology engulfs you with every possible sensory experience so you feel what the artist felt; you become the artist—at least as much as is possible."

Heidi let her words linger for a few long seconds before saying, "Well, what do you think?"

Eyes opened slowly, everyone's mind filled with images and possibilities.

Lillie studied her hands, clasped in her lap. She blew out a long stream of air. "Extraordinary. This is the kind of thing we've been searching for: how to move our museums' missions from being custodians of important artworks and artistic heritage, to that of creating an experience that will engage our visitors with every piece of art in our museum."

"If I were to summarize your eloquent thesis, Heidi, could I simply say, this takes the visitor from having a passive experience and puts the guest in the artists' shoes?" Finn looked from Lillie to Heidi.

"Perfect, Finn. That is an excellent synopsis." Heidi beamed.

"It sounds as if this combines AI, virtual reality, augmented reality, QR codes, nanotechnology… I could go on, but I'm running out of tech words." Philip shrugged. "Remarkable. Michael is quite the big brain, isn't he?"

"He is, and he makes Gabe happier than I have ever seen him." Freddie smiled for the first time in a while.

Lillie carefully gauged Heidi and Freddie's mood and decided to press. "Was it in your plan to introduce Michael's technology at the opening of the Berlin Musée Des Beaux Arts?"

"Ja, that—" Freddie began but Heidi interrupted.

"That is all we have been talking about and one of the reasons we have been anxious to firm our relationship."

Lillie arched her brow at Philip and smiled as if to say, "I believe you owe me a thousand pounds."

Believing the moment was exactly right, Philip rose and stood in front of Freddie. "At the very least, Baron," he said with formality, "I believe we should shake on it." He extended his hand.

Freddie rose and, locking eyes with Philip, grasped his hand in a firm grip.

"Thank goodness we have Champagne at the ready." Heidi strode to the sideboard and pulled a chilled bottle from the ice bucket. Luckily, each person had an empty glass at hand, ready to be filled. When the bubbles were poured, Heidi took Freddie's hand and walked him to stand next to Philip. "You two do the honors." She raised her phone to capture the moment on her camera. "Well, somebody make a toast," she ordered.

Taking the initiative, Philip raised his glass. "To the future of the von Bassewitz Foundation Laney Musée des Beaux Arts Berlin. How's that for a long name!"

"Perfect." Genevieve caught Philip's eye and they grinned at each other. She could hardly wait for the party to wind down so she could get him alone and find out what happened in the garage. *Who knows what I might have to do to get information out of him,* she thought, and her heart did a little dance.

CHAPTER 32

BY THE TIME the clock in the great hall chimed twelve o'clock, too many Champagne bottles rested upside down in the copper wine cooler. Throughout the evening, every time Max brought a tray of cheese, meat pies, pears and whatever else he could find in the kitchen, the tray was picked clean before he could bring the next round. Drinking, mourning, lying, suspecting and planning were all hungry pursuits. The group retold every detail of the last twenty-four hours several times until finally the party started to break up. It was time to call it a day.

"I absolutely think the winds are dying down," Lillie said as she stood and straightened her arms above her head in a luxurious stretch. She hoped she was right and morning would bring sunny skies and snow-melting temperatures.

Finn slipped his arm around her waist, pulled her to him and said, "I know it hasn't been as long as it seems but it's been long enough. My office is doing far too well without me. I need to get back and show them how indispensable I am."

"I could say the same thing but everyone on my staff thinks they are totally fine without me." Lillie covered a yawn.

"What do you think, G? This could be the chance to give Lillie the axe and save a boatload of money at the Foundation." Philip winked at Genevieve, snuggled next to him, her feet pulled up under her.

"I think we should show a little mercy and let her continue to toil for us for the time being. We can always fire her later." Genevieve was enjoying the light banter.

Totally unthreatened, Lillie threw a kiss to the room. "Good night, one and all. Fingers crossed for a bright and sunny day tomorrow."

The last four watched Lillie and Finn leave the room hand in hand.

"Those youngsters," Freddie said. "No stamina."

Heidi offered an exhausted smile to the other three. "Nightcap, anyone?"

"You Austrians!" Philip shook his head violently. "We Yanks cannot keep up with you."

"Oh, I think you did pretty well with the bubbly, old chum," Freddie said in his best British accent.

Philip stood and held out his hand to Genevieve. She took it and heaved herself off the sofa. "It's been a challenging day, Freddie, Heidi. As Lillie said, tomorrow the sun will shine, the snow will melt and life will be a little brighter."

Heidi and Freddie stood and everyone exchanged kisses on the cheek and wishes to sleep well.

Philip and Genevieve made their way to the great hall and up the stairs in silence. He closed their bedroom door, turn the lock and when he turned around, she had clamped her hand over her mouth.

"Do you have something to say?" he asked casually.

Genevieve's eyes were so wide he thought they might pop out of her head.

"Speak, oh crazy one, but do it quietly." He pulled his sweater over his head and draped it over a chair by the fireplace. He placed a few pieces of kindling and three logs onto the grate and lit them. The flame caught and he sat. "Well? Shall we swap stories?"

"Do you think we should text Lillie and Finn?"

"I think we can wait till morning. When we call Darlington, we can bring the three of them up to date at once."

For the next hour, they shared their adventures with each other. Sitting across from Philip, Genevieve told about finding the tech room and insisted it was an integral part of the art theft and the murders, though, she admitted, she had no idea how all of that technology could be involved or who was using it.

When it was Philip's turn, she interrupted him before he began. "Wait, wait. Let me tell you what happened when I heard you and Freddie in the corridor." Her muscles taut, she leaned toward him, eyes bright and anxious. "I was on my way out and just about to step into the hall when the lights came on and you two started walking toward me." Her story came in such a rush

Philip stared at her lips so he could catch every word. "I switched my flashlight off and plastered myself against the wall inside the cavern. I was certain you could hear my heart pounding when the two of you walked by." She stopped to take a breath. "Thank goodness you were laughing and talking, otherwise I might have passed out. I kept thinking: what if I had been walking toward you when the lights went on? What would I have done? Although I must say, I've gotten pretty good the last couple of days, making up stories on the spot. But I don't know what I would have said if you two had caught me there. Honestly, Philip. There were several parts of our plan that weren't very well thought out."

Not knowing if she was finished, Philip continued to watch and listen for several seconds until she collapsed back into the chair. He gave her a quiet moment before he said, 'You're right. There were several things we didn't consider that could have been disastrous. You just named one. Another was because Freddie wanted to show me the collection, we had no control over where Max was."

"Exactly!" Genevieve squinted an accusation at Philip. "When I came out of the cellar, Max was in the great hall and naturally asked me what I was doing." She toed off her shoes and pulled her legs up under her, then wiggled into the down cushions.

"Oh, damn, Genevieve." Philip's mouth stretched into a smile. "What did you say?"

"I said I was hoping to catch you before you left on your big trek. I just needed to tell you something but it appeared you were already on your way to the garage."

"Quick thinking. I see what you mean about developing your lying skills in the last twenty-four hours. Well done."

Genevieve puffed up. "I'm calling it developing my spycraft. That sounds much better."

"It does and it's a perfect segue to the critical part of my story. Get ready. We may need more of your craft. And, darling girl, there is a spoiler alert, so fair warning."

"Spoiler alert?" Genevieve leaned forward, her face open and eager. "I can hardly wait."

Philip waggled his eyebrows. "Well, pretty girl," he said in a Groucho Marx voice, tapping a pretend cigar, "Let me tell you." He inhaled and sighed. "I found number 247."

Several seconds ticked by before Genevieve registered any understanding of what Philip had just said. But when it dawned on her, she again slapped her hand over her mouth. When she removed it, her mouth was a perfect O.

"Where was it?" she whispered. "Does Freddie know you saw it? Where is it now? Did you open it yet?"

Philip held his hands in front of him in surrender. "Whoa. Let me tell the story and you just listen. Fair?"

"Fair. Go!" she ordered.

"Here's the spoiler, pretty girl. I told Freddie I wanted to buy the XKE and give it to you for Christmas."

Lines popped between Genevieve's eyebrows. "Is the spoiler that you don't want to buy the Jag?"

"G." An exasperated growl caught in his throat. "The spoiler is that you now know what you're getting for Christmas."

"Philip!" She squealed and jumped out of her chair. "The 1970 signal-red Jaguar XKE with biscuit interior is mine?" She draped herself across his lap, wrapped her arms around his neck and planted a robust kiss on his laughing lips.

"No. It is not yours. At least not yet. But that's not the important part of the story. Would you please put yourself back in your chair and listen to what I'm saying?" He pulled her arms from around his neck and gave her bottom a gentle shove. "You're making this story much longer and more difficult than it needs to be."

"I'm so sorry," she said, realizing she had lost sight of the important part of his story. "But it's not every day a girl gets her lifelong dream car."

"And today's not that day either."

She grunted slightly as she stood, then walked back to her chair. She pulled a wrap from the back, tugged it around her shoulders and sat. "I promise, I'll do better. Please go on. You told Freddie you want to give me the car for Christmas." She couldn't hide her thrilled smile. "And then what happened?"

"He said he would be happy to sell me the car."

Still smiling, she hugged herself and shivered with excitement.

"Genevieve."

She heard Philip use her full name and said, "Sorry, sorry."

He started again. "Freddie said he would be delighted to give you the car himself but didn't think I would be happy about that. I confirmed he was right."

She grimaced at the idea of Freddie giving her an expensive gift.

"I told you he has a crush on you, but I digress. He went into the office to pull up the records on the Jag and I went to look at it more closely. I'm certain it's in mint condition, but I wanted to sit in it and see if I could get out without a crane." He chuckled.

"And?"

"I did but I don't think you'll have to worry about me driving it too often. I popped the trunk. You know it has a lever under the dashboard."

"Mm-hmm. I remember from my dad's XKE. Gosh, I loved that car."

"I didn't think you'd be able to get even a small suitcase in the trunk. I was completely absorbed in you and your luggage so when I lifted the lid and saw a wooden crate, I was flabbergasted. I put the lid down, looked to make certain Freddie was still in the office then lifted it slowly as if the crate might jump out. That's when I saw the number. 247. You can imagine what a tough time I had pretending I hadn't seen anything."

"I don't know how you did it, darling. What happened next?"

"Freddie finished in the office, came out and we talked about the car. He showed me the provenance, all the restoration bills, the maintenance bills and the whole time I'm waiting for him to open the trunk, but he didn't. He even said, 'The trunk is larger than you thought it would be, isn't it?' There's no question he has no idea that crate is in there. And, of course, we still don't know that it's a piece from the Gardner Museum."

"You may not know, Philip, but, after what Karl Friedrich said to me—that it would make our museum the most famous on earth or something like that—I am absolutely certain it's a piece from the Gardner. In fact, I know it's the Vermeer. I feel it in my bones. So we have to go back and get it." She stood, threw off the wrap and headed to get her coat.

She stuck her hand in her pocket to get her gloves and pulled out the flashlight. "Oh, good. I didn't put this back. For once, that was a good thing." She walked to the door and with her hand on the knob, turned back to Philip. "I'll go to the kitchen and get the key. Meet me on the landing to the cellar stairs."

"I just need to find a heavier sweater, make a pit stop and I'll be down."

Across the room, they held each other's eyes, Genevieve's full of excitement and Philip's full of caution.

CHAPTER 33

AS THEY CREPT down the first long flight of stairs, they moved in silence with their hands on the railing, cautious not to make a misstep. They reached the landing and stopped for a moment, to calm their nerves then, with Genevieve lighting the way, continued.

"It's so much nicer doing this with you," Genevieve whispered. "I was pretty nervous down here by myself. Though I have to say, the dungeons are remarkably clean and I only saw one spider, one rat, and no bats."

"Lucky for you." Philip stopped, grabbed Genevieve by the arm and pulled her to a stop as well.

"What's wrong?" She turned the flashlight up so their faces were in the beam.

He cupped her chin, leaned down and brushed her lips with his. "I just wanted to say, Genevieve Warwick, life is never dull with you." Their foreheads met and they lingered there for a moment before Philip kissed her lightly again, and they pressed on toward the other end of the hall.

With his words still ringing in her ears, Genevieve smiled all the way down the corridor and up the stairs at the other end. "Here, hold this please." She gave Philip the flashlight then fumbled in her deep jacket pocket until she felt the key ring. The key slid into the lock and turned smoothly. She eased the door open, felt for the panel and switched the lights on.

They blinked at the brightness and Philip switched the flashlight off. "You stay here. I'll get the crate." He strode into the rows of cars straight for the Jaguar.

"Can't I come see my car?" Genevieve bounced on her toes with pent-up energy.

Philip turned and pointed at her. "Stay there. I won't be a moment." He leaned over the car door, pulled the lever and Genevieve heard the lovely thud of the trunk latch releasing. He walked to the back and lifted the lid. "Genevieve, come here, please."

Without a second invitation, she was there in an instant. "What is it?"

"Take a look," he said, pulling her around so she could see in the trunk.

Squinting into the small storage compartment, Genevieve was confused. "What the hell?"

"What the hell, indeed," Philip confirmed.

Genevieve hesitated but the question had to be asked. "You're certain you saw a crate in here?"

"What do you think?" Philip said, clearly annoyed.

"Of course you did. Should we look in any other trunks?"

"I can't imagine someone would have removed it from this car and put it in another. Would that make any sense?"

"Probably not." But she couldn't resist walking a few cars down and lifting the trunk lids. As Philip predicted, the trunks were empty and immaculate.

"Come on, G, we need to get out of here." He reached out his arm and took her hand. "Let's go," he said, and pulled her toward the door.

"Well, that was disappointing."

"And we don't have our cover story if we encounter someone."

"You're right. I'd better start thinking up another lie—I mean, story."

They slipped back out of the garage, down the stairs and through the corridor. As they passed the cavern entrance, Genevieve stopped abruptly. "Philip, let me show you the tech room. Maybe you'll see something I didn't."

"Why not? We're here. As the Brits say: in for a penny, in for a pound."

Passing through the arched entry to the vaulted room, Genevieve swept the flashlight beam across the ceiling, saying hello to the spider she had seen earlier. The spinner still sat center stage, her lacey web stretching across the cold stones. Genevieve refocused the light ahead of them and they moved through the cell block to the end of the hall.

"Are you ready for this?" Genevieve said, her hand on the knob, ready to reveal the room full of technological gadgets.

"There's a lot of stuff in here."

Though Genevieve buzzed with anticipation, all Philip said was, "Sure," with no enthusiasm at all.

She turned the knob but the door resisted. "Are you kidding me?" she said under her breath. She tried again but the door was clearly locked. "I can't believe this. It wasn't locked before." Her hopes dashed, Genevieve gritted her teeth with disappointment.

"Aren't there other keys on the ring besides the garage key?"

"You're right," she said with renewed excitement. She jingled the keys out of her pocket and held them in the flashlight beam. Four keys. She nudged aside the garage key and looked at the labels on the other three. "Wine room", "art vault", "office". It certainly wasn't the first two, so she held the office key between her thumb and forefinger and worked it into the slot on the handle. It slid in easily. She held her breath and turned. The latch clicked, and this time when she twisted the knob, the door opened. "Eureka!" Her breath whooshed out in triumph.

In the dark room, LEDs blinked and winked as data flowed into computer servers and blue screens waited to be roused from hibernation. Little green lights held steady on equipment resting on the rows of shelves, announcing it was charged and ready for use.

Genevieve swung the flashlight to the left and caught the light switch in its beam. Philip clicked the rocker switch. "Damn!" he said, the moment the overhead lights came on.

"What?" Genevieve's head swiveled from one side of the room to the other, from one set of shelves to another.

"There." Philip pointed. "In the chair."

"You've got to be kidding." Genevieve sucked in a breath.

There, in a low-backed office chair, they could see the side of a wooden crate and on the side in black ink the number 247 was stamped.

CHAPTER 34

By the time Philip and Genevieve closed their bedroom door and turned the lock, they were both sweating from the exhilaration of finding the crate and secreting it back to their room without being discovered.

Philip laid the box flat on the coffee table and went straight into the bathroom in search of his utility kit. Since his sixteenth birthday, when his grandfather gave him a leather toiletry bag filled with essentials every young man should have, he'd never traveled without it. In that bag was his cherished Swiss Army knife, which he could use to pry the staple-like cleats from the crate's soft wood.

While she waited for him to return, Genevieve tugged two logs from the firebox and tossed them into the fireplace, where coals barely glowed. Within seconds flames lapped at the dry wood and heat wafted into the room.

Suddenly parched, she poured a glass of water from the carafe sitting on the side table and gulped noisily. Though she was still keyed up, she could feel her adrenaline waning. Just in case she had trouble sleeping later, she took a bottle of Tylenol P.M. liquid from the drawer and put it next to the carafe, then dragged herself over to the chair next to the fireplace and collapsed into it.

As he came back into the bedroom, Philip held the Dopp kit over his head like a trophy. "Tada!" He unzipped the side compartment and produced his fifty-year-old Swiss Army knife, his traveling companion for as many years. "Are you ready for this?"

Genevieve nodded.

He stood the crate on one end and began to pry up the cleats. The Swiss Army knife was the perfect tool. "You realize if this piece of art isn't from the Gardner Museum, we're going to have to re-staple it and return it to the tech room, don't you?"

"I hadn't thought about that. But you know what else?" Genevieve said.

"What?"

"I still have the keys in my coat pocket. I guess I'm making one more trip downstairs one way or the other." Too tired to get up, Genevieve stretched forward as far as she could until her fingertips barely touched her coat, which she had thrown across the sofa. She caught the tip of the wool collar between two fingers and groaned as she pulled the coat off the sofa and into her lap. Slipping her hand into the left pocket, she felt her phone and pulled it out just as her text tone sounded. Lillie's picture flashed on her screen next to a text that said, "You awake?"

"Yup, and your timing's perfect. Creep on over," she texted back. "That was Lillie. I think they, or at least she, is on her way over."

"Well, her timing's good."

Before Genevieve could get to the door, they heard a soft knock. She turned the lock as quietly as possible, pressed the handle down, and pulled the door open about a foot. Both in their pajamas and robes, Lillie and Finn sidled in and closed the door silently behind them. Half asleep, Finn shuffled to the nearest chair and collapsed, but Lillie was wide awake. "Have you noticed the winds have died down? And the snow has really tapered—" She interrupted herself. "What's going on here?" She realized Philip and Genevieve were still in their clothes. "You two haven't even gone to bed yet, have you?" Then, finally, her focus landed on Philip tugging staples from the crate and she whisper-shouted, "Where did you get that?"

All of a sudden, Finn was awake, alert, and interested.

"Genevieve, fill in these two latecomers," Philip grunted, struggling with a fastener that refused to give.

"Right." She narrowed her eyes, thinking. "Hmm. Where to begin?" She started her tale with her solo trip to the cellar, during which Finn and Lillie had kept Heidi and Freddie occupied, and gave them a blow-by-blow. As she approached the finale, Lillie and Finn sat on the edge of their seats, hanging on every word. "By the time we got back here, we were so jazzed on adrenaline, we were hyperventilating," she said, ending her story as Philip pulled the last staple from the crate.

"Okay, kids," he said, flipping the blade back into the red-lacquered body of his beloved knife and slipping it into his pocket. "Any bets on what we're about to see?" He pointed to Genevieve. "G?"

"You know what I think," she said. "There's no doubt in my mind this is the Vermeer."

"Lillie?" He cocked his head and waited.

"I think it's going to be the Vermeer because Angelina said the Vermeer was here."

"Finn?"

"Not only did Angelina tell the Met the Vermeer was here, but she had photographs. I'd love if it were the Vermeer or at least some piece from the Gardner Museum. That would be extraordinary. What do you think, Philip?"

"I agree with you. I'd love it if it were a piece from the Gardner, but I can't imagine how that could have happened. After more than thirty years, how in the world did it end up here?"

The four people stood in a semicircle, looking down at the wooden box. With great ceremony, Philip cracked his knuckles, shook his hands and slowly lifted the crate lid. Gasps filled the room and silent O's rounded everyone's lips as Philip, Genevieve, Lillie, and Finn feasted their eyes on one of the few works of one of the greatest painters of the Dutch Golden Age.

CHAPTER 35

"WHAT DO WE do now?" Overcome with awe, Lillie longed to run her fingers over the brushstrokes, but the curator in her wouldn't allow it. "I, um, I can't believe this is actually Johannes Vermeer's *The Concert*, probably the most valuable stolen object in the world." She pulled her phone from her robe pocket and took several photos.

"It's incredible to believe we're looking at his work, right here in this bedroom." Philip gulped the last of the water in his glass.

"Maybe we aren't," Finn said.

Water sprayed from Philip's nose and he coughed and choked until his face was crimson and tears streamed down his cheeks. "That hadn't occurred to me. Can you imagine?" he said when he stopped coughing and could finally speak. "What if we've been going through all this for a few brushstrokes painted by an art school dropout—a fake, a fraud?"

Lillie's brows scrunched together and she leaned so close to the canvas that her nose almost touched the paint. "I suppose that's a legitimate concern. Certainly, the authenticity will have to be verified, but when it gets back to the Gardner Museum, they will be able to do that easily. In the meantime, I suggest we assume it is the genuine article. So I ask again, what do we do now?"

"We need a good hiding place." Genevieve's eyes roamed the room. "It has to be someplace no one can find the painting but somewhere safe, somewhere climate and humidity controlled."

"Back in the art vault?" Finn said.

"That's… that's absolutely brilliant." Genevieve perked up.

"Do we even know where it is?" Lillie said.

"We do."

"Surely it's locked and alarmed," Finn said, thinking about the problems of returning the painting to the vault.

"When we were coming from the ski room…" Philip stopped to think. "Was that just yesterday?"

"Considering how late—or early—it is right now, it was day before yesterday, because right now it's actually tomorrow." Genevieve giggled as she tried to keep track of time.

"Anyway," Philip continued, "when we were coming from the ski room, we ran into Max, who was coming from the art vault. There is a lock on the door from the corridor and an alarm on that door. Beyond that, we have no idea what security there is between there and the inside of the vault."

"Ah." Lillie stuck out her lower lip. "Disappointing."

"That's too bad," Genevieve agreed.

"Plan B?" Philip resumed scanning the room for a hiding place.

"Oh, ye of little faith." Finn walked to the credenza by the fireplace. "Have you forgotten your secret weapon in all this?" He pulled the crystal stopper out of a facetted carafe, splashed scotch into his glass, and threw it back with a swagger. When he got no response, he said, "Come, you lot. This is not a difficult question."

"What are you suggesting, darling?" Lillie said.

"I'm not just suggesting. I am stating emphatically that there is not a lock or alarm system in Schloss Friedrichstein I can't get around. Did all of you forget I am a security expert? The art vault is the perfect place for this very old painting to be, so that's where Philip and I are going to put it. Right, Philip?"

"Whatever you say, Finn. There's nothing I want to do more than fumble around this creepy castle with a stolen painting, looking for a place to put it. And lucky for you, Max admitted to us the security system is lacking so it may not be as challenging as we three think." He threw his head back, stretched his arms overhead and yawned, then said, "By the way, has anyone else considered the two corpses outside, frozen like popsicles, might be dead because they knew about the stolen painting?"

With her elbow on the arm of her chair, Genevieve rested her chin in her palm and tapped her fingers on her cheek. "From what he said to me at dinner before he died, I'm certain the elder Baron knew the painting was here. Maybe Elsa was his accomplice and someone murdered them both because they were going to tell us the stolen painting is here. Philip, you're suggesting that we four are in danger, aren't you?"

"As you may or may not recall, darling girl, Duncan pointed that out when we talked to him earlier." Philip pushed out of his chair and paced between the three people watching him, riveted, hanging on his every word. "Outside of the four of us, there are five other people in the schloss. It seems very likely to me that at least one of them is a murderer and/or a thief. Assuming the blizzard is over in the morning, we either need to get Darlington and his people here or we need to get the hell out. And until one of those things happens, we must all be fabulous actors. None of the five other people can have even an inkling of what we've found or what we suspect. Is that clear?"

Eyes wide, and unnerved, Genevieve and Lillie nodded.

"I think you're right on the mark, Philip. In the meantime, are you ready to go, mate?"

Energized by his own speech, he was more than ready. "I am," he said, "but don't you want to put some clothes on? Do you really want to go downstairs in your jammies, like it's Christmas morning?"

"I'm quite comfy, thank you. Am I going to embarrass you?"

Philip snorted a laugh. "Not in the least. If you're happy, I'm happy. I have the flashlight. Should we take my Dopp kit?"

"I doubt if we're going to need toothpaste and a toothbrush. As long as we have your Swiss Army knife, I think we have everything we need."

"Excuse me, boys," Genevieve said, stopping them in their tracks. "I know you think you can MacGyver your way into the vault, but as long as we have them, you might as well take the keys. Then the only thing you have to deal with is the alarm." She tossed the ring to Philip and he snatched it neatly out of the air.

"She's not just a pretty face, is she?" Finn threw a smile in Geneieve's direction.

"Not by a long shot," Philip said, as Genevieve blew him a kiss.

Finn put his hands on the upholstered arms of Lillie's chair and loomed over her.

She tilted her chin up and raised the corners of her perfect bow mouth. "Have fun disarming the alarm system," she said, grinning at him.

"You know I will." He leaned in and kissed her parted lips. "Don't wait up." He chuckled.

She echoed his words: "You know I will."

"Oh my god, you two." Philip combed his hands through his hair. "We're only going down two flights of stairs. We're not going down the Nile on a raft. We'll be back in fifteen minutes."

"Maybe twenty," Finn corrected.

With Finn hugging the crate and Philip manning the flashlight, they eased into the hall and made their way to the stairs in the dark. At the top of the flight, Philip turned on the beam and they crept downward step by step, hoping the old staircase wouldn't creak or moan. When they arrived at the bottom, Philip pointed to the far side of the great hall and noticed for the first time the green diodes dotted here and there high up on the wall near the vaulted ceiling.

"Are those surveillance cameras?" His whisper sounded too loud.

Finn nodded and hoped no one was monitoring the screens that would show them wandering the schloss in the middle of the night.

On the other side of the great hall, they snailed their way down the corridor until they came to the wooden door where Philip and Genevieve first encountered Max. Philip shone the light on the lock and keypad. In the glow of the flashlight, Philip saw a grin stretch across Finn's face. Without hesitation, he punched eight numbers into the keypad followed by the number 1 and they heard the single beep announcing it was disarmed.

"The key, Philip. Where's the key?"

Philip pulled the ring from his pocket, found the one labeled "art vault", and slipped it into the lock. To his relief, it turned and he opened the door.

Holding the handrail, Philip went first down the next flight of stairs. Unlike the stairwell going to the cellar, this one looked new. The walls were covered with sheetrock and painted a creamy white that reflected the flashlight beam and made it easy to see their way down. When they got to the bottom, the vault door was directly ahead of them and, much to Finn's delight, had the same alarm keypad. He punched in the same eight numbers then 1 and they heard the happy beep. Philip slipped the key in the lock and they were in.

"I am going to have to have a serious talk with Freddie about their security," Finn said the minute the door was closed. "This is absolutely appalling."

"How did you know what the code was?"

"Eight of the buttons on the keypad are worn."

"But how did you know the order of the numbers?"

"Because, Philip, the numbers are 12345678. An enormous percentage of people keep the default code, fearing they won't remember anything more complicated."

"Wow," was all Philip could say.

"Shall we?" Finn held up the crate and Philip swung the light around the large room. Vertical wire racks lined one wall. Philip pulled one out and a gasp caught in his throat.

"Finn, look at this. This is an Edvard Munch landscape."

Finn set the crate on a table in the center of the room, walked over to Philip, and took the flashlight. "I hate to state the obvious, but we are not here to admire the art. We are here to hide a piece of art in plain sight." He shone the light on the opposite wall where large cubbyholes held crates. Each crate had a stamped number. He found an empty slot between 246 and 248 and, in an instant, slid the 247 crate into its spot and was ready to go.

Taking a last longing look around, Philip motioned to Finn that he was ready to go. As they retraced their steps, they were careful to lock the doors behind them and rearm the alarms. When they were back in the great hall, Philip pulled Finn close to him and whispered in his ear, "We have to put the keys back on the board in the kitchen."

Finn nodded and they made their way across the great hall, through the dining room, pushed open the door to the kitchen, and froze. There, with his head in the refrigerator, was Freddie.

CHAPTER 36

As he rooted around in the refrigerator, Freddie swayed his hips and pumped his shoulders. It didn't take a minute for Philip and Finn to realize he was wearing earbuds.

Slowly, they backed up, holding the swinging door as they went, praying the hinges wouldn't squeak. The second the door was closed, they turned and fast-walked back through the dining room and the great hall. They dashed up the stairs, taking them two at a time, and, as quietly as they could, sprinted down the hall to Philip and Genevieve's room, where they fought to get through the door first then collapsed into chairs on either side of the fireplace like two ragdolls.

Curled up on the sofa, Genevieve and Lillie had been waiting impatiently for their return but hadn't expected it to be so dramatic.

"Success?" Looking at Philip, Genevieve knew he was spent. His lanky body melted into the deep cushions and he looked at Genevieve through heavy-lidded eyes.

The two bone-weary men bobbed their heads in unison.

"No problems at all?" Lillie moved from the sofa to Finn's chair and sat on the wide, rolled arm.

"I don't know if you'd call it a problem. What do you think, Philip?"

"I'd call it an almost-problem rather than a problem."

"I don't care what you call it. What happened?" Genevieve snapped, fatigue starting to take its toll.

Finn's brows arched. "Do we need a nap, Genevieve?" he said, then continued. "As you know, the last thing we had to do in our little caper was to return the keys to the kitchen. But when we pushed through the kitchen door, guess who was there?" An exhausted smile barely raised the corners of Finn's lips.

"Heidi?" Lillie squeezed Finn's neck, trying to ease his taut muscles.

"That's lovely. Please don't stop." He moaned and rolled his head in small circles. "No. It wasn't Heidi. Freddie was there with his head in the fridge."

Bug-eyed, Genevieve looked to Philip for confirmation. "That really happened? You burst in on Freddie? What did you say?"

"We said nothing." Philip's blinks were getting longer and longer. "He was wearing earbuds. So we reversed course and left him rooting around in the refrigerator. Jeeze, let's hope the refrigerator door doesn't close on him so we have another body in cold storage." He leaned forward, put his hands on the chair arms and shoved himself to stand. "Okay, kids. Out. I have to go to bed. We have a lot to do tomorrow—actually, later today—including getting the keys back on the board. And, of course, filling Darlington in." Realizing he didn't hear the wind roaring, he asked, "Do you two know what's happening outside?"

"We do." Genevieve perked up. "While you were gone, we actually opened a window and got a firsthand look. The snow has stopped and there is almost no wind. Fingers crossed Darlington can get to us by this afternoon. Aha," she held up her finger. "I forgot to tell you: I texted him and said, 'The von Bassewitz collection is extraordinary,' just what he told us to do. That will be quite a surprise when he wakes up." She smiled at the thought of him reading her message in a couple of hours.

"Okay, Lillie, my pet." Finn put his hand on Lillie's knee. "If you can pull me out of this chair, we shall leave these good people."

Lillie dragged herself off the arm of the chair, stood in front of Finn, and offered both her delicate hands. He took them and groaned as she tugged him from the depths of the cushions, then wrapped his arms around her and kissed the top of her curly head.

"Good night, all." Genevieve urged Finn and Lillie to make their exit.

Before the door was closed, Philip was out of his clothes and brushing his teeth. "Will this day never end?" He stared at himself in the mirror and weary eyes stared back.

"It's almost over. We're almost at the finish line," Genevieve said, already under the duvet and nearly asleep.

Though her eyes were closed, she could tell the light switched off in the bathroom. Philip slipped under the covers and stretched out his leg, feeling for Genevieve with his foot. When he found her and planted his frigid toes on her ankle, she squealed and pulled her leg away. "Stop it, you bad man. Go to sleep." But she could already hear his deep, steady breathing. She propped herself up on her elbow, stretched toward him and gave him a kiss. "Sleep fast, darling boy. Tomorrow's going to be a hell of a day."

CHAPTER 37

From somewhere in her deep slumber, Genevieve heard the ping of her phone and, ignoring it, wriggled further into her cozy cocoon. When it pinged a second time, Darlington popped into her mind and she clawed her way to consciousness. Next to her, Philip's rhythmic breathing was a comfort. She fluttered her eyes open and smiled at the sun peeking through the opening in the curtains. Never had she welcomed a cloudless day with such pleasure. She propped her pillows against the headboard and shimmied her shoulders into the comfy pile, then reached for her mobile on the side table.

When she tapped the screen, her favorite picture of Philip and her popped up and much to her surprise, the time display said it was ten o'clock. It was late. When she hit the text icon, Darlington's message came up.

Incredible! I read your text three times before I could believe what you were saying. How brilliant to take the painting back to the vault. Call me as soon as you are awake. Anxious to coordinate plans for today.

After reading the message several times, she wondered if she should call him now or wait for Philip? She should probably wait for Philip to wake up.

She tapped out a rapid response and hit the send arrow. *Philip is still asleep. Will call as soon as possible. Hope you and your team can make it to the schloss today. The sooner the better.*

Immediately he texted back: *Our team is organizing everything. We plan to get to you early this afternoon. Talk soon.*

Trying to wake him, she tickled Philip's nose. He swatted her hand away. She did it again and he rolled over, taking his nose with him so it was out of her reach.

"This is a waste of time," she said, and decided a hot shower would do her a world of good. She threw off the covers, slipped her feet into her woolen slippers, tugged on her robe and headed into the bathroom. Within minutes, the room was filled with steam and she was under a beating stream of hot water. When she first smelled the Rose Otto, she thought it was the shampoo she was working into a lather. She plucked a few bubbles from her hair and sniffed them. Jasmine and sandalwood. Yet the Rose Otto surrounded her, more intense now.

"Charlotte, are you here?" she whispered. "Charlotte?" She spoke louder this time, trying to keep her voice calm, steady. Opening her mouth to speak again, she felt icy fingers touching her neck, though hot water still pounded on her head and back.

The steam in the shower billowed and rolled in waves, making it impossible to see through the glass doors into the room, then abruptly it was gone. The steam vanished and the shower doors cleared. Only the droplets of water from the showerhead trailed down the surface.

She turned off the water, reached around the edge of the door for the towel on the door rod and buried her face in the deep pile. Rose Otto filled the shower stall, thick, heavy. She pulled the towel over her head and rubbed her hair until it stood on end then wrapped the towel around herself, tucked the end into the front and leaned back against the warm, wet tile. Her head dropped forward and she stared at the glistening floor.

"Charlotte, are you warning me? What are you trying to tell me?" She sobbed the questions. "Just tell me." When she lifted her head, something on the mirror caught her eye. She squinted. She shoved off the tiled wall and moved to the glass door, blinked, blinked again and wiped her eyes with the back of her damp hand. On the mirror, Charlotte had written her answer: *"TREACHERY."*

When the bathroom door opened, Genevieve jumped and nearly slipped on the wet tiles. "Oh my god, Philip. You scared the wits out of me. Look! Close the door and look at the mirror." He turned away from her and there, in the steam on the mirror, the word *"TREACHERY"* was disappearing into little rivulets and dripping into the sink.

"Charlotte?" Philip guessed instantly.

"Yes." Genevieve's voice quivered. "Rose Otto, icy fingers, the works. The old girl's clearly trying to warn us."

Philip plucked her thick terry robe from the hook on the door and held it open for her. "Come on, G. Get out of there. We need to get downstairs."

When she opened the shower door, the cold air from the room poured in, making her shiver. She plunged her arms into the robe Philip held for her, wrapped it around her and tugged the belt tight. "Drat. I should have taken a picture of Charlotte's message before it disappeared." She swiped across the mirror with her towel, leaving only a moist film on the surface. "Before we go downstairs, we have to talk to Francis."

Already naked and in the shower, Philip said, "I'll run down, get coffee, and see if I can sneak the keys back on the board. Somebody's going to look for these, if they already haven't. I'll tell Heidi and Freddie we'll be down as soon as we call Duncan. He's a perfect excuse. And it's not a lie because we do need to call him."

"Lots to tell. Lots and lots to tell." With the hairdryer blowing, Genevieve and Philip were practically yelling at each other to be heard.

Clean, tense, and worried about the day ahead, the two Warwicks gave each other a morning kiss and set about their missions. Philip headed downstairs and Genevieve sat on the sofa, cross-legged. Ready to start the conversation with Francis Darlington, she punched his number and he picked up before it rang at her end.

"I was getting rather worried. Is everything all right?"

"I'm sorry, Francis, but we didn't get to bed until about four-thirty."

"I noticed you sent your text around four. I almost called then. I truly can't believe you have *The Concert* there at Schloss

Friedrichstein. I am absolutely gobsmacked. Did Philip get it back in the vault?"

Genevieve regaled him with Philip and Finn's adventure, ending with their almost-run-in with Freddie, which brought a laugh on the other end of the line.

"That was certainly a lucky break that the Baron was absorbed in his music."

"It was." Hearing a tap on the door, Genevieve hustled across the room to open it wide enough for Philip to get through. "Aha. Philip has just arrived and he's carrying a tray of coffee and something to nibble on. Darling, Francis is on the phone," she said, and closed the door. "I told him about last night and we haven't started discussing the Met's plan for today, so your timing is perfect."

"Good morning, Francis. Are you ready for the big bust and rescue?" He set the heavy silver tray on the coffee table. "Coffee, G?"

"Yes, please. Let me do it. You sit." Steam wafted from the spout of the silver thermos and Genevieve inhaled the rich aroma of the coffee she knew would be deliciously rich and strong.

"If I may, I'd like to go over the plan."

"By all means." Philip took the cup and saucer from Genevieve and popped a sweet, flaky cookie into his mouth.

"First, there's excellent news from Lech. The municipality has been working on the roads since the snow tapered off at about midnight. The last report from my people was that the city is doing a fine job. Do you have any idea if the drive up to the schloss is passable? Legally, the homeowner has a limited time to clear any walkways or drives on their property."

"I'm glad to say I do know something about that. Max, the elder Baron's man, is on the plow as we speak. I don't know how far he's gotten, but he's anxious to get a clear path so the police can get here and address the two corpses we have next to the kitchen."

"Of course," Darlington said with a rueful sigh. "The local police are more than interested in the two bodies, I'm certain."

"So what's the plan and the timing?" Taking a drink of coffee, Philip sighed, savored its warmth and richness.

"The plan for you is to keep your game faces on until we arrive. Can you do that?"

Trying to draw on her usual optimism, Genevieve said, "Sure, Francis. But it's becoming more difficult by the minute." She caught Philip's eye and mouthed, "Charlotte?"

Not wanting to share anything about their ghost, he shook his head. "Noooo," he quietly shouted, then said to Darlington, "We'll be very 'Philip and Genevieve' until you get here with the cavalry. And Lillie and Finn will do the same, be themselves. We'll all do our best to act normal."

"Yeah, whatever that means," Genevieve scoffed.

Philip rolled his eyes at Genevieve. "Francis, we know what *we* have to do, now tell us how your team is going to get us out of this place."

"As you can imagine, this case is complicated with many jurisdictions involved, each one vying for ownership. Really, what police force doesn't want to be known as the authorities who found a piece from the Gardner Museum heist? You'll have to excuse me for just a minute," Francis said. They could hear a mumbled conversation, then the rustle of papers shuffling. "Sorry about that." He refocused on their conversation. "At this point, everybody is involved: the FBI, the Met, INTERPOL, and the BK—Austria's Criminal Intelligence Service, their equivalent to the FBI. Until this morning, when you told me you had *The Concert,* nobody was giving us the time of day. Now, every agency is falling all over themselves to get in on the action. Right now we're waiting for the paperwork from the BK. And you're not going to believe this. The York police department is sending DCI Fields to be here. He's on his way from Innsbruck Airport."

"Really?" Genevieve and Philip said at the same time.

"That's really something."

Darlington heard the delight in Genevieve's voice. "It's logical," he said. "He was the one who started the ball rolling when he connected Angelina von Bassewitz's calendar appointment with Scotland Yard. Without Cecil, none of this would be happening."

"So we have him to blame," Philip said with a laugh.

"You do, indeed." Darlington's office chair creaked as he shifted positions. "Now, I don't want to alarm you, but as I said, at this point everyone wants in."

"Is that a problem?" Philip said.

"Only in that there are going to be a lot of agencies and their officers coming to Schloss Friedrichstein. Think Normandy, presumably without the casualties."

"Okay," Genevieve drawled. Her mind raced, envisioning helicopters landing, SWAT teams swinging from the schloss towers, officers in winter camouflage crawling on their bellies through the snow.

"I'm kidding, of course." Darlington chuckled. "A couple of Austria BK agents, posing as Lech officers, will come to the schloss to investigate the two dead bodies. Though they don't really need it, they will have a search warrant. Once they're in, another team of BK agents will enter, along with the representatives from the other agencies, including Cecil and me."

"Considering everything that's gone on—you know, a murder in England, two corpses and a stolen artwork here—that sounds remarkably easy; very straightforward." Genevieve was heartened.

Darlington agreed. "When possible, simple is best. What questions do you have for me?"

"Do you have any idea about timing?" Philip looked at his watch and it was already 11:30.

"It's hard to give you an exact time. From our end, we're ready to go as soon as all the paperwork is in order. The moment I know the first group is heading to the schloss, I'll text you. Philip, Genevieve, are you all right? You feel okay?"

A spark flashed in Genevieve's eyes. "I feel so much better, more confident, now that we know what's going on from your end, Francis. I think this is going to work."

"Good," he said. "Philip, is everything good?"

"I think we're set. We'll fill Lillie and Finn in and just be our charming, usual selves. Right, G?"

"Our charming selves it is."

"G, we need to get downstairs. If there's nothing else, Francis, we'll see you soon."

The line went dead and they were ready to go.

CHAPTER 38

By the time Philip and Genevieve walked through the dining room door, Freddie, Heidi, Finn and Lillie were seated around the table stacking cold cuts, cheese and tomatoes on rolls, fresh from Frieda and Christine's oven.

"Mimosa?" Heidi held a flute in the air.

Genevieve's stomach churned at the idea. "Ooo, tempting, but no thanks Heidi. Last night was rather late and I'm still recovering."

"It just seems appropriate," Heidi said, "given the fact that the blizzard is over and Max is plowing us out. The powder is going to be amazing. Who's up for hitting the slopes? When I called the ski line, they said the double lift will be open at one o'clock."

"Aren't we expecting the police?" As far as Philip was concerned, no one was going skiing. No one was setting foot off this property. "In case anyone needs reminding," he said, his tone aggressive, "there are two corpses outside in the snow."

"Mein Gott im Himmel! I completely forgot." Heidi's hands flew to her cheeks. "Oh, Freddie, I am so sorry."

Reaching across the table, Freddie took her hand. "Heidi, Schatz, these have not been normal days. It is difficult to remember what day it is, much less what happened when."

"But Papa was—" she started to say, but Freddie interrupted her.

"Papa was very old. It was his time to leave us." Interlacing his fingers with hers, Freddie continued. "It's fine, my darling. And poor Elsa? We may never know what happened to Elsa."

Philip and Genevieve shared a glance that said, "Oh, I bet we will."

"Excuse me." Philip rose. "I'm going to go thank Frieda and Christine for keeping us fed the last few days. That can't have been easy."

Finn watched him go, assuming Philip's mission was to replace the keys on the board in the kitchen.

Feeling the moment was right, Lillie said, "Freddie, I've been thinking. Rather than worry about the new museum right now, wouldn't it be better to wait until after the new year? You and Heidi could come to Paris, see the new exhibition and we could all spend the weekend at Château Beaulieu to finalize the details." She smiled at Genevieve. "If that's all right with you?"

"That's a lovely idea, Lillie." Genevieve's caring smile showed no hint of her fear that somewhere in Schloss Friedrichstein, perhaps right in front of her, was probably a thief and possibly a murderer. "You two name the date and we'll show you a wonderful time, I promise."

"That's an excellent idea," Freddie said. "That will give us time to get approval from the Foundation's Board for the donation."

"And get through Papa's funeral, the holidays, all the estate issues, and, and, and…" Heidi added.

For the first time since meeting her, Genevieve thought Heidi looked exhausted. *And why wouldn't she?* she wondered. She took a sip of tepid coffee, shivered and realized she had forgotten to put on a sweater before she came down. Her silk blouse was hardly warm enough. "Excuse me," she slid out of her chair and stood. "I'm going to run upstairs and grab something warmer. I'll be right back."

"Here, Genevieve." Heidi pulled a wrap from the chair next to her. "You don't need to go upstairs. You can use this." Heidi stood and walked toward Genevieve, holding the small blanket in each hand, ready to wrap it around Genevieve's shoulders.

Already at the door, Genevieve turned around. "Thanks, Heidi, but I need to get my phone as well. I left it on the charger. I'll be right back."

Cold air smacked her as she opened the dining room door and walked into the great hall. "What a weird few days," she mumbled under her breath and trotted up the stairs. "I am not going to be sorry when we're on our way home, safely away from this place." The moment she stepped on the top stair, she was surrounded by the smell of Rose Otto. "What, Charlotte? What is it?" She was more annoyed than surprised. "What's the point of all this Rose Otto and icy fingers if you're not going to tell me anything? A single word, treachery, doesn't give us much to go on." The fragrance whirled around her, a gentle tornado, lifting the ends of her hair, spinning, spinning until she arrived at their bedroom door. "Okay, you're telling me something but I don't understand what. What is this supposed to mean? You're scaring me."

She reached for the doorknob but couldn't push her hand beyond the whirlpool of fragrance. "Are you trying to keep me out of my room? Cut it out, Charlotte," she snapped, her temper thoroughly piqued. "As they say in the south, you are getting on my last nerve." At that, no trace of Rose Otto lingered, no air spun around her. All was calm. Reaching for the doorknob, she held her breath. The knob turned and the door opened a crack. She pushed it gently and it slowly swung, wider, wider. Nothing appeared to be amiss. "So what was that all about, Charlotte?"

As she walked toward the closet, she glanced this way and that, antennae alert for anything disturbed, out of place. The bed was unmade as they'd left it. Philip's clothes from last night were draped over the armchair by the fireplace. Four glasses still sat on the coffee table and the tray from this morning's coffee waited to be taken back to the kitchen. "I'm beginning to think you just want attention, Charlotte." She flipped the closet light on, flooding the generous walk-in space with blue-white florescent light. She dropped to her knees in front of her suitcase and began riffling through it, searching for her sweater, when she heard the bedroom door close. "Philip," she called. By the time she had taken everything from one side of the case, she was swearing under her breath. Where could her damn sweater be? She put everything back and started on the other side. Another noise caught her ear. "Philip," she said, sharper this time.

"It's not Philip, Genevieve."

Startled by a voice she vaguely recognized but didn't expect, her head whipped around to see who was behind her. Her eyes shot wide, her jaw dropped, and she pushed herself to stand. "Michael! What are you doing here? You're supposed to be in New York."

He smiled pleasantly, his chubby cheeks blooming even fuller. "That's what everyone thinks. And yet, here I am."

"What in the world are you doing in our room?"

"Actually, Genevieve, I'm interested in retrieving something you stole from me."

"Wha…!" She coughed a laugh with no response.

"Where is it?" he said, a menacing edge creeping into his voice, his charm morphing into malice. "Don't miscalculate, lovely lady. I am not a patient man. You and Philip have completely upended a perfectly good plan." Perspiration dotted his upper lip. "Believe me when I tell you, I'm quite annoyed about that. Just look what happened to Angelina and the Baron. That's the last thing I want to happen to you. You can make amends by simply telling me where you put the Vermeer. That's all I want," he snarled, his eyes narrowing to fiery slits.

Genevieve couldn't believe what he was saying. Was he really telling her he killed Angelina and Karl Friedrich? Was this the same lovely man she and Philip had entertained at Wilmingrove Hall recently? The love of Gabriel's life?

"I need the Vermeer, Genevieve," he said through clenched teeth. With his hands fisted at his side, he took a menacing step toward Genevieve.

Her heart raced, her head swam, and a wave of nausea engulfed her. Teetering on the brink of fainting, she staggered, tripped over her suitcase, fell back and hit her head on the plaster wall with a loud thunk. Pain shot through her skull and her body slumped to the floor, her back against the wall, her chin on her chest.

"Are you kidding me?" he hissed. He squatted beside her and, in an attempt to rouse her, smacked her cheek with one light slap. "Genevieve." He shook her by her shoulder and her head wobbled back and forth on her chest. "Genevieve," he seethed, and slapped her again, harder this time. No response. With a grunt, he pushed his bulk to stand and stomped into the bathroom.

Her eyes slitted open, she watched him leave the closet then scanned the small room, looking for something she could use as a weapon. When she spied a boot jack just out of reach, her heart raced. From the bathroom, she heard running water then the tap squeaked off. She had only seconds. Stretching as far as she could, her fingertips touched the boot jack. She gave one more effort and her fingers wrapped around one of the wooden prongs. In an instant, she repositioned herself, just as she had been, this time with her sweater covering her hand and her weapon.

She sensed Michael standing in the closet doorway. Feeling his eyes boring into her, she willed herself to keep hers closed, feigning unconsciousness. His raspy inhale and exhale were the only sounds in the room. Or maybe the thundering rush of blood in her head made it impossible for Genevieve to hear anything else. If he stood there staring much longer, she was going to scream. She lifted her lids just enough to see Michael's feet and legs in front of her and tightened her grip on the boot jack.

Just as she readied herself to spring, he screamed, "Wake up, you thieving bitch!" and doused Genevieve's head and face with cold water.

Gasping and blinking water from her eyes, she went from frightened to furious in a nanosecond. With a death grip on her weapon, she pulled her legs up under her, into a squat and with a mighty inhale, shoved herself up, ramming the boot jack between Michael's legs.

His eyes rolled upward in agony and he fell back, sprawling on the floor, clutching his throbbing crotch.

Looming over him, she bared her teeth and snarled, "Who's the bitch now, Michael?"

She watched the fear in his eyes as she raised her hand over her head and came down with a mighty thwack, hitting him on the side of the head with the boot jack. With great effort and much grunting and groaning, Genevieve rolled his tubby body onto his stomach and grabbed two silk scarves from her suitcase. She pulled his hands together, and drawing on her summers at sailing camp, tied a bowline knot around them. Satisfied his hands were secure, she repeated the knot around his ankles. Then, for good measure, she grabbed another scarf, bent his knees and tied his ankles and wrists together. By the time she finished, her adrenaline was racing, fueling her breath and making her giddy.

She dropped to her knees and, nose to nose with Michael, grinned an almost hysterical grin. "What kind of idiot are you?" A disturbing giggle bubbled in her throat. "You have everything in the world—money, someone who loves you, prestige, intelligence. What did you think you were going to do with one of the most…" Her voice trailed off as she heard the bedroom door open. "Philip?"

"No, Genevieve, it's Heidi. I came to tell you the police are here. Is everything all right?" She pushed the door closed, leaned against it, then reached behind her and turned the lock.

"Oh my god, Heidi!" Genevieve jumped to her feet and burst out of the closet, "You're not going to believe—" The rest of her words caught in her throat.

Lounging against the bedroom door, Heidi seemed remarkably comfortable holding a small, exquisite pistol straight at Genevieve. "You are quite wrong, dear friend. I believe it all."

Heidi's smile sent a chill down Genevieve's spine and her mind raced, not understanding, searching for some sense of what was happening so she could figure out what her next move should be. She took a cleansing breath then let it slowly escape through her nose.

"So, is it true? Did Michael kill Angelina and your father-in-law?" Impressed with how calm she sounded in spite of her racing pulse, she went on. "Do you know he got his hands on the Vermeer from the Gardner Museum robbery thirty-five years ago? Do you have any idea what he's planning to do with it? Do you think he realizes he can't sell it to anyone?"

Heidi pushed away from the door, walked toward Genevieve, and waved her pretty little Sig Sauer Rose pistol. "Sit over there," she said, pointing with her gun to a chair by the fireplace.

Genevieve watched Heidi's every move, clueless why she was waving a pistol, looking for an opportunity to outsmart or overcome the taller, younger, very fit woman she had thought was her friend. In the meantime, she did as she was told.

Heidi walked to the closet and snorted a laugh when she saw Michael out cold and hogtied on the floor. "Well done, Genevieve." The steely-eyed beauty strolled back to the chair opposite her prey and sat down. "We don't have much time. The local police have just arrived to deal with our two corpses so we need to move this along. But first, I must disabuse you of the notion that Michael was anything but a willing tool in either murder, though he did secure the Vermeer." She crossed her long, elegant legs.

Confused, Genevieve frowned. "He didn't kill Angelina? Or Karl Friedrich?"

"He did not."

"Then who did? And what about Elsa?" Genevieve's questions came faster, now.

Heidi's flawless skin wrinkled between her eyes in a frown. "I have absolutely no idea what happened to Elsa." She looked down at the pistol in her hand as if she were surprised to see it there, then smiled up at Genevieve. "Very strange, indeed. I wonder if we shall ever know why she was frozen in the snow. I do, however, know about the other two. I don't think you'll expect this. Wretched Angelina was eliminated by none other than your own darling Andrew Frasier." The words hung in the air like a mic drop.

Disbelieving, Genevieve couldn't speak. A thousand new questions flooded her mind, but nothing came out of her mouth. Then it dawned on her. "That's why he resigned right after the grouse shoot."

"That surprised you, didn't it?" Heidi's eyes sparkled with

delight. Still holding her gun, she rested her hand on her thigh.

Finally focusing on one small part of the huge picture, Genevieve said, "You have to be lying. None of this makes any sense. Why would Andrew kill Angelina?"

"Money and flattery. It's amazing what several hundred thousand pounds and a little flirting can get you." She looked pleased with herself.

"You mean you wanted her dead? He did it for you?"

"Actually Karl Friedrich wanted her dead and asked me to take care of it. So I did. You see, Angelina had become the bane of the Baron's existence."

"What did she do to the Baron? Why would he want her dead?"

"Angelina found out about something Karl Friedrich did years ago and she was going to tell you and Philip. Actually, she wanted to tell the world about it. The Baron could not let that happen."

"What could be so terrible that Angelina had to be murdered?"

Buzzing with energy, Heidi leaned forward, elbows on her knees. She could hardly wait to answer. "Several months ago, Karl Friedrich sent documents to Angelina that she needed to complete a transfer of property the von Bassewitz family gave her in the divorce settlement. As we told you, the elder Baron's behavior was becoming erratic. Sometimes he was his brilliant self, other times he had no idea what he was doing." Heidi's eyes misted. "It was a sad thing to watch." She sniffed and blinked her tears away. "Certainly by accident, in the documents Karl Friedrich included a letter he had written years ago but never sent."

As Genevieve was about to clarify, her phone pinged a text.

"Is that Philip?" Heidi said.

Genevieve tapped her blank screen and Philip's text popped up. "It is."

"What does he say?"

"'Where are you? The police are here.'"

"Give me your phone," Heidi said, her left hand outstretched, her right hand holding the Sig Sauer. "You have text to talk?"

Genevieve nodded.

Heidi pressed the microphone icon and spoke into the phone, "I'm in the bedroom with Heidi. She's telling me about Michael and the Vermeer. All very interesting. We'll be down in a few minutes." She hit send, leaned forward and put the phone onto the coffee table. "That buys us a few more minutes. I believe I was telling you about the letter."

"Yes." Genevieve rolled her shoulders to release the tension building in her neck. "You said the Baron wrote a letter to someone, never sent it and recently Angelina saw it?" Genevieve felt as if she were listening to Heidi describe the plot of a novel. "What was in the letter? Who was it written to?"

"The letter was written to Jonathon Laney, the 12TH Earl of Crosswick, Philip's cousin. It was an apology for causing the accident that made the Earl a paraplegic and changed the course of his life."

"What?" Genevieve bellowed, nearly coming out of her chair.

In an instant, Heidi brought her gun back to attention, aiming at Genevieve's heart. "Relax, Genevieve. You and Philip really owe Karl Friedrich a debt of gratitude. If it hadn't been for him,

Jonathon would have married, had children, and Philip wouldn't have inherited the Crosswick fortune and title. So wasn't that a happy accident?"

With every revelation, Genevieve was more incredulous. How could any of this be true? "I know the story of his terrible skiing accident, but how in the world did the Baron cause it?"

Heidi looked around the room for a water carafe. "I'm parched. Don't you have any water in here?"

At the mention of water, Genevieve almost laughed and sucked her lips into her mouth to keep from grinning. "I don't have still water but I have some flavored sparkling water. Let me get you a glass." Commanding herself to be calm, she strolled to her side table uncapped the bottle of seltzer left from the day before, unscrewed the liquid Tylenol P.M. she had left out in case she couldn't sleep, and poured equal parts of both into a tall glass. With her finger, she swirled the mixture until it was a pale purple.

"Here you go." She handed the seltzer water to Heidi and hoped she would drink it, though she couldn't imagine it would taste good.

To Genevieve's shock and delight, Heidi drained the glass in one fell swoop, gasping for breath as she gently set the glass on the table next to her. "Thank you, Genevieve. Now where was I?"

"You were telling me how the Baron caused Jonathon's accident."

"Oh, ja. It was 1958 and he and Jonathon were in Sun Valley, Idaho, skiing together." As Heidi spoke, she shifted her little gun from her right hand to her left and relaxed it on the arm of the chair. "Apparently, they were outrageously competitive with one another so it was not surprising when one of them challenged the other to a race from the top of Bald Mountain to the bottom. According to Karl Friedrich, he thought it would be a great joke to loosen Jonathon's binding. It would also, of course, ensure his victory. He never intended to ruin his friend's life. It was a rather a vicious prank that went horribly wrong. You can understand that such a proud man could never allow such a thing to become known. So when Angelina threatened to expose him, as you can imagine, something had to be done." Angelina's matter of fact tone made Genevieve's shiver.

"But Heidi, the Baron and you had Angelina murdered. Murdered! I don't care how proud a person is, normal people don't murder other people. And the police can't figure out how it was done. DCI Fields and his team are absolutely stumped."

"Oh, Genevieve, it was so clever. Andrew fitted a firearm to one of the drones he uses to train your spectacular birds of prey. He shot Angelina when she went to the moor."

"Wait a minute. How did Andrew know she was going to be on the moor? That was pure happenstance, wasn't it? DCI Fields surmised that her dog jumped out of the car and she ran after him. Andrew couldn't have known that would happen."

Heidi smiled, shook her head. "That is not what happened at all. Andrew contacted Angelina, told her about the dinner party, and said it would be a good time to confront you and Philip with everyone there. He told her he would meet her on the moor afterwards to give her a video of what had happened and she could send it to the press. She was very excited about that. Of course, instead of meeting Andrew, she met her maker." Heidi couldn't help but chuckle.

"That's an outrageous and appalling story, but what does that have to do with the Baron's death and the Vermeer?"

"Ah, yes, the Vermeer. Angelina was involved with that as well. She was a partner in a gallery in Munich—very high end, very posh, very nouveau riche. But her partner was a bit shady, you know—contacts with the wrong people, that sort of thing—so it wasn't surprising that he got wind of an opportunity to get his hands on *The Concert.* The person in possession of the painting knew the FBI was closing in on him and contacted Angelina's partner. He was anxious to get rid of the painting at any cost. Angelina overheard their conversation and wanted their gallery to have nothing to do with stolen art. She told Michael about it and asked him to help her extract herself from the gallery. Instead, Michael bought the Vermeer."

"Why on earth would he do that?" Genevieve couldn't possibly be more shocked.

"Oh, there's a very good reason." Heidi's head bobbed up and down for several long seconds. "One word. Love."

"Love?"

"Love. Michael is deeply in love with Gabriel."

"Everyone knows that. Obviously, there's more to the story." The longer Heidi talked, the more confident Genevieve was that soon—very soon—Philip or the police would crash through the bedroom door.

"Of course. There's always more to a love story, right, G?"

Genevieve cringed. No one called her G but Philip. Absolutely no one. Forcing herself to smile, she said, "I'm certain you could say that about you and Freddie. But finish your story. You were telling me why Michael needs the Vermeer."

"Ah, ja." She smiled a mysterious smile Genevieve couldn't interpret. "You know Gabriel."

"I don't really know him. I've only met him a couple of times, but I like him."

"Ja, Gabriel is easy to like."

"So?" Genevieve encouraged.

Much to her relief, it seemed to Genevieve their captive-captor relationship was morphing back into their previous friendship, the mood genial and the conversation easy in spite of the subject matter. Rather than Heidi clutching her pistol, it nestled between her legs; a precarious position, Genevieve thought.

"Gabriel has many very expensive habits. You know about some of them, I am certain: his polo ponies, his yacht racing, but I don't imagine you are aware of his greatest expense. He gambles."

"A lot?" Genevieve asked, not particularly surprised.

"If you consider owing some very bad people three million euros a lot, then, yes. I'd say he has a problem."

"So how is the Vermeer going to solve his problem?"

"Michael bought *The Concert* from the thief of the thief of the thief, for three hundred thousand euros in order to return the painting and retrieve some of the ten-million-dollar reward."

"Clever," Genevieve had to admit. "Then he pays off Gabriel's gambling debt and saves the day."

"Exactly." Heidi coughed and cleared her throat. "Do you have any more of that delicious seltzer?"

"I do." In a flash, Genevieve snatched the glass and was at the side table mixing the Morpheus cocktail. This time, Heidi drank only half of it but Genevieve was thrilled, nonetheless.

Heidi licked her lips then wiped them with the back of her hand, very un-Heidi-like. She chuckled, laid her head back against the soft chair cushion, and closed her eyes. For a moment, Genevieve thought Heidi was well on her way to dreamland until Michael groaned loudly from the closet and Heidi's eyes flew open.

"What was that?" Her hand was on her gun and she was ready for anything.

Doing her best to hold her composure, Genevieve raised the corners of her mouth. "It seems Michael's waking up. Shall we leave him in the closet or should we invite him to join us?"

"No, no. This is a nice little chat between girlfriends, don't you think? Besides, as soon as you tell me where you and Philip put the Vermeer, we certainly don't need… um… Michael—that's right, Michael—any longer… do we?"

As the Tylenol began to take effect, Genevieve watched Heidi's energy fade. She would only be awake a few more minutes and Genevieve needed answers to a few more questions. "Heidi. You were telling me about Gabriel's expensive habits and how Michael is going to get money for the Vermeer."

"Mmm. Ja. I remember, but I am so tired, Genevieve. I think I need a little nap." The pistol slid from her hand and dropped to the carpet.

"I might have gone a little heavy on the Tylenol," Genevieve mumbled. She stepped the short distance to the other chair and picked up the gun off the floor. Heidi's eyes were closed and her breath soft and steady. "Never mind the Vermeer," she said and patted Heidi's cheek. When her eyes fluttered but stayed closed, Genevieve patted a little harder and leaned so close to the Baroness that they were nose to nose. "Hey!" she yelled and Heidi's startled eyes popped open.

The Baroness felt the arm of the chair for the gun. She looked at one hand then the other, on the cushion between her legs, but there was no gun.

"Are you looking for this?" Genevieve sat back down, rested her elbow on the arm of her chair and aimed the gun right between the two frightened eyes staring back at her.

"Never mind Michael. He can tell us all about the painting himself. Before you pass out, I want you to tell me about Karl Friedrich. Did he die of natural causes or was he poisoned?"

"What do you think?" Each time Heidi blinked, her eyes stayed closed longer.

"Just tell me."

"I did Karl Friedrich a kindness. I just helped him along." She eased her head onto the back cushion, looking at Genevieve with hooded eyes.

"So you poisoned him."

Heidi smiled. "I did."

"Why? Why would you kill a man who will soon die?" This woman was insane, Genevieve was certain of it.

"Timing is everything."

"What do you mean, Heidi?" Her eyes were closed again. "Oh, no you don't." Genevieve wasn't having it. She loomed over the sleeping woman, grabbed her shoulder and shook her awake. "You are not sleeping until I understand what your evil little mind was thinking." She slapped both cheeks and threw her back against the cushion. "Now tell me. Why did you kill a man who would die soon?"

Heidi sighed deeply. "It is all very logical. Last week, the Baron changed his will yet again. In this latest version, I inherit everything. With control of the von Bassewitz fortune, I can leave dear, insipid, stupid Freddie and live anywhere I like, somewhere that is not old and depressing. Somewhere that is glamorous and beautiful. I can enjoy my life without all these pathetic, needy von Bassewitz men hovering around me all the time. The Baron has done this before—made me his heir. Then a week later he changes his will back to his boys. This time I was not going to let that happen. I decided to help Karl Friedrich move on before he changed his mind again. It is as simple as that." Her eyes slid shut, her head rolled to the side, and Genevieve heard a soft snore as Heidi's breath hit a deep rhythm.

Her phone vibrated on the table next to her and Philip's face filled the screen. She hit accept and put the mobile to her ear. "G, what's going on up there? You and Heidi need to get down here. The police are everywhere including Darlington and Cecil. Finn took them to the art vault and they have the Vermeer." His words poured out in a continuous stream. Genevieve just listened, loving the sound of his voice.

When he took a breath, she seized the opportunity. "Darling, you need to bring Darlington and DCI Fields up to our room.

There has been a lot going on up here."

"Wh—?"

"Just do it, please. Immediately." Her tone was insistent and she knew he would be there soon.

From deep in the closet, Genevieve heard Michael's pathetic moan and felt a pang of guilt. What had she done? He had saved a treasured painting the world had been searching for for years and she probably gave him a concussion, and maybe neutered him, for his trouble. "Michael," she said, trying to sound comforting as she walked into the closet and squatted beside him. "If what Heidi told me is true, I'm sorry I hurt you, but I thought you were going to kill me."

Lying on his belly, his arms and legs trussed behind him, he could barely lift his head to look at Genevieve. From a jagged cut where Genevieve whacked him with the boot jack, blood trickled down the side of his face and into his right eye. "Oh, Michael, I really whacked you, didn't I?" She jumped to her feet. "Let me get a damp cloth and wipe the blood out of your eye."

As she headed to the bathroom, the jangling of the doorknob diverted her. "I'm coming. I'm coming," she yelled, as someone began pounding on the door.

"Genevieve!" Genevieve, are you in there? Open the door," Philip commanded from the other side.

When she flipped the lock, the door flew open and Philip, Darlington and Fields pushed into the room. At the sight of her husband, the person she trusted most in the world, the man she had shared her life with for forty-five years, all the composure Genevieve had maintained for the last half hour shattered. She threw her arms around his neck and squeezed until he gasped,

"G, I can't breathe."

Holding on to her shoulders, Philip held her at arm's length, looking for injuries. "G, are you all right? Are you hurt?"

When she shook her head and sobbed, "No, I'm okay," he pulled her back into his arms and held her close.

The three men scanned the room, saw Heidi snoring in the armchair, heard moaning from the closet, watched Genevieve clinging to Philip and couldn't imagine what had been going on here.

"You're certain you're not injured?" DCI Fields patted her shoulder and Darlington looked at Philip, his eyes filled with concern.

"No, no, I'm fine," Genevieve assured them, Easing her hold on Philip. Though she could have stayed buried in Philip's arms forever, she had stories to share.

"Hey, could somebody please untie me?" a pathetic voice called from the closet.

"I'm fine, fellas, but I think Michael probably needs some help."

Philip smiled down at her then kissed her forehead. "I can't wait to hear this story, darling girl."

"Oh, it's a doozie," she said, stretched up on her tiptoes and gave him a noisy kiss on the mouth. "It's a real doozy."

EPILOGUE

"**T**UTU, TUTU!"

Sitting at her desk in the library, Genevieve braced for Alex and Ella to race into the room, bursting with all the exuberance a nine and eleven-year-old have at Christmastime. She swiveled in her chair, turning away from the view out the soaring library windows. The massive blizzard that had buried them in Austria last week had left only a few inches of snow on Wilmingrove Hall's manicured lawns, just enough to add to the festive spirit.

All wide eyes, giggles and long legs, her grandchildren threw themselves on their grandmother and she was glad she was sitting down. With her arms wrapped around the two children, she hugged them tight, blowing raspberries on both their necks until they squealed like piglets.

"Tutu, come on," Ella begged. "Mrs. MacIntosh said to tell

you drinks are served in the drawing room." They grabbed Genevieve's hands and pulled her to stand. "Let's go, Tutu. Everybody's already there waiting for us."

"Finn and Lillie brought us presents but we can't open them until you come," Alex said as they strolled out of the library door, Genevieve in the middle and a child on either side, each holding a hand.

"So the truth is out. You only want me in the lounge so you can open a present, you little mercenaries," Genevieve teased.

As she walked through the grand salon, the lovely smell of roses wafted around the grand hall. Genevieve didn't know if the fragrance were from two enormous arrangements of red roses, dark blue hydrangeas and white lilies on the sideboard next to the staircase, or perhaps from Charlotte letting her know she was nearby. Either way, she welcomed the comforting scent.

"Wait," Alex said, halting them just outside the closed door. "Let me announce you like Wallace does, Tutu."

"How very elegant. Thank you, Alex." She stood to the side of the door so she could make a grand entrance after her introduction.

He opened the thick, paneled door, took two steps into the room and cleared his throat.

"Lords and ladies, ladies and gentlemen," the eleven-year-old said as he had heard his father and grandfather announce so many times over the last two years. "It is my great pleasure to introduce Lady Crosswick, the Countess of the House of Crosswick and my Tutu… tada."

Genevieve entered, smiling with the pleasure of being home.

She loved this room, cheerfully elegant with its buttercup moiré taffeta walls, polished mahogany furniture and comfortable down-filled sofas and chairs. Though she hadn't chosen her evening's attire to blend with the drawing room's decor, her muted-yellow plaid dress was perfect. As she walked to where Philip sat on a tapestry loveseat beside the fire, her skirt swished just at the top of her polished mahogany ankle boots. With a grin and a happy sigh, she sat next to Philip and slipped her hand into his.

"You okay, Lady Crosswick?" Philip patted her knee.

With a grin still on her lips, he cupped her chin. For several seconds, his gaze roamed over her lovely face, the face he had adored for four-and-a-half decades. He leaned in and kissed her, softly at first, then deeper. For a moment, he lingered, then, as he pulled away, he mouthed, "I love you."

There was not a moment of any day Genevieve didn't feel his love, but Philip rarely said the words, so this was special. Feeling a warm glow, she squeezed his hand and tried to swallow the lump she felt rising in her throat. Looking down at her hands, she felt the sting of tears and tried to will them away.

"My lady," Wallace said, standing in front of her. "Champagne?"

She looked up into Wallace's caring eyes just as two fat tears ran down her cheeks.

"My lady, are you quite all right?" he asked, as he handed her the flute of pink bubbles.

"I'm wonderful, Wallace," she said, wiping the drops away with her knuckle. "I'm just so glad to be home."

"And, my lady, we are all very glad you and Lord Crosswick

are home as well." He gave her a solemn nod and moved back to his post by the door.

Across the room, Alex and Ella waited for their presents, not so patiently, on either side of Lillie. The moment Finn handed them over, paper ripped and flew in all directions. On Lillie's left, Alex was the first to unwrap his prize. He threw the reindeer-covered gift wrap into the air and squealed, "A ski chalet LEGO kit! I love it! Thank you, Lillie." He threw his arms around her neck and planted a big kiss on her cheek, then bounded off the sofa and plowed into Finn, hugging him fiercely.

On Lillie's other side, with the wrapping paper long gone, Ella dug deep into her cardboard box and pulled out something big, heavy and swathed in bubble wrap. As fast as she could, she yanked the bubble wrap from around her prize and there was a statue. She looked at Lillie then she looked at Finn. "This is Jolie Fille and me, isn't it?" She stared at it as if it might come to life. "You made a statue of Jolie Fille and me."

Finn moved to the sofa and sat in Alex's vacated spot. "It's a wonderful likeness of you and Jolie Fille, isn't it? You see your tiny riding boots and your helmet? And look at the white markings on your horse's legs and forehead. The artist loved doing this piece, knowing it was going to a young lady named Ella who loves her horse."

Ella put her small hand on Finn's cheek and smiled into his eyes. "Thank you, Finn." She turned to Lillie and kissed her cheek. "This is the most wonderful gift anyone has ever given me." She thought for a second. "Except, of course, when Bumpa gave me the real Jolie Fille."

"Out of the mouths of babes," Finn laughed.

Philip stood and walked to the fireplace. "On that happy note, I would like to propose a toast."

"I was wondering how long it would take you," Genevieve teased him. "We've been in the drawing room almost ten minutes without a toast, Philip. You're slipping."

"Very funny, Genevieve. I think everyone will welcome this particular toast so here goes." He raised his glass. "I would like for us to drink to the new Laney Musée des Beaux Arts, Berlin." The room erupted in cheers. "It's actually going to happen and, let it be known, I owe Lillie a thousand pounds."

Though delighted at the prospect of adding another museum to the foundation, David was surprised it was going forward. "After everything that happened with the von Bassewitz family, how did you pull this off?"

Her curls bounced as Lillie tossed her head. "Elementary, my dear Watson," she said with a sly smile. "Actually, it was easier after Freddie took over than before the Baron died. Though Karl Friedrich told Heidi he had changed his will, he had not. Freddie and Gabriel inherited everything and Freddie is hell-bent on making the Berlin museum a reality. And with Michael's new technology, the museum is going to be extraordinary."

"Damn," David said. "You mean Heidi poisoned the Baron for no good reason?"

"Is there ever a good reason to poison someone?" As a doctor, Julia was curious.

"Good point, Julia," Duncan agreed.

"Okay," Becca jumped in. "We've heard most of the story but I still have several questions."

Philip lowered his glass. "Ask away, Becca. My toast can wait."

"Before you go on, Philip…" Julia left her chair and walked toward the door. "Alex, Ella, why don't we go to the kitchen and see if you two can sit in there and have your dinner? Good idea?"

"Yeah, Mom. I'm starving." Alex couldn't leave fast enough. He snatched his LEGO set and made a beeline for the door.

"I want to take my statue." Ella cradled the porcelain gem in her arms and followed her brother.

"My lady, allow me to take Master Alex and Lady Ella to Mrs. Lomax," Wallace said, holding the door as the two walked out.

"Thank you, Wallace. Little ears don't need to hear our conversation, do they?"

"Certainly not," Wallace agreed, and closed the door behind him.

"Good call, Julia. Okay, Becca, fire away." Though he had not made his toast, Philip took a drink of his Champagne.

"First, I haven't heard anything about Elsa. Have the police discovered what happened to her?"

"Oh, you're not going to believe this." Genevieve sat forward on the loveseat. "The police found a note in her pocket."

"And?" Becca waited.

"As Freddie told us, for many years, Elsa was one of Karl Friedrich's closest confidants and trusted retainers. But since he became irrationally abusive, he had treated her horribly. So she decided to put a laxative in his wine in hopes that he would shit himself at dinner and embarrass himself in front of his guests. When he died at the table, she thought she had killed him, so while everyone was rushing around dealing with his death, she wrote the note explaining what she had done, took a bottle of paracetamol, and walked out into the blizzard."

"These people are insane," David said. "Are you absolutely certain you want to have them involved in the museum? As your solicitor, it's a question I need to ask."

Genevieve appreciated David always looking out for their interests. "Absolutely, David. One of your many jobs is to try to keep us from going down the wrong path—which is not always easy, we know—but we think Freddie is going to be an extraordinary partner. And with Michael's invention, I don't think we can miss."

"Mom," Duncan said. "I want to tell you, I am in awe of what you did." The room broke into applause. "I've always known you're clever and tough, but I never imagined you'd have to disarm a woman with a gun and almost neuter a man you thought wanted to harm you. You are something else and I'm so lucky to have your genes. Yours too, Dad, but... whoa, Mom!"

Thoroughly pink with embarrassment and pride, Genevieve grinned at her son. "I only hope Michael will someday forgive me for assaulting him. I really gave him quite a wallop."

"I bet he'll be very careful around you from now on." Duncan squirmed in his seat at the thought of what his mother had done to the poor man. "One more question about Michael. Is he home scot-free?"

"Yes. He is," Philip said. "His only offense was to buy stolen goods, but since he bought the painting with the intention of securing its return to the Gardner Museum, he won't be charged with theft, and he will receive a portion of the reward."

"And what about Gabe? Do you think he'll continue to gamble?" Duncan asked.

"Who knows?" Philip shrugged. "And before you ask, Gabriel won't be involved in the foundation or the museum at all. He's entering a program for chronic gamblers and Freddie has asked Max to be Gabe's constant companion. If anyone can keep him on the straight and narrow, Max can. And, of course, he has Michael. What he did to bail Gabriel out of debt was quite extraordinary. He loves Gabriel and we all know what love can do, which brings me back to my toast."

Groans rippled around the room.

Having returned from handing off his two charges to Elsie Lomax and the kitchen staff, Wallace moved around the drawing room filling empty glasses and topping off those that weren't.

"As I was saying, we need to toast the Laney Musée des Beaus Arts, Berlin but not for the reason you think. The House of Crosswick has a long, illustrious history—a history Genevieve and I have grown to cherish over the last two-and-a-half years. My ancestors did an extraordinary job of building and protecting this magnificent legacy. Stepping into the role of Lord and Lady Crosswick, the Earl and Countess of Crosswick, Genevieve and I had many anxious moments, terrified that we would be the generation that would let everyone down."

Genevieve joined Philip in front of the fireplace, slipping her hand into his. "Lord knows it hasn't been easy."

They smiled at each other and Philip continued. "I speak for both of us when I say that, with the help of all of you, we no longer worry." He pointed at Duncan and Julia. "The next generation of Crosswicks is thriving with another right behind it. We have great confidence that the House of Crosswick will grow and flourish in the coming centuries. The Berlin museum is a metaphor for our future. Our legacy has been difficult to achieve but well worth the effort.

"For the last two and a half years, we've endured one overwhelming event after another. Through it all, we've drawn strength from each other and emerged unscathed, surviving the inheritance of extraordinary wealth, attempted murder, attacks on our friends and family, attacks on our reputation, threats to our vineyard, loss of a dear friend, terror of kidnapping, and much, much more. It's been an absolute frenzy."

Philip felt a lump in his throat and took a deep breath to calm his emotions. "Somehow, through everything, we knew we would endure, coming out the other side happy, safe, and still very much in love with all of you." He raised his glass high. "To Berlin, to all of you..."

"And to Charlotte," Genevieve added.

"Oh, yes," Philip agreed. "To Charlotte, our ever-present muse. Cheers, and santé!"

Everyone stood. "Cheers and santé!"

"I have one last question," Becca said. "What about Genevieve's XKE? Is it going to be under the Christmas tree?"

"You'll just have to wait until Christmas morning and see," Philip said, then leaned over, gave Genevieve a warm kiss on her lips, and swatted her bottom.

Cheers and Santé!

Legacy, Tragedy: A Lord and Lady Crosswick Prequel,
Available Exclusively at tanalhboerger.com

AND SO IT BEGINS

I'M QUITE SURE my first memory is floating in moist darkness, waiting for something extraordinary to happen. And then it did. I remember my surprise at the waves that rhythmically ebbed and flowed. The longer it lasted the more it annoyed me and just when I decided I'd had enough, the biggest wave of all shoved me against an elastic band. Of course, I didn't know at that time what an elastic band was, but in retrospect, that's what it felt like. And then, another big shove through a small hole, and I was blinded by bright lights bouncing off white walls, white uniforms, white sheets, white faces. I think I was upside down, though, again, I have to say, I didn't know what upside down was. I whimpered, but when someone smacked my bottom, I gave them what they were asking for—a big, fat wail. I remember thinking, "What a set of pipes!"

That was 3 August 1921. I've been telling that story since I was four and every time I do, someone pats me on the head, well, not so much anymore, since I'm, well, dead, but they used to, and they would say, "What a funny story, you clever boy." I would roll my eyes knowing, even at four, that they didn't think I could possibly remember my time in the womb and my journey out into the world. But I did.

And I remember my mother. She always smelled of roses. When I was six, she told me that Rose Otto was her favorite perfume because my grandmother Lady Caroline, had given her a vial of the treasured scent on the day she married my father. Our family believes in tradition and Rose Otto was a tradition that began with my great-grandmother, the magnificent Charlotte Chaubert, the toast of Paris and London. According to my mother, who loved to tell a lively story, Charlotte was my grandfather's passion. Lord Philip adored her, denied her nothing, but in the end, the love of his life was taken from him far too soon.

Sometimes I wonder if I had heeded their story as a warning, could I have veered from the events that took my life down a path I did not choose, or want? It's a bit late to ponder these things, but sometimes my mind still goes there.

The London Times, August 6, 1921

THE COUNTESS OF CROSSWICK HAS BEEN DELIVERED OF A SON

The Countess of Crosswick was safely delivered of a son at 05:26, 3 August, at Columbia-Presbyterian Medical Center, New York City, New York. The baby weighed 7lbs 2oz.

The Earl of Crosswick was delighted to greet his first child.

Lord and Lady Crosswick will reside with their son, Jonathon William Wallace Laney, at their home, Margrave House, Kensington, upon their return to London.

And so I was announced to the world. An auspicious beginning, to be sure. A proper English babe wailing his way into the world, not in the serene, shaded lanes of Kensington, London, but into the noisy, brash streets of New York City, surely a harbinger of how I would live my life.

I'm not certain that my parents wanted more children, or actually any children at all. It seemed to me they were delighted with each other and would have been perfectly happy to live their interesting lives surrounded by artists and musicians rather than a brood of young savages. Regardless, I was the only savage they produced, and it suited me that they stopped at one, as long as I was it.

It was said that I was a bonnie baby, but that was my mother and my granny speaking. I doubt if my father said the same. I believe he preferred the attractive swirl of paint on canvas more than the red face of a newborn. He tended to avoid me in my early years until I could ride well enough to join him on The Hunt at Wilmingrove Hall, our family seat in Yorkshire. Or when I could give him a good run for his money on the chessboard. Then he began to take an interest in me and my development.

I had a nanny I loved nearly as much as I adored my mother, but my nanny was my friend and my mother was, well, someone I worshiped. She was a charming, brilliant, and stunning woman who never tired of bringing life and laughter into our home. No matter what I did, she delighted in it. If I colored a picture for her that was nothing more than a few scribbled lines on the paper, she would declare it to be the work of a burgeoning young talent. If

I made a mudpie and insisted it was a plum pudding, she would pretend to eat it all and insist it was worthy of a Michelin star. She read to me. She tutored me in the vast and spectacular art collection that was my parents' pride and joy and because she loved it, I loved it.

And she told me stories. The night she told me the tragic tale of my great-grandmother, Charlotte, the wife of the 9th Earl of Crosswick, it was raining and cold. I was six. My mother and I huddled together on a small sofa in my father's study, which would one day be mine. I remember how cozy we were with a lap robe tucked around us and a fire crackling on the hearth. My hands cradled a cup of hot cocoa, and my mother kept stealing sips, smiling at me each time she did, a little cocoa mustache painting her upper lip. The smell of cocoa still reminds me of my mother. The smell of cocoa and Rose Otto.

"Your great-grandmother was a beauty," she began. "Everyone adored her, but no one as much as your great-grandfather." As she spoke, my mother's forehead nearly touched mine. Her voice was so quiet, I watched her lips to make certain I didn't miss any words. "It was your great grandparents' fortieth wedding anniversary, and this house was filled with guests who were here to celebrate with them." My mother's hand was cool on my cheek. "Everyone gathered at the bottom of the staircase, waiting for Charlotte to make her grand entrance. When she appeared, she was stunning in a shimmering silver dress with a train that curved around her feet. Even at sixty-four, she was breathtaking." My mother looked deeper into my eyes. "You have her eyes, darling boy." And she kissed the tip of my nose, then went on. "The 9th Earl raised his Champagne glass and said, 'To my magnificent bride of forty years. No one else has ever walked the earth, whom I could love as I love you.' At the end of the toast, the band struck up Charlotte's favorite song 'Oh You Beautiful Doll' and Charlotte blew a kiss to the Earl." My mother's eyes were glistening with tears. I didn't understand why she was crying. "When she started down the stairs, the toe of her shoe hooked on her gown's silver train. She tried to grab the banister but missed and tumbled head over heels down the stairs. By the time she reached the bottom, she was…." My mother's voice trailed off, but I understood.

"One day, darling boy, I'm sure you'll meet her," she said. I know my mother intended to comfort me, but when she saw my eyes, wide with fear at the idea that I was going to run into an old, dead lady, perhaps in the middle of the night when I got up to go to the loo, I'm certain she realized she had miscalculated. She quickly tried to recover, pulling me close, kissing my forehead, and laughing. "Don't worry darling. I just meant we'll talk about Granny Charlotte again, and the more we talk about her, the more you'll feel you know her."

I didn't believe her, and for the next year, I lived in fear of great granny jumping out of my wardrobe, every evening when I opened the door to get my dressing gown. Other six-year-olds were frightened of monsters or goblins. I was terrified of my beautiful, kind, dead great-grandmother. And then I learned, purely by accident, that Granny Charlotte was a ghost.

JOIN TANA'S NEWSLETTER
TO DOWNLOAD THE
WHOLE STORY, FREE:

WWW.TANALHBOERGER.COM

OTHER BOOKS BY
TANA L.H. BOERGER

Money, Murder, Mayhem
Art, Wine, and Crime
Vengeance at the Vineyard
Fortune's Final Frenzy

FORTUNE'S FINAL FRENZY CHARACTERS

Alexander Laney Warwick – Philip and Genevieve's grandson, age 9.

Andrew Frasier – Falconer.

Angelina Haufman – Freddie's first wife.

Karl Friedrich Hauffman, Baron von Bassewitz, the elder – Patriarch of the von Bassewitz family.

Captain Bruni – The Warrick's pilot.

Charlotte Camille Chaubert – Philip George Winston Laney's wife who fell to her death in 1913 at Margrave House. She is the House of Crosswick ghost.

David Spencer Frederick Weatherington – The Warwick's solicitor and close friend

DCI Cecil Fields – York head of detectives.

Duncan Philip Warwick – Philip and Genevieve's son.

Ella Hayden Warwick – Philip and Genevieve's granddaughter, age 7.

Elsie Lomax – Head Cook.

Finnegan Mountbatten – Head of Mountbatten International Security, Lillie's boyfriend. Philip and Genevieve think of him as a second son.

Francis Darlington – Detective Chief Inspector of the Metropolitan Police Services' Arts and Antiquities Unit.

Friedrich Gerhardt Hauffman, Baron von Bassewitz, the younger – Freddie to his friends and the Baron's older son.

Gabriel Johannes Haufman – the Baron's younger son, and a charming playboy .

Genevieve Hayden Warwick – Philip's wife.

Heidi, Adelheide Christiana Hauffman's – Freddie's second wife.

Jonathon William Wallace Laney – 1920-2018 – Philip's cousin from whom he inherited. Skiing accident in Sun Valley 1957.

Julia Whitney Warwick – Duncan's wife, a physician.

Lillie Langdon – Executive Director of the Laney Museum of Fine Arts Foundation.

Lottie and Claire – Kitchen staff.

Max Klein – Baron von Bassewitzes' driver, valet, and friend.

Michael Andersen – Gabriel's partner and a brilliant inventor. He has created a technology that will revolutionize the museum experience.

Mrs. MacIntosh – Head housekeeper at Wilmingrove Hall.

Philip Jame Warwick – Lord Crosswick – Heir to the House of Crosswick fortune.

Rebecca (Becca) Harris Conway – David's wife and owner of an American Bourbon distillery.

Reginald Wallace – Butler at Wilmingrove Hall.

Sean Harrington – Estate manager.

William – Young purser on their helicopter and plane, doubles in The Hall when needed.

ACKNOWLEDGMENTS

FOUR YEARS AGO, I gave birth to Philip and Genevieve Warwick. When Philip responded to the question, "What would you change about your life if you could pick anything?" and said, "Absolutely nothing," I knew he and Genevieve were about to jump on a speeding train they would ride for several years to come—and I had my hand on the controls. What a heady realization.

Deciding during the pandemic to write a novel was a seminal decision that changed my life. As a fledgling writer, I had a grand goal of creating an entertaining mystery series, challenging feat, indeed. Writing "The End" on the last page of the fourth and final book, is fraught with emotion. Getting to that point has been a journey overflowing with sparkling people offering unexpected insights, encouragement, and endless creative energy. I have met and pulled into my orbit, a team I would never have known, much less called friends, if I hadn't decided to write.

To Rosie Walker, my editor and touchstone. What a lucky girl I was when our stars crossed. From the first book, *Money, Murder, Mayhem,* I knew you were my perfect editor, with your gentle but firm hand. With each book you have helped me become a better writer. Onward and upward.

To Caerus Kourt, designer extraordinaire. If the cover doesn't grab a reader, you're sunk. Fortunately, I don't have to worry about that with Caerus. Not only have they created consistently perfect covers that tell a story and link one book to another, but they understand the importance of the book's interior and deliver a rich experience for readers as they turn the pages of each book. Caerus, you constantly amaze.

To Jane Ryder, our master marketer. You are sharp-witted, smart as a whip, a dear friend, *and* you deliver sales. What more could anyone ask?

To Jay Calendine and Cal Saltzman, two tech-brilliant fellows who guided me through drone technology and offered great counsel on just what drones can and cannot do.

To Alana Davidson, my sister, who has yet to disown me even though I ask her to read and re-read the words I have endlessly assembled and rearranged until, at last, I hit "Send" and the manuscript flies through cyberspace to Rosie's inbox.

To my best boy, Tom Boerger, my tireless sounding board. How often do we laugh at the fact that we never tire of talking about plot twists, character arcs, who should die, how they should die, and what grand places we need to explore for the next book. In addition to your consistently valuable critiques and suggestions, this time you handed me a pearl that enriched the story and gave me a plot-point twist. For that, you get an extra smooch.

To our son, Trevor. Thank you for insisting the title wasn't right until it was. I can always count on you to hold my feet to the fire…in a good way.

To Cody and Stella, my grandchildren who always know the right questions to ask and never fail to offer the most creative ideas.

And to you, my readers. For those of you who have been with Philip and Genevieve from the beginning, haven't we had fun? And for those of you who have started with book number two, three, or four then gone back to the others, thank you for joining Lord and Lady Crosswick and their chronically endangered friends and family on their crazy sleuthing adventures.

Now that the Warwick's final chapter has been written, I'm excited to see what story is waiting to be told in the glamorous world where I spend my writing moments. There's a tale already bubbling in my head. It's making me smile, making me shiver with anticipation, and making me anxious to get back to my computer. Until then, pour yourself a special beverage, cozy into your favorite reading chair and plunge into *Fortune's Final Frenzy*. I'll be thinking about you.

ABOUT TANA

DURING THE PANDEMIC when Tana started her debut novel, she had no idea she would turn out to be a mystery writer until halfway through *Money, Murder, Mayhem*. She also had no idea that four years later she would have completed a mystery series. But now, with four books under her belt, she finally feels comfortable calling herself an author, and she loves the genre. In her Lord and Lady Crosswick Mystery series, Tana draws on her years of travel with her husband, Tom, her passion for art, antiques, fine food, beautiful wine, inspiring places, and interesting people, to create crimes with culture. Now that she has written Philip and Genevieve Warwick's last rollicking adventure, she is teeming with ideas for her next novel…it's going to be a doozy!

WWW.TANALHBOERGER.COM

f TANALHBOERGER